THE DARK
RUNNER

THE DARK RUNNER

Gilbert L. McLeod

CITIOFBOOKS, INC.
3736 Eubank NE Suite A1
Albuquerque, NM 871113579
www.citiofbooks.com
Hotline: 1 (877) 3892759
Fax: 1 (505) 9307244

Ordering Information:

Quantity sales. Special discounts are available on quantity purchases by corporations, associations, and others. For details, contact the publisher at the address above.

Printed in the United States of America.

ISBN13:   Softcover   979-8-89391-415-3
                      eBook   979-8-89391-416-0

Library of Congress Control Number:

TABLE OF CONTENTS

PART FOUR

The Fateful Meeting: Midsummer 1811

PART ONE

The New World

CHAPTER ONE

Kuntamba left his home near the source of the Niger River long before sunrise. He was on a journey to visit his elder sister who lived three hundred miles away in the coastal town of Monrovia. It was an easy journey, starting in the central mountains of his homeland and taking him south to the lowlands that joined the African continent with the warm Atlantic waters. His stride was a long, comfortable gait that consumed the miles, leaving his mind free to enjoy the familiar landscape and to contemplate the vastness of an ocean he had never seen.

On the sixth day, just as the sun gave its warning that darkness was about to give way to light, Kuntamba stirred on his bed of dry grasses. He smelled the cool air and thought he detected a hint of saltiness in its bouquet. Rising to his feet, he stretched his long, lean legs with a special deliberation. He was determined to arrive at the port of Monrovia by mid-afternoon of the next day. He hoped to have enough time to buy his sister a gift and find her home before nightfall.

The early part of his trek had been leisurely. Suddenly, his eagerness to see his only living relative, the sister who had raised him, combined with his desire to look upon the vast life force that is the ocean. He quickened his steps and lengthened his stride. For the first time since leaving his highland home, his nostrils flared ever so slightly. The beat of his heart broke from its slow, methodical rhythm and began pulsing with the motion of life and the perfection of a physical efficiency that was bequeathed to him at birth. The endurance and precision with which Kuntamba ran were birthrights inherited from a long line of formidable ancestors.

His forefathers, whose minds and bodies were only truly alive when in full stride, found a soothing peace in the labor of motion that enabled them to transcend physical effort. Kuntamba sought to enter this same trance-like state, a place where time, distance, and fatigue did not exist. Today, Kuntamba's mind refused to surrender his consciousness to the motion of his steps. His thoughts ranged ahead of him, and he visualized his sister's smiling face, remembering his childhood and the love she had shared with him.

As the day wore on, the sun tested his resolve for a speedy journey with a relentless heat and seemingly shadowless light. Beads of moisture began to collect on his wide forehead. The prevailing onshore wind resisted his progress, catching the drops of perspiration and forcing them up into his tightly knit hair. The wetness clung to his scalp and to each coiled hair, capturing the heat that radiated from his head before releasing the excess warmth to the hot wind, leaving him cool and refreshed. The wind, born of motion, poured against his chest and thighs, cooling his muscles and circulating blood, bestowing the gift of tirelessness on Kuntamba.

The faint blue line that had been the ocean gradually widened into a swath of blue-green decorated with white spots. Soon Kuntamba was able to see the rolling waves easing themselves up on the shore. Beyond the shoreline, far out to sea, one small fleck of white was defying the wind and the waves, traveling parallel to the coast.

In an instant of recognition, Kuntamba's heart paused. His muscles labored as his heart received the message that only a life and death emergency can initiate. His steps took on a new urgency, increasing in power and force. His lungs began to pull in great drafts of air. His relaxed, pleasant expression suddenly transformed into a focused intensity.

Kuntamba's eyes searched the shoreline for his sister's town as his bare, callused feet slipped between sharp-edged rocks and moved over sandy pits with the unerring sureness of a bat flying through a dense forest at midnight.

Kuntamba's face twisted harshly as the strange object that challenged the ocean's current enlarged into a sailing ship. He knew of the fast sailing clipper ships that visited his land from the far side of the world. He also knew that if the ship's decks were loaded with barrels of rum, the slavers would be on the hunt. This vessel, with a dark blue hull and three white masts, had nothing on its decks. A dreadful premonition washed through Kuntamba.

The strange ship with a red, white, and blue flag was heading west. Kuntamba wondered if it had stopped at Monrovia and traded rum for slaves. His stomach tightened in fear.

It was dark when Kuntamba entered the port city his sister called home. The streets were illuminated by a faint wisp of light flowing from a new moon. The huts' dim, flickering candles reflected an emptiness that overflowed with the pain of eternal separation. The vacant shelters told the story of the clipper ship and a day of horror.

From nearby fields, the dark runner heard parents crying out for sons and daughters whose voices they would never hear again. He cringed as the sobs of mothers separated from young children reached his sensitive ears. Tears of compassion blurred Kuntamba's vision as he saw the broken bodies of men and women who had fought bravely to protect their families.

He searched through the chaos. When he finally reached his sister's shelter, all he found were ashes. Turning toward the ocean, he studied the distant skyline. He wanted to know whether the sailing ship had headed out to sea or up the coast. Quickly, Kuntamba sprinted to the top of a nearby rise, his eyes fixed on the line that divides water and air. He remained motionless and unblinking for several minutes. Abruptly, he turned and ran. He had seen the tip of a ship's mast reflected in the moon's faint light just before the vessel slipped below the horizon.

Kuntamba ran all night. Sometimes his feet found the sandy shore. Other times, his tireless legs carried him unhesitatingly up steep inclines. As his feet slapped softly on the hard ground, he found the cadence that balanced his breath, pulse, and stride. Stilling his mind, he slowly entered the sacred trance. His respiration became deeper as he revitalized his body with the life force that inhabitants of distant lands call *Chi* or *Prana*. In this state, Kuntamba saw beyond the darkness and the convolutions of the dirt path beneath his feet. He heard more than sound. He sensed plaintive moans and cries and the fall of a whip that had not yet been raised. He was engulfed in a passive alertness that made approaching him without his knowledge impossible.

The weak light that preceded dawn illuminated Kuntamba's steps and the trance faded, leaving him refreshed in body and mind. Looking seaward, he saw the ship he had pursued throughout the night. He shivered suddenly, the salty air moistening his skin. He knew he was being watched. He caught the glint of the sun on glass. At sea, two additional sails unfurled, the west-blowing wind catching the sails. The ship's prow leapt forward as it churned the water, cutting strongly through the swells.

Kuntamba shortened his stride while increasing leg speed. As the ship rounded the rocky point, it moved closer to shore. The dark runner saw the outline of a stranger on board, staring in his direction. The foreigner's body seemed tense, fearful. Kuntamba could not know that the man who watched him through the spyglass feared the unknown. This fear, whose roots were in the realm of all that is possible, stemmed from not knowing what the pursuing African's intent was. Kuntamba knew, as the ship moved farther away, that he and the foreigner were not done with each other.

CHAPTER TWO

Aboard ship, the stranger turned and left the deck. He was a man whose frugality had matured into greed and an all-consuming hunger for wealth and power. Rum and gold had satiated his lust for the objects that money could buy, yet he only felt truly powerful when the hold of his ship was crowded with human cargo harvested from the coast of Africa. Absolute control over the lives of others had sustained his dark ego for years. Yet somehow during this trip, for the first time, his exultation in his own mastery over his living freight began to needle him.

Captain Bernard Stouvall, master of the *Ocean Breeze*, had left Portsmouth, New Hampshire, in the early fall of 1810. The holds of his ship were packed with barrels of rum. Even his deck was stacked with the liquid that made slavery profitable. He had personally raised and harvested the sorghum, which produced the rum.

He was thirty-five days into his journey; thirty-five uneventful days. Stouvall was bored, restless, and angry. Promises had not been kept. His manacles were not full. Precious time was being wasted tacking against the wind. The Ivory Coast was just one day away. The additional time, along with two days in port, could be critical. The hurricane season was fast approaching, and the ship faced an added threat—pirates.

Bernard Stouvall was an impatient man. He did not like delays. He still had rum stored below to trade for slaves and gold. He was worried that an early winter in New England could force him to spend precious months away from his holdings. The African native running on the beach bothered him. He didn't know why, but the visual image of the black runner unnerved him.

The sun had just begun to light the sky when Captain Stouvall, drawn by an inexplicable impulse, once again fixed his optical eyepiece on the shore and searched for the racing native. It only took a moment to find him. For over an hour, the ship's captain studied the strange African. His concentration was so intense that the several hundred yards that separated the two men almost ceased to exist.

Stouvall's mind was full of questions: he wanted to know why the African was running and if he was following the ship. Perhaps, Stouvall thought, he is racing ahead to warn his countrymen of the ship's approach. Was it coincidental that their paths were on a parallel course? Stouvall needed to be sure. "Unfurl all sails," he called to his first mate. Within minutes, the ship surged forward as the wind caught the sails and drew taut.

Stouvall raised his telescope and studied the shore. To his amazement, the African matched the *Ocean Breeze*'s increased speed with a seemingly tireless stride. Stouvall noticed that the African's head was canted seaward. The captain snorted with anger. How dare this African, a member of a slave people, challenge him, a captain and wealthy property holder, to an undefined competition.

Stouvall's boredom was suddenly gone. In its place grew a surging desire to master, defeat, and humiliate the African. The captain hurriedly retreated to his cabin to think. At first, he thought the native was running to warn family and friends at the next port, but he dismissed the notion. The slaves he would be trading for were already confined in guarded holding pens.

Paranoia gripped the captain. What if, he considered, the mysterious dark runner was hunting him, Bernard Stouvall? He hurried on deck, took out his telescope, and looked toward the shore. As he adjusted the lens, the African came into view. This time, the African's eyes met Stouvall's through the intimacy of the glass, deep brown penetrating eyes full of strengths and secrets. Stouvall's stomach tightened, but he refused to turn away. The spasm spread up into his chest. Unable to endure the pain, he broke the locked gaze, lowering his telescope. The physical pain subsided immediately. He shook his head, trying to clear his thoughts. What if the dark runner was a witch doctor or practitioner of black magic. The sailors' stories of spells and death curses rushed through his mind.

Hearing footsteps behind him, Stouvall quickly turned. It was the first mate.

"Pardon me, sir, but we have a problem in the galley. Some of our meat has gone bad. Several sailors are suffering from stomach cramps." The first mate was surprised to see the odd expression of relief that washed over the captain's face.

"Give them all a laxative. We'll pick up more meat at the next port."

His fear of the supernatural partially relieved, Stouvall began to devise a plan to capture the native who refused to tire. Had the master of the ship's thinking been sharper, he might have immediately suspected that the African was pursuing the contents of the ship's hold. This would have simplified his plan. He could have waited for the African to come to him, but the captain's mind was twisted by greed and a desire to punish the dark runner for his insolent stare. Stouvall had made this trip many times before. He planned to use his knowledge of the African coast to capture the running African.

Stouvall knew that, just a few miles ahead, the shore disappeared into a steep cliff face. This would force his pursuer inland across some extremely rough terrain, delaying the native's arrival at the next port. The captain planned to arrive at the next stop ahead of his imagined foe and position his men for a quick capture. Believing that the African was all but in his manacles, the ship master relaxed. He could not wait to drop anchor the next day and set his trap for the brazen African.

To Stouvall, Kuntamba was an African rather than a man. It was the distinction of different skin color and culture that enabled the captain to capture, chain, abuse, and enslave the Africans. He equated them with animals, refusing to acknowledge their minds, bodies, and actions were almost identical to his own.

Next morning, the soft fog hung just above the water and land in the moments before dawn. Captain Stouvall ordered a rowboat lowered. Six of his most experienced slave hunters were making final preparations for the capture of the dark runner. Within thirty minutes, the men of the *Ocean Breeze* were concealing themselves in the sparse cover on the wind-blown coast. The captain smiled. He anticipated bending the dark runner to his will.

Taking his spyglass, Stouvall studied the shore and the narrow road that led to the pier. At first, he saw nothing. He was elated. His trap had been set in time. Suddenly, his breath caught in his throat. Fixing his glass on a single shadow, he held steady until the first rays of the rising sun revealed the identity of the African. As the image became clear, Stouvall found he was staring into the same eyes that had plagued him for the last twenty-four hours.

The captain slightly fearful, considered sending the first mate to handle shore duties, then changed his mind. He needed to bargain with the African slavers in person, which made staying aboard ship impossible. Leaving the rowboat, Stouvall tried to remember where his men were concealed. Perhaps the dark runner was already surrounded. He studied the area. He didn't have to wait long. The African bolted from his semi-concealed position with two seamen in close pursuit. The native was racing straight up the middle of a rutted path toward the location where the first mate and the ship's carpenter had hidden.

The *Ocean Breeze's* master watched anxiously as his four men closed in on the African. They misjudged his speed and, in doing so, sprang their trap before Kuntamba was completely surrounded. Stouvall's anxiety turned to anger as the long, lean runner easily accelerated past the slavers. The chase was short. Soon the seamen were gasping for air as legs, conditioned only to the pitch and roll of the clipper ship, collapsed in exhaustion.

When the captain's anger finally cooled, he began to ponder the dark runner. An idea began to grow. He recalled how southern boys loved to race their horses. He had seen enormous wagers placed on the outcome of a single race. Plantations could be won and lost by the response of a horse to his master's whip. Those same southerners treated slaves like beasts of burden, cattle to be used and slaughtered on a whim. Stouvall also knew that if he had not seen the African run, he could have easily been lured into a wager that pitted a slave on foot against a mounted white man. Knowing this, Stouvall was convinced that the southern boys, with their fine horses and need to impress each other, could be enticed into a competition with the slave who had outrun the *Ocean Breeze* in full sail.

But first things first...he needed to capture the dark runner.

Once the captain's logic linked the dark runner to potential profits, he began to analyze the situation. "Why," he mused softly, staring out over the ocean, "has the African followed my slave ship?"

Rowing back to the *Ocean Breeze*, the answer flooded over him and lifted his sour spirits. The runner was looking for someone, he must be, and that person was chained in the hold of his ship. The captain renewed his plotting to capture the African, stumbling only when he realized that he did not know which slave the African was interested in. A wife? A child? Father? Mother? Only one solution, a cruel one, came to the captain. He would have the slaves brought up on deck one at a time. Stouvall was pleased. He knew it was just a matter of time until the African ran no more.

As his first mate and the African slaver chief boarded the clipper ship, Stouvall called them over, wanting to know if the chieftain was able to communicate with the dark runner. The slaver nodded apprehensively.

Through his interpreter, he told the captain that the African runner was considered to be one of the few truly holy men to ever walk the earth. The natives regarded the dark runner as a spiritual guide called "runner with the spirits." The villagers believed that Kuntamba was able to communicate with other holy ones over great distances and could plant thoughts in the minds of anyone he chose. Stouvall also learned, although he did not accept it, that the holy ones rarely ingested food.

"Is there anything else I should know?" Captain Stouvall pressed the slaver.

The chief turned his back to the beach and Kuntamba before muttering a response. "I know only the rumors spread by the old ones passing legends into the impressionable ears of the young."

"What are these legends?" asked Stouvall, irritated.

"The man who runs with the spirits can heal the deathly ill, and when necessary, he can be in two places at once," the chief replied.

Outwardly, the captain dismissed the fantastic claims, but doubt remained in his mind. The dark runner did seem to be beyond the bounds of human endurance. Maybe there were two of them, which would explain the legends and the dark runner's ability to outrun the *Ocean Breeze*. Stouvall remembered staring into the African's clear, dark eyes and wondering if the dark runner could read his mind. He swore out loud so all could hear. "There are no holy men," he shouted. "It is the fantasy of children and old women, and I will prove it to you!"

The captain paused. How could one twin tell his brother, who was miles away, where to go? Could one mind communicate across space and time with another? Shrugging, he dismissed the idea as absurd. There had to be a logical answer.

"Tomorrow at noon," he ordered his first mate, "Bring the slaves up on deck, two at a time and lay two lashes on each."

He grinned. He knew the holy man didn't plant that particular thought in his head.

Standing motionless just beyond the lap of the waves, Kuntamba snapped out of his focused meditation. "Tomorrow I will see if my sister lives," he whispered. He feared she was injured or dead because his mental probe had not found her receptive mind. Kuntamba hoped it was only his sister's preoccupation with the suffering of those around her that made telepathic communication difficult.

CHAPTER THREE

High noon arrived to the sound of clanking chains. Paired slaves gulped fresh ocean air as they turned light starved eyes away from the sun. Stouvall stood quietly, not watching the human misery paraded on his deck. His spyglass was fixed on the dark runner's face. He waited, watching for a sign of recognition to flash in the African's eyes. The burly second mate, who had willingly agreed to lay the whip on each slave before sending him or her below, lay rolling on the deck in pain for no apparent reason. When another crew member eagerly took the whip, his first lash caught the sail, tearing a large rip in the cloth.

Stouvall looked back at the dark runner. He saw a glint of light in the African's eyes and the hint of a smile pulling at the corners of his mouth. The captain's first instinct was to lay the lash on the slaves himself, but something held him back. Rationally, he knew he must stick to the business at hand, but fear of the unknown and the dark runner's possible power caused him to cease the public whipping of the slaves. He emphasized the word *public* to the crew, inferring that the whipping could wait, before he glanced at the slaver chief. He knew it would be unwise to anger the chieftain and his hunters by lashing the women and children without cause. The last thing Stouvall wanted was a skirmish on the deck of the *Ocean Breeze*.

As the slaves marched before him, Stouvall continued to study Kuntamba's face. The African's expression was immutable, refusing to yield the slightest clue of his feelings to the ship master.

Slowly, the procession of slaves completed their time on deck. Each individual turned and looked longingly at the homeland he or she would never see again; each memorizing the land, the sea, the retreating mountains, and the holy man who waited on shore.

Although the dark runner remained still while the slaves were paraded on deck, Stouvall still believed that he still had what the dark runner sought. The African was bound by the same unbreakable familial threads of kinship that Stouvall himself had hungered for in his own childhood. He knew that all he had to do was wait, but the captain was an impatient man. He wondered what the African would do if the *Ocean Breeze* set sail across the sea, but greed and the promise of the wealth the African could win forced the captain to act. He ordered his first mate and the slaver chief, who spoke several languages and sold his enemies and neighbors into slavery, to meet with the dark runner.

As the emissaries rowed back to shore, Stouvall went below deck, deep into the bowels of the pain-filled hold. Fleeting images of his youth, when honor and truth mattered, raced across his mental screen. It made him question his motives, accusing his sensitivity. But logic intervened. "It's better that I carry these primitive creatures across the ocean. I will feed and water them. Other captains are not so generous. On my ship, most will live to sleep on dry land." His religious training reinforced his reasoning, adding, "At least they will have access to religion and an opportunity to become civilized."

Shaking his head to regain focus, he began to study the dark faces that were exposed by his flickering lantern. His sight probed for similarities or characteristics that would reveal a relationship with the dark runner. He tried to look into the eyes of his human merchandise, chained in horizontal rows. Unsuccessful, he left, damning the dim light and the unknown captive who made the dark one run.

Waiting on the beach, Kuntamba had seen the misery of the imprisoned and recognized an opportunity. His life had been lived in reverence and meditation, a meditation in perfect harmony with his body, mind, and soul. On two occasions since leaving home, Kuntamba had unsuccessfully tried to see what the future held for him. He suddenly understood why the sacred trance refused to reveal his destiny. He realized that his life was about to change. Fate would carry him across the ocean to a strange land. He willingly accepted the inevitability of his capture and a miserable life below the deck of the blue clipper ship. Kuntamba watched as his African brother with the flashing teeth drew near. He saw the soulless eyes of the chieftain and the concealed pistol hidden behind his back.

Before the couriers spoke, Kuntamba said, "I will trade myself for the ten African women chained in the ship's hold on one condition. I will only serve the leader of your ship, the man who watches me through the tube capped with glass. I will be his servant for two years. At the end of that time, he must free me." Although Kuntamba doubted that the captain would release him at the agreed time, the verbal commitment would suit his purposes for the present.

Kuntamba's message was translated and communicated to the captain as the dark runner watched and waited on the beach. On board the clipper ship, Captain Stouvall began to pace. His lust for money and the dark runner's offer presented a difficult choice. The idea of releasing ten prime and healthy females back into the African coast where they were likely to be caught by the next ship to visit the area was repugnant to his business sense. He had seen auctioneers blaspheme when thin, sickly slaves were driven onto the block. He knew that the dark runner, with his slim build and gaunt appearance, would fetch only a pittance. Stouvall understood the system and the cold logic of men who bought and sold human flesh.

Stouvall's pacing slowed as his confounding dual greed was overruled by his need for recognition. He was not a handsome man, and his personality was caustic as a bucket of lye. His need to bask in the esteem of others, to have at least the outward respect of the wealthy and powerful, was the motivation that drove him to compete in the most profitable venture of the era—the slave trade. His success in financial affairs had brought him neither fame nor admiration. Instead, recognition came to him from connivers, liars, and thieves.

In the dark runner, the ship master saw not only a chance to find favor with his countrymen, but an opportunity to watch them bend their knees to the power of his riches. Because he found no fault with himself or his actions, his inner vision was balanced on the scales of justice. With the thought of easy money flooding his mind, the captain made his decision.

He would gamble that the African would keep his word. Turning to Shepherd, the first mate, Stouvall ordered jubilantly: "Release the females on shore and ask their patron to return to the ship with you."

"But, captain..." Shepherd began to object.

The captain silenced him with a threatening glare.

An hour later, two rowboats ground their prows into the sandy shore. Ten African women jumped over the skiff's sides into the shallow water. The women moved slowly ashore, looking back frequently, unsure of what was expected of them. They grouped together, questioning, not sure if the hand-held weapons that killed from a distance were meant for them. When no motion was made to harm them, their confusion became tinged with baffled hope.

Kuntamba's sister broke into a run, the nine free women quickly following. Only she understood what was happening. Only she and her brother knew that the slavers waited to recapture them just beyond sight of Stouvall's clipper ship. Instead of running inland toward the arms of the slavers, she took an unlikely route straight up the rocky coast. Miles later, her would-be captors far behind, she and the other women turned inland toward the safety of her childhood home.

As she ran, she thought of Kuntamba, the captain, the sea, and the chains. At first the joy of her newfound freedom was tainted with concern for her brother. She worried that the sailing ship would carry him beyond her touch forever. During her life with Kuntamba, she had come to know many things. She understood that her brother's surrender was merely a prelude to a greater destiny. The knowledge lifted her spirits and enabled her mind to receive Kuntamba's thoughts and love. Kuntamba would thrive. His sister knew the power of his unraised hand and unspoken words.

She thought back to the moment when she had stepped from the rowboat, briefly meeting Kuntamba's eyes as she passed. She had felt a oneness cross between them, a brushing of kindred hearts which left a memory that neither time or distance could dim. It was that connection, and a lifetime of memories, that would allow them to touch each other's consciousness across the vast ocean.

CHAPTER FOUR

Captain Stouvall waited impatiently for the dark runner to step into the rowboat. Kuntamba stood quietly for over an hour. Finally, he turned and walked to the waiting rowboat. Stepping into the boat manned by Mr. Shepherd, the dark runner stood straight and stared out to sea, moving with the shift of the boat and the waves' rolling motion. As the small vessel glided across the shifting sea it looked, to Captain Stouvall, as if the dark runner was walking on water.

In that fleeting instant, Stouvall realized that his relationship with the dark runner who dared to negotiate with slavers would be far different than any he had experienced with other human beings. He winced inwardly, realizing he had classified the dark runner as human. He shrugged, blaming the English language for its lack of nomenclature and definitions.

Subconsciously, a new insight was bubbling and stirring. In time, it would find its way into the captain's thoughts. Eventually he would learn that, by negotiating with the dark runner, he had entered a situation that was only partly within his control. He was caught in a quandary that only men who plot and are driven by dishonest motives find themselves entwined in. Stouvall saw the dark runner as a possession to be guarded, concealed, and cared for. He desperately wanted to be in total command of the African's life, but if he starved or injured his prize asset, the dark runner might sicken or die. Stouvall debated whether the African should be chained below in the darkness, or if he should be brought up on deck where he could exercise and maintain his conditioning. It did not take Stouvall long to resolve his inner dilemma. The African would be given access to most of the ship. After all, there would be no escape once the *Ocean Breeze* reached the open sea.

Uneasy, the ship master looked up at the expressionless face of the native he would one day call Kuntamba. Diverting his stare, Stouvall wondered at his own discomfort, the same uneasy feeling he had felt when his clipper ship had been unable to outdistance the dark runner. He was gripped with restlessness, as if he was in a competition without rules.

Kuntamba nodded his head in assent when pointing fingers ordered him below deck. He didn't protest when Mr. Shepherd approached, dragging the chains that would secure his legs in an iron grip. After the first mate left, the dark runner looked around. He was in the hold, surrounded by the chained men, women, and children of his country. Dark eyes stared at him. Destined to be sold into slavery, they wondered why the holy man had permitted himself to be captured. Others disdainfully denied his sanctity. A few prayed silently for Kuntamba's blessing.

Wanting to comfort them, Kuntamba spoke. "Soon they will free me. In time, I will be able to help you. But know this: my life and yours have changed forever. The future is dark, but your children's children will thrive. You are the parents of a new people. Your pain, and that of succeeding generations, is the anguish of partition. Be courageous and of indomitable will and the foundations of our people's future will be unshakable."

Less than a day later, the frowning first mate returned, unlocked Kuntamba's leg irons and led him up on deck. This time, the ten foot chain was tethered to the forward mast. Kuntamba examined the painful weight of the iron chain. He wondered about the minds of men who could fashion such a merciless device. Twisting his body to face the wind, he heard the sounds that only chained humans can make.

A deep sadness washed over him as he realized that the ten women he had helped to free had been replaced with other villagers. He watched helplessly as they were pushed and dragged from sight.

For the first time in his life, Kuntamba questioned the god who lived within him and filled the universe. He wondered if god's law and purpose could be fulfilled by evil actions. His higher mind whispered to his doubting consciousness, telling him that there were no mistakes in a cosmos born from perfection. He learned that all experiences teach and test. He was reminded that in the fullness of time, all debts would be paid and that his task was to always follow his inner wisdom. He was left with a deep sense of knowing, his spiritual balance at the midpoint between deep sadness and elation.

This time, Kuntamba was the one who felt the probing stare of the captain as he tried to read the dark runner's reaction to the capture of the replacement slaves. Instead of anger or frustration, the ship's master saw deep misery in the dark runner's face. The weight of Kuntamba's expression almost forced the captain to step back. Captain Stouvall could not possibly know that a voiceless struggle between good and evil had begun deep inside of him.

CHAPTER FIVE

Hours later, Captain Stouvall guided his clipper ship into the north easterly flowing equatorial currents before directing Mr. Shepherd to take the helm. Stouvall had not felt the open ocean under his feet for three days. Looking seaward at the endless swells and the deep blue sky, an expansive sense of freedom washed over him. But it was tainted. His thoughts turned to the dark runner and the chains that held him. Pivoting abruptly, Stouvall walked over to Kuntamba, bent down, and unlocked the leg irons. Kuntamba stood quietly, acknowledging his release with a nod of his head. Rejecting the offer of food and water, Kuntamba turned, opened the hold, and eased himself back down into the squalid world of chained misery.

On deck, seamen noisily protested to the first mate. They were afraid that the dark runner would free his countrymen and bathe them in the blood of rebellion. When confronted, Stouvall submitted to their demands, arming himself and his men with pistols.

Having appeased the crew, the captain retired to his quarters. Lying back on his cot, he savored his financial success. His hold was full of living, breathing wealth. He had traded ten females for thirty young, strong slaves. He had no more rum to bargain with and the holy man would, if Stouvall's plans came to fruition, make him wealthy beyond his dreams. Yet something he could not define poisoned his feelings of accomplishment. He was the master of his own ship and he had the power of life or death over his living cargo. Only the dark runner seemed to be beyond his sphere of influence, yielding only because he chose to, not because he was moved by force or fear.

In the confining hold, African men, women, and children were crowded together. The *Ocean Breeze* was not designed to carry slaves, but to haul bulk goods whose mass made the ship sit low in the water, stabilizing the vessel in rough seas. Now the *Ocean Breeze* cut the water with more of her hull exposed. Consequently, the vessel rocked and pitched, throwing the captives against each other while testing the length of chains and tightening the hard iron against muscle and bone.

On deck, where fresh air, sunlight, and unlimited vistas were part of life on the sea, Stouvall wondered why the dark runner preferred the sunless, stagnant confines of the hold to the open sea and salt air. He worried that his prize property might become ill, but he couldn't bring himself to force Kuntamba up on deck. The captain saw the dark runner occasionally, and each time the African appeared to be in perfect health.

Stouvall's ruminations were interrupted by a shift in the wind and the flapping of sails as they went slack. He remembered how ships sailing the Ivory Coast sometimes paid an unexpected tariff for their cargo when the counterclockwise circling winds, born just north of the equator, blossomed into storms that chased ships across the sea. Many of the sailing vessels never again returned to home ports.

The feel of the air, the change in atmospheric pressure, and even his exhaled breath, told the captain that a storm front was approaching. Sounding the bell, he summoned all hands to the forward deck. The master of the ship ordered his crew to prepare for high winds and a raging sea. The sails were secured, decks cleared, and the portholes and holds were battened down.

In the dark interior of the ship, only chains and iron held the precious cargo in place. With the rise and fall of each swell, bodies tumbled and rolled as thrashing arms locked together for security. Others bent over as if trying to touch their toes, with only their hands locked on cold iron, desperately trying not to be thrown about. Amid the human upheaval, Kuntamba made his way through the twisting legs, passing the blood-drenched ankles and the staring, pleading eyes. He saw questions and fear, but the most dominant energy was anger.

When small ankles had lubricated circular bands of iron with blood, Kuntamba freed a foot or compressed a hand into a cylindrical shape so it could clear the iron bond and escape. He knelt to pass healing hands over open wounds and, with his voice, stilled their fears and calmed their anger. As the wind raged outside, he told them his story and why he was free of the chains. He told them the storm would pass and that he and nature would heal their wounds. He promised his food and water would be theirs. He advised his countrymen to expend their energy, anger, and determination in an effort to survive.

Finally, he said, "Humankind is on an eternal journey. Sometimes, when one race has the power to dominate another, the pace of the journey slows until wisdom is brought into balance with intelligence."

He continued. "We are the dominated race and are caught in a period of social ignorance and greed which will spread our people to every land. Our task is to learn, grow, and survive. If we are to thrive, we will have to learn new ways and strange languages. But what we must learn and imprint on the consciousness of our children is to never imprison or take advantage of another person for profit or any other reason." Kuntamba looked at his companions in bondage and saw only confusion and blank stares. His instructions had fallen on ears that were not ready to listen.

Abruptly, the *Ocean Breeze* lurched forward as its sails caught the wind that blew out of the west. Kuntamba was thrown back, causing him to dance a quick series of short steps. Just as he recovered his balance, the *Ocean Breeze* listed to the port side as a swirling gust caught the sails obliquely, driving the ship over on its side and testing the strength of the masts. Onward the clipper sailed, cutting a path through the surging waves. Sometimes the craft's port side rail was breached by the rising sea, causing her timbers to moan and creak in recovery.

Kuntamba listened to the sound of the ocean's water splitting and breaking over the decks and starboard side. The sea sounded like a hungry beast trying to either devour its prey, or to eject it from its fluid body. He timed the slap of the swells as they cut diagonally across the *Ocean Breeze's* profile, prompting the ship to groan in distress. The dark runner felt the motion of the sea with its mountains and shifting valleys of wetness. He found himself wanting to run, to stretch his legs and fill his lungs with the ocean's cool breath, but the desire passed quickly.

The dark runner knew that now was not the time to dream of running across the African countryside. He turned his attention to those around him, treating lacerations caused by chafing irons and wounds that exposed bone. He struggled against the diseases that plagued people who are forced to lie in their own excrement.

CHAPTER SIX

The ocean continued its sadistic motion, settling into long respites of relative stillness before exploding into a lifting twist of fury. Kuntamba forced open the hatch during one of the quiet lulls, letting in a blast of cold air and a flood of healing salt water. He went on deck to wash bloody garments and scavenge a few scraps of food and fresh water. The galley was empty. He filled his arms with dried meat and bread, returning to the hold where the hungry Africans huddled. Finishing his task, he returned to the deck. He wanted to watch and study the men who manned the ship and dared to confront the ocean's power.

What he saw was a paradox. The sailors, who treated slaves and sometimes each other with disdain and cruelty, were working together, risking their lives for the common good. Kuntamba wondered how bodies and minds could survive in the dual worlds of cowardice and bravery, brutality and sensitivity. He listened to the seamen's words, watched their body language, and he learned.

The dark runner's attention was drawn to the captain, the man he had bound himself to for two years of his life. Captain Stouvall knew he was being studied, but was too busy and tired to care. He was in a life or death struggle with the ocean, the winds, and the intermittent periods of driving rain.

One hundred miles to Stouvall's stern, an expanding mass of turbulent air was pulling strength from the warm, equatorial waters. The tempestuous atmosphere was pushing, almost chasing, the *Ocean Breeze* as the ship fled on an erratic course that, by the will of god or chance, mirrored every adjustment Captain Stouvall made in his course. The captain searched for a cross-current of air, hoping it would catch his sails and carry him farther north to quieter waters and safety. He worried that the storm's wake might usher in the unmoving air of the doldrums, leaving the ship's sails limp and the *Ocean Breeze* hostage to the ocean's whims.

Deciding to gamble, Stouvall spun the helm hard to starboard, guiding his ship across the equatorial current in a north-by-northwesterly direction. As Mr. Shepherd relieved him at the helm, Stouvall ran from one side to the other of the *Ocean Breeze's* heart-shaped midsection, listening to the strain on the sails and rigging.

The *Ocean Breeze* was a Baltimore clipper. She was fast and maneuverable, but she had never been tested in seas tormented by 75 mile per hour winds. Captain Stouvall did not relish pitting his investment, and the wealth of human cargo in his hold, against a violent, fickle, and inexhaustible sea. As the *Ocean Breeze* fought the relentless waves, the skipper questioned one of his earlier decisions. Normally, his ship's 255 foot length required at least thirty-five skilled sailors to man her around the clock. He had settled for twenty-eight men, of which eight barely knew port from starboard. With an approaching gale tormenting every timber of his ship, he hoped that his hunger for profit would not come back to haunt him.

Exhausted, Stouvall wondered if the storm born off the coast of Africa could be connected to this slave who had traded himself for the freedom of ten women. He remembered the African slaver saying the dark runner was a holy man with strange, mystical powers. A thought crossed the ship master's mind. Could the African be conjuring up this storm? A second thought suggested that maybe the dark runner should be thrown overboard where nature and the lashing sea could test the supposed holy man's powers. But his guile reminded him that casting the dark runner overboard might invoke the full fury of the storm gods, if they existed. Suddenly, as if the heavy seas wished to authenticate the captain's contemplations, a great swell lifted the *Ocean Breeze* high up on its crest before plunging the tiny vessel down into a valley surrounded by moving mountains of liquid death.

Turning to check on his helmsman, the captain bumped into Kuntamba. "Get out of my way," he yelled angrily as he shot out his left arm and open hand, catching the dark runner in the chest. To Stouvall's amazement, his 225 pounds barely moved the African's 145 pound body. Pretending he hadn't really tried to push his mystical captive out of the way, he demanded, "What do you want?"

"Food for the hungry," Kuntamba replied.

The captain was stunned. He didn't know that the dark runner spoke English. He also wasn't aware of the African's ability to apply a near perfect concentration in order to surmount any problem or task he chose to undertake. Cursing into the wind, Stouvall bristled, "Take what you need, and not one crumb more!"

The African watched as the burly captain took the helm and sent Mr. Shepherd forward to check the main sail. Kuntamba wondered if he could convince the captain that it was wiser to care for the living slaves than to let them die. If the captain agreed, that might indicate that the tiny spark that was the captain's soul could, over time, be encouraged to grow and light a new path. Time, circumstances, and the sea would determine Stouvall's final chance.

In the dimly lit area below deck, Kuntamba walked among the sick and injured. He dispensed dry bread, a chunk of salt pork, small green limes, and hope. With each visit to the hold, he succeeded in freeing a few more captives from the restraining irons and, with each visit, the health and value of the captain's hostage cargo increased.

Back on deck, the dark runner studied his captor with new intent. The captain had traded ten captive women for him and had allowed

Kuntamba to feed and care for his countrymen. Kuntamba wondered why a man, whose only motive was profit, would negotiate with him and no other person, black or white.

Seated on the damp deck, Kuntamba began to meditate. Slowly his subconscious mind produced a vision of his foot-race with the blue clipper ship. He saw the sails gulping the wind and the captain staring at him through a spy glass. Almost like a fog lifting, the captain's thoughts and intentions began to disclose themselves. Stouvall wanted to match the African's speed and endurance against men and their animals. Kuntamba now understood the captain's ultimate purpose in trading one slave for ten, yet a singular question remained.

What would any man gain by pitting a slave against a man or beast? Captain Stouvall couldn't claim the victories as his. It had to be something that fit in the white man's world, a world where liquid poison could buy another man's life.

CHAPTER SEVEN

Kuntamba looked out at the sea as a series of rolling waves assaulted the *Ocean Breeze's* port side. As the deck under his feet was forced deeper into the water and the entire ship was twisted by the convolutions of the immense waves, the dark runner realized the clipper ship could lose its struggle against the shifting ocean.

Moving nimbly across the wet surface, he watched crew members struggle to keep their balance on deck and battle the rush of sea water charging back into the ocean. He stared at other seamen as they fought sails that flapped dangerously in high winds. Turning quickly toward the sound of the aft lug sail ripping loose from its spar, Kuntamba watched in fascination as the sail curled around and up the jib, twisting in the wind, its thick cloth shredding like paper in the gale. The dark runner felt the pressure of the cascading sea and the ship's motion as its buoyancy fought the water's weight and the pull of gravity. He recognized the workmanship, skill, and planning that built a vessel that an angry sea could not dominate.

A new realization sprang from his observations. The captain had a depth that reached beyond greed and a need to dominate others. Kuntamba's opinion of the captain slowly gained perspective, which brought new questions. The captain's large body stood at the helm, fighting the sea for possession of the *Ocean Breeze*. The African wondered how a man could be cowardly enough to follow society's standard in the slave trade yet stare with unyielding courage and determination into the fury of the storm.

The captain seemed to have a quality that transcended mere survival. His uncompromising courage seemed undaunted by the possibility of death. Kuntamba recognized a stamina that could fight a raging sea for three days and nights with nothing to sustain that captain's body but a drenching wetness, salty water, and determination. Kuntamba wondered what past circumstances had forged Captain Stouvall's early life.

The dark runner worried about his countrymen below deck. He alone understood the trials, pain, and sorrow that lay ahead of them. He wondered if they would find the fine line that divides a callous hardness and affection. Would they separate courage from violence, or would his countrymen become hardened to the world around them?

Looking up, Kuntamba's attention fixed on a seaman who had dared to climb the aft mast in a foolhardy attempt to untangle a twisted lug sail. The sailor hugged the mast in a death grip as the *Ocean Breeze* tilted precariously to the port side. The dark runner prayed as an immense wave tore at the seaman's body with tons of rushing sea water. He was truly amazed that the fragile body of the seaman not only survived the oceanic attack, but immediately returned to the task at hand.

The anachronisms of courage and responsibility confused Kuntamba's understanding of right and wrong. He had difficulty comprehending how even a shred of goodness could survive in minds and souls darkened by greed and insensitivity. What kind of surroundings could so condition the slave traders that the misery, pain, and death of their prisoners did not awaken a glimmer of compassion in their hearts?

Kuntamba stared at the captain's shadowed body as the wind and rain pounded him relentlessly. Standing with one hand just below the mizzen course and the other gripping the spanker's rigging, the African began to move his body with the motion of the ship. Eventually he found the sea's rhythm and harmony, enabling him to see more than the captain's physical features.

As Kuntamba found a oneness with the vessel, an image of a young boy plowing a field without end slowly filled his vision. Looking closer, he saw the boy dragging bags of feed twice his size from a barn to waiting animals. As Kuntamba's vision changed, he saw the great hulk of a drunken man stagger toward the sleeping boy. Massive arms raised in anger mauled the cringing boy who would grow to become Captain Stouvall.

It surprised him that the boy refused to cry out in pain. He just seemed to endure. Kuntamba was uneasy. How could someone who had suffered so much inflict a lifetime of slavery on others? He began to understand how, in the captain's world, life was hard and unforgiving by its very nature. He had endured his lot in life; others should endure their own.

Captain Stouvall relaxed his grip on the helm. He had succeeded in guiding the *Ocean Breeze* out of the storm's main track. Peripheral winds still buffeted his ship but the worst was behind him. For the first time in days he thought of food and rest, but denied himself those luxuries until his inspection of the ship was complete.

Looking about, he saw the dark runner pointing at him. Inexplicably, the captain's mind churned back to his youth and the preachers who verbally expelled vile soliloquies that promised eternal damnation in a pit of fire. He remembered the long, bony, ecclesiastical fingers pointing, accusing, and identifying. He saw the burning eyes of religious fervor that had frightened him as a boy. From the preachers' zeal flowed an energy that spoke of superiority, dominance, and the power of belief. As a child, the captain had retreated into a frightened silence during the fire and brimstone sermons.

Kuntamba's pointing finger awakened an anger in Stouvall that had lain dormant for decades. The anger carried an almost tangible urge to inflict pain on anyone who dared to accuse him. The captain swore, his need to punish carrying him toward the unmoving figure of Kuntamba. Coming closer, Stouvall realized the pointing finger was not fixed on him, but on the sea.

Turning his tired body, he expected to see one of his drowned seamen being dumped overboard. Instead, he was met by a mountainous wave that crushed him into the deck, submerging the *Ocean Breeze* to her rails, a creaking moan from her hull unheard by all but the captives below deck.

As the inundating torrent of water flowed back to the sea, the clipper ship rebounded, driving much of the water from the *Ocean Breeze's* deck. The surge did not, however, go empty-handed; it carried six seamen in its froth and hungrily pulled at the captain's fallen body. The force of the wave pressed Stouvall against the rail, where the churning water struggled to lift his bulk and sweep him out to sea. The captain fought, but the water was everywhere. It smothered the motion of his arms, obscured his vision, and filled the air he was trying to breathe.

Stouvall began to flail about in search of an anchor, but instead of wood or a woven rope, his fingers found a long thin arm with a narrow hand and slender fingers. The seemingly fragile fingers tightened in an inescapable grip that held him until the *Ocean Breeze* finished its upward motion and settled at the waterline. Slowly the hand relaxed, and the captain looked into the dark eyes of his savior.

It was an almost impossible moment for the master of the ship. His captive, the dark runner who was not quite human, had saved his life. He didn't know whether to honor, praise, or ignore him. Slowly, the captain's strength returned and with it a host of old memories. Stouvall recalled a slave ship lost at sea and captive Africans chained and starving to death on a ghost ship without a living captain.

The captain refused to let reasoning intervene. He thought, "I know why the dark runner rescued me. He needs to survive for his countrymen and himself." Stouvall turned sharply away, not thanking Kuntamba or even giving him a glance of recognition. But Kuntamba knew that when the still calm that follows every storm had turned crashing waves into gentle splashes and the full moon filled the water's surface with reflected gold, the captain would rethink his actions.

In his cabin, Stouvall puzzled how the thin African whom he had never seen take a mouth full of nourishment could, with just one hand, prevent his 220 pounds from being dragged overboard by the rush of hundreds of thousands of cubic feet of water being sucked back into the sea. A strange force had held the dark runner in place while their two hands were locked in an embrace. With the questions came doubts in his own belief system and a curiosity that would someday seek the source of Kuntamba's strength.

CHAPTER EIGHT

After the storm, the *Ocean Breeze* settled back into its rhythmic response to the tides and trade winds. The ship was headed towards the Carolinas. Stouvall was now short-handed, having lost six seamen in the storm. He prayed his ship and the remaining crew would not have to endure another struggle with a hurricane's colossal power.

The captain started to go below deck to check on his living cargo, but Kuntamba, standing by the hold's door met him and said, "All is well below. They are alive and they are healthy." Normally the master of the ship would have pushed aside any man to see for himself, but the dark runner's eyes and the ring of his voice somehow disarmed Stouvall's ability to question or challenge him. What the captain did not know was that, in the belly of the ship, more than one hundred slaves moved about unimpaired by chains or tethers.

For the crew, it was finally time for relaxation. The course was set and the sails were full. Once again, the *Ocean Breeze* practically sailed herself. Captain Stouvall continued his observation of the dark runner. He watched as members of the crew intentionally bumped into the African, then cursed him for causing the contact. He watched the slave turn, answering insults and abuse with an expression that reflected the understanding of a wise parent to a mischievous child.

As the weeks passed, the ship's master noticed that his sailors had come to accept the dark runner's presence. They began to move out of his path when he glided silently toward them. Some of the crew even lowered their eyes slightly when Kuntamba looked in their direction. Captain Stouvall himself began to feel a respect for his captive that surpassed the slave and master relationship. He didn't know it, but his study of the dark runner had caused his feelings for Kuntamba to move from a quiet respect to a begrudging admiration.

Recognizing the subtle changes in the captain, the dark runner wondered if the unseen tendrils of the ship master's nascent humanity could survive under the glare of slave traders in the marketplace and auction blocks. Would greed and insensitivity further darken his heart when the bidding began? Only the gods knew, but it did not matter because the captain was caught up in a series of events that he had already set in motion.

It was impossible for Stouvall's greedy mind to understand the forces his meeting with the dark runner had released, and if he had, he would not have comprehended their meaning. But his experiences with Kuntamba and his observation of him were stirring questions of right and wrong deep in his subconscious. The questions were still seeds that would one day birth a hunger for wisdom in his barren soul. The seeds, if they survived, would mature into a spiritual quest that had no strength, just potential. Only time and the tests born of existence could cast the first light of wisdom on the captain's dark soul. The time was approaching—the coast of South Carolina had just been sighted.

The sun returned to the task of warming the western horizon while dragging behind its shadowy tail an exact measure of darkness that would not be repeated for another year. The *Ocean Breeze's* anchor clattered on the deck before it sank into the still water and bit into the ocean's bottom. Stouvall looked toward shore. A low settling fog obscured his view.

Tomorrow was Monday. Stouvall knew that when the sun rose, the auctioneer who made a living from his commissions, the blacksmith, and the disguise artists would have already spent several hours preparing the slaves for sale. Phony medical certificates authenticating each slave's perfect health, or explained that a limp was only temporary, were being stuffed into the pockets of various sea captains. Captain Stouvall, waiting offshore, would not be able to take advantage of such deceits.

Determined to check on the condition of his cargo, Stouvall climbed down into the hold. He entered what should have been a world of misery, but instead of darkness there was a world of flickering candles. He saw empty manacles and African eyes staring at him with trepidation. Turning to his left, the captain bumped into Kuntamba.

Startled, he stepped back, pushing a stabbing fear from his mind. He was alone. There were many slaves, free of their chains. If they chose, they could kill him quickly. It was a moment of acute vulnerability. Then logic returned. The slaves had nowhere to go. Members of his crew, as well as other slavers on shore, would relish killing rebellious slaves just for the excitement it would give them.

Looking up toward the deck, Captain Stouvall called, "Send down the iron worker." Spinning around, the ship's master studied the waiting faces and shifting forms in the flickering light. Before he could clear his throat to speak, Kuntamba's words interrupted him.

"For as long as I have cared for my African brothers and sisters in the bowels of this ship, they have been free of the iron that cuts and scars. They will not run! They do not know in which direction home lies. They desire freedom, but know the endless waters stand between them and freedom's gifts. I have told them their suffering will be great and their homeland will be visited only in the stories of their descendants. They know they are captives and they expect a lifetime of labor and cruelty."

"Still they long for the sun's bright warmth, the sight of the clear blue sky, and they hunger for the feel of mother earth under their feet. I have told them that the most precious stones are born deep beneath the earth where the weight of the mountains slowly forges its beauty and value. They know the burden of oppression may bow their legs and bend their backs. Their only prayer is that adversity will not darken their souls."

"They understand they are entering a period of trials that will either find them wanting, or hone them into men and women whose souls will commune with the gods while fulfilling their destinies, which is to become more than men and women. Instead of chains, bind them with rope."

Kuntamba, reacting to the captain's manner, said, "Women will admire your humanity and men will marvel at your courage and the power that must belong to a man whose slaves do not challenge his authority."

The dark runner watched as the captain's eyes took on a new expression, his chest puffing out ever so slightly. In a gruff voice, the captain replied, "Have it your way, but if one slave bolts, you will be the first to die."

In his heart, the captain knew it was a lie. He would not kill Kuntamba, and the African knew it, too. Behind the captain, the ship's ironworker clattered down the ladder into the hold. He started to address his captain, but was cut off by Stouvall. "Go back to your original task," the captain said.

The captain stood on deck facing the shore. His first mate, Mr. Shepherd, approached and waited for direction. "Take three men and go ashore," Stouvall said. "Claim two holding pens. If they are dirty, clean them. I have lost too much good property in those disease-ridden, urine-soaked cages." He added self-righteously, "Some captains only feed the maggoty remains of rotting flesh in a flour and water gravy to their goods."

Mr. Shepherd stared at the captain, puzzled. Since when did the captain care what happened to the slaves? As Shepherd walked away, it occurred to Stouvall that he never had been concerned with the cleanliness of the holding pens before, but he shrugged it off. It was just good business sense, he told himself.

As Shepherd and three other sailors prepared to go onshore, Stouvall called them over, changing his first order. "Forget the pens. Spread the word to all potential buyers that the *Ocean Breeze* will dock at midmorning with a hold full of the most healthy, well-fed, unscarred slaves ever to arrive in South Carolina."

"Tell them," Stouvall said, "that if they want the best, they'll have to pay accordingly. The auction will take place on the *Ocean Breeze's* deck at dusk." Stouvall preferred the twilight hour because he knew its obscuring light would hide the rigors of capture and the arduous sea journey.

As he watched the first mate and three sailors row ashore, it occurred to Stouvall that everything about this voyage was different. He had not once closely examined his captives since the beginning of the trip home, a practice that was conducted daily in the past. His last brief visit to the hold had revealed nothing about the health of his cargo. He had only Kuntamba's word that his captives were in good condition. That would have to be good enough because the appraiser was due on board ship soon.

CHAPTER NINE

Later that evening, the ship's gang plank was lowered. Across its length walked 22 prospective buyers. They saw a sparkling clean deck and a raised platform surrounded by chairs. After everyone was seated, the hold's heavy door was intentionally thrown back so that it crashed loudly against the deck. The sharp sound added an element of fear and expectation to the flickering lantern light and the sound of a loose sail flapping mournfully on a nearby ship.

A woman had joined a group of the patrons onboard, drawn by the promise of excitement. Others came out of fear and morbid curiosity. Only one woman, an elegant lady, came to care for the sick and the dying. Her skin was white, but the blood of Africa could be found in her veins.

Knowing his buyers were all men, Captain Stouvall selected a young female with ample charms for his first offering. Her round dark eyes strained to see in the darkness. A push of the first mate's hand sent her into a crouch that a jungle cat would have admired. The patrons could see every detail of her musculature. She possessed a sensuality that hypnotized whether she was in motion or poised for defense.

The bidding was breathtakingly fast and furious. The air was palpable with passion and frustration. Captain Stouvall had created an aura of expectation and mystery in order to maximize his profits. He had hired an auctioneer who was experienced in the slave trade, capable of anticipating buyers' questions and exploiting their appetites. Immediately, he reacted when a patron leaned in for a better view, prodding the dark flesh so that it could be more closely appraised. He knew when a buyer's hand raised spectacles to the bridge of a nose, signaling a heightened interest which would soon turn to cash.

The second offering brought on deck was also a female. She was tall and statuesque. As she climbed up onto the platform, the lantern light surrounded her and illuminated her magnificent physique in a smoky, ethereal haze. She slowly raised herself to her full height and took three steps forward, looking down into the eyes of those who would buy her body.

As she moved forward, chairs scraped backwards, retreating from her dominance. Even the auctioneer was dumbfounded, but he leapt to his task. Instinctively he turned toward the section where the middle-aged gentry sat. His voice rang out. "Bidding starts at 500 dollars." Before his words could die, the opening bid was met and raised until silence ended the bidding at 3300 dollars.

Before the purchasing agent's servant went to claim the statuesque African, his master admonished him. "Treat her well. Let no man touch her, and do not mark, brand, or scar her. She will be traveling inland where her services will bring me a continuous income for many years." The new owner of the elegant slave had an interest in a brothel. He knew that his investment would be returned within thirty days.

As she was led away, her eyes sought Kuntamba, her heart listening to his unspoken words. "You are on a journey into the white man's world," he told her, his heart heavy with sadness. "It is a place where imbalance rules. You may travel the low places, but if you always remember that your body is the instrument of your soul, your divine inner spirit, you will endure. Others' actions cannot tarnish the perfect. Your life may be decided by others, but never will they touch the real you." With one last look at Kuntamba, she turned toward her future with fearless sight and the knowledge that the slave was more than the master.

The dark runner looked down and closed his eyes. He saw the future and felt a slight tremor move the length of his body. His mind was dark with ominous clouds that obscured his vision. Slowly his emotion and feelings quieted, allowing his spirit to look further into the future.

His revelation beheld an ocean of pain that men and the slaves they controlled were rushing toward. The sea of pain invited those who lived for the conquests of the present into limitless pits of despair. Willingly, with outstretched arms, white and black men alike embraced the endless lake of darkness and were devoured in its soulless depths.

The vision left Kuntamba shaken. His sensitive being felt the pain that would be endured. It momentarily overwhelmed him, radiating outward. The people standing nearby inadvertently felt its pulse and withdrew, their minds suddenly full of woe, fear, and impending disaster. When Kuntamba stirred, he stared into the hazel orbs of Matilda Jones, the white-skinned woman who had come to heal and comfort the sick. Intuitively, she knew why the captives had remained healthy and she knew she was looking into the face of a holy man.

Captain Stouvall saw something in the woman's expression as she made visual contact with Kuntamba. Was she interested in buying the African or was it something else? Responding to her attention, Stouvall made it clear that Kuntamba was not for sale. He had other plans for him.

Overhearing the captain's words, the auctioneer immediately paused in his rhetoric and said, "We have a contract. My fee is based on the sale of the entire shipment." Stouvall flinched as if he had suddenly been drenched with ice water. He sprang from his seat, pushing toward the agent.

Frightened, the auctioneer backed away, his frail frame shaking. "But," he equivocated, "Your harvest is of such high quality that the commissions I have already earned make it possible for me to overlook one thin slave."

It wasn't the auctioneer's words that stayed Stouvall's hand, but the sudden silence of the buyers and their female companions that turned the captain back. Stouvall nodded brusquely at the auctioneer, lowered his glaring eyes and sat down. He slowly began to relax, wondering if the dark runner possessed a hidden power that controlled him. He reassured himself that his only interest in Kuntamba lay in the money the dark runner would win in foot races, no more.

But another image tingled in the back of his mind—the memory of the woman who came to minister to those who were about to be sold into slavery. When she looked at Kuntamba, something happened. Stouvall reviewed the image several times, trying to understand what had taken place, but the meaning escaped him.

Stouvall shrugged impatiently, allowing his greed to resurface. The dark runner was not for sale because the southern gentry will soon discover what would happen if they dared to pit their horses against the African. The captain reluctantly admitted to himself that Kuntamba was a most unusual individual. As his mind cleared, Stouvall leaned back and closed his eyes. Once again, Matilda Jone's face floated across his mental screen.

Stouvall tried to resist the recurring pictures of her, but his memory revealed more than her compassion. He recalled her unadorned beauty, as striking as a brilliant sunset. He pushed her from his mind, knowing from past experience that women were not interested in him as a mate. A few had won his affection, only to leave in the middle of the night with a sizable portion of his wealth. Their actions confirmed Stouvall's lifelong distrust of women, beginning when his mother deserted him at an early age. His distrust of women was blinding him to the soft knock of love in Matilda's understanding hazel eyes.

The auctioneer stared at the burly captain, uneasy. His discriminating observation fell on Kuntamba—a fixed and penetrating stare. The African felt the probing glare and knew the man possessed a power, but it was a power from the darkest regions of his soul.

The agent was not alone in his questioning. Everyone onboard the ship wondered what protected Kuntamba from the auctioneer's hammer.

Only Matilda, possessed of a maturity of spirit that allowed her to see beyond mere physical appearances, understood. She knew that the dark runner was a holy man whose mere presence could uplift those who were beginning to tire of life's competitive drive for wealth and property.

By the standards of the time, Matilda was considered a spinster. Her father was a minister, and her mother a mulatto. Matilda had lived in the north where her father had attempted to immerse her in teachings of the bible. Where he saw the letter of the law, Matilda saw truths concealed in parables. He claimed the right to interpret the bible because of his training in theology. She did not interpret—she knew. Her religious foundations were rooted in a participation in universal law, while her father's insights clung to cliffs that rose from fear and spiritual myopia.

When Kuntamba looked into her eyes, his heart beat faster. Not because he thought he had found a life mate, but because he had discovered a kindred spirit whose very presence shattered the spiritual isolation he had endured all of his life. In Matilda he found a fellow traveler on the path of enlightenment, another soul that had pierced the veils of materialism and worldly pain.

He instantly knew that their paths were merely crossing and that they would only experience each other's nearness in their minds. He understood that her life embodied service and compassion while his physical journey encompassed observation and guidance that would silently stir the consciousness of those who were ready to embrace the awakening divine fragment that lives within all humankind.

Rising from her seat at the edge of the auctioneer's stage, Matilda approached Captain Stouvall and complimented him on the health of the slaves. She then asked him an odd question. "Do slaves have souls?"

When he didn't answer, she smiled and returned to shore, but not before checking the *Ocean Breeze's* registry. She sensed that the captain was on the verge of entering the unseen world of self-mastery, a place where inner turmoil, regret, emotional distress and loneliness dominate.

If Stouvall was strong enough, he would discover that his passions, greed, and fears were nothing but bars imprisoning his soul. Matilda would wait until his inner battle had ended and a more enlightened man was forged. Not until then would she allow the tremor she felt when she saw the ship's master mature and ripen into love. She accepted the captain's dark past as a harvester and trader of slaves just as she understood his relationship with the lean slave would result in his becoming a better man. She knew that evil is a darkness of the soul and it cannot exist in the presence of inner light.

The water lapped against the rowboat. Matilda felt the cool, dark air against her body. Time would tell, she knew, and was content to wait.

CHAPTER TEN

The *Ocean Breeze* sat high in the water. The holds were empty and the crew was celebrating onshore. Released from his responsibilities as a caregiver, Kuntamba was restless. He approached the captain and asked permission to speak. Stouvall nodded. Kuntamba said, "I need to run and feel the heart of this new land pulsing through the soles of my feet. I need to reenergize my body with its sweet air and recapture the feeling of motion that arises from my own effort."

"I give my word that I will return and fulfill my promise. Do not worry. No hands will capture me and no lead ball will find my flesh. When the morning sun rises, I will be standing on this vessel in the exact same place."

It was not in Stouvall's nature to trust anyone. Still, the dark runner had saved his life, enriched his purse, and although he would not admit it, Kuntamba was the first person in his life that he did not mistrust. Stouvall believed the dark runner's words when he promised to return, but it was Matilda's question, "Do slaves have souls?", that enabled him to give the African a night of freedom.

With a wave of his hand, the captain set the dark runner free to race across the land. For a fleeting moment, Stouvall did not care if the African came back or not. When he looked around, the African was gone. Across the gangplank and down the dock, a quick spirit carried the dark runner into the thick underbrush. With a great inhalation of fresh air and a sense of exhilaration, he faded into the darkness.

During the night, teenagers ran in Kuntamba's wake, spewing hateful epithets. When adults called out, "Runaway slave!" the words were followed immediately by the report of badly aimed rifles. But before the weapons could be reloaded, the elusive target slipped from view, leaving some wondering if an actual escaped slave had really crossed their field of fire or if it was simply their imagination

Once free of the aura of corruption that permeated the harbor, the slave pens, brothels and bars, Kuntamba felt an almost ecstatic sense of freedom. With the unbridled liberty came thoughts of his homeland. He recalled the stories of the old ones who spoke of humanity's beginnings in a time beyond the reach of imagination, beginnings that led to a long history of migration, cultural development, war and destruction. The ancient energy had survived the ages, still thriving in Kuntamba's time. From it sprang the misery of women who had little control over their own bodies, birthing brutal tribal kings and forcing them to welcome greedy foreigners. But in this new land, the air was still charged with a vitality that exists when nature's harmony is undisturbed by man's greed and spiritual blindness.

Kuntamba ran all night. He ran in a great, sweeping arc that carried his revitalized body through virgin hardwood forests, across tumbling streams, and down into lush, green valleys.

Early the next morning, Captain Stouvall stepped on deck and looked across the bow of the *Ocean Breeze.* Standing in the shadows, he saw Kuntamba. He studied the African carefully. The faint light seemed to make more of the details of his body and expression visible than the pre-dawn light should have allowed.

He was pleased that Kuntamba had kept his word, but his pleasure had two roots. The first was an unspoken internal satisfaction in the African's presence, and the second lay in the world of gambling. During the night, Stouvall had engaged in a wager that only the dark runner could honor.

The word *honor* loomed in the captain's mind, demanding a definition. Stouvall knew if he had been a prisoner who had been freed for a night, he would not have returned. Yet the dark runner had kept his promise in spite of what waited for him; enslavement and being the property of another. For an instant, the big captain thought he understood honor.

Just as quickly, his thought process fragmented. He visualized the dark runner in a strange land without friends or family. Kuntamba had to return after all, Stouvall rationalized. Preservation of life was the strongest instinct.

These concepts made the captain uncomfortable. He had just admitted that slaves have families who would help in the time of need, and he had used the word *human*. He tried to retreat from the realization he had just touched on, but its truth could not be denied. Stouvall felt strangely depressed. One of the foundations of his internal world had just been fractured, leaving his frame of reference in a position of uncertainty.

Kuntamba stood nearby, silently prompting his captor with unspoken wisdom. He understood the duality of the captain's inner struggle. The dark runner knew Stouvall would either remain in the world of ignorance or find the courage to seek new truths and stand alone. The captain had partially surrendered the shield of superiority that permits one man to blind himself to another man's misery. He was beginning to think of Africans as human, as part of a family, yet he still struggled with the concept of slaves having souls. Subconsciously, he knew that if he had a soul, so must slaves. He missed the love of the family that he never had.

Out of the silence, Kuntamba spoke. "Do you wish me to run today?"

Stouvall stared at Kuntamba, collecting his thoughts. "Yes," he replied, wondering how the dark runner knew a wager had been made.

After the slave auction onboard the *Ocean Breeze*, Captain Stouvall had joined several of his men in a saloon on land. Everyone in the area already knew the big captain of the *Ocean Breeze* had received more money for his African harvest than any other slave ship that had ever docked in South Carolina.

Thieves, gamblers, and outright robbers all came to the saloon in search of their own harvest. They didn't know that most of the revenue earned from the auction was locked in a safe in the captain's quarters. They also didn't know that Captain Stouvall was a master in the art of deceit.

The captain and Mr. Shepherd were seated in a dark corner where they could watch the crowd without being fully observed. Scattered around the dingy, foul-smelling structure, the *Ocean Breeze's* remaining seamen positioned themselves for a long night of drinking and watching.

At first, the captain and Shepherd spoke in careful, whispered tones. When the sound level of the saloon fell, they knew they had an audience. A few hours later, after many drinks had been served and tossed back, their conversation grew louder. Captain Stouvall began to brag in slightly slurred speech about a horse he owned back in New England. He boasted of its speed and stamina, loudly proclaiming that there wasn't a horse in the South that could keep up with his gray mare. Shepherd pretended to openly challenge the captain's assertion, yielding only when Stouvall's swaying hulk glowered down at him.

Sitting a short distance away, Scarsdon, a gambling man, listened carefully to Stouvall and Shepherd's conversation. The gambler prided himself on his knowledge of horseflesh and his riding ability. He owned a string of horses, among which was an extraordinary stallion that was currently stabled in the livery down the street from the saloon. He believed with good reason that his five-year-old stallion was the finest steed in the Carolinas, and possibly the South.

Scarsdon had amassed enough wealth racing his stallion to refurbish his plantation and purchase an additional fifty slaves. When he heard the big captain gloat, he turned toward Stouvall's table and said in a friendly voice, "Captain I could not help but hear you speak about your mare. Would you be interested in a little wager?"

Stouvall considered the tall, wiry man who addressed him and replied with feigned drunkenness. "Come a little closer so I can see your face." Then the captain added, "Sadly, High Socks died a year ago this very night."

Seeing an opportunity to engage the captain in a wager had just evaporated, Scarsdon replied, "It's a sad day when a man's prize race horse dies. Such a shame. She might have been the perfect broodmare for Irish Whiskey. I named him that because I traded a case of the best Irish liquor money can buy for him when he was just a yearling."

Stouvall studied the man. "Your stallion—European stock, eh?"

Squinting in the dim light to see the captain's face, Scarsdon almost spit out his answer. "He's from the purest bloodlines ever produced in Europe or America."

Leaning forward, Stouvall replied, "Oh, yes. My mare ran some of that European stock right into the ground. As soon as they hit the hills and rough terrain, they folded. No guts, no stamina! In fact, I had a slave back home whose only job was to care for High Socks. He used to cut across country on foot just to watch High Socks outdistance those blooded horses."

Scarsdon started to answer with heat, then hesitated, smelling a wager. He had several animals in his string that could work cutting stock and herding cattle all day long. He had ridden them at a gallop from sunrise to sunset. Analyzing the situation, Scarsdon laid his trap. "I've never seen a man or slave who could wear down one of my cutting horses."

Stouvall rocked back on his chair and laughed. "Hell, I've seen nigra women fleeing the slavers who could outlast and outdistance cutting horses."

Scarsdon was hooked. The suggestion that a black subhuman slave could outrun a white man on a fast and well-conditioned horse was more than his pride could endure. Scarsdon smelled money and longed to teach the Northerner a lesson. His voice lost its friendliness. "I have the horses and a plantation with one hundred and ten slaves working my fields. I am willing to wager everything I have against the money you collected at last night's auction. You produce the slave, male or female, and I will ride against your entry myself." Scarsdon's voice was deliberately loud, knowing that the idea of a large wager would excite the locals and make it difficult for the captain to refuse without loss of face.

The captain's crew gathered nearby. Several of them became angry. One seaman declared, "Captain, if you throw our money away on an impossible bet, you better be prepared to sail the *Ocean Breeze* all by yourself."

Stouvall's face was dead serious. He rocked his chair down hard, jamming its front legs into the wooden slats that passed for a floor. He looked at Scarsdon for a long, long moment, then turned to his seamen. "You signed on for the round trip. If you are not on board the *Ocean Breeze* when she's ready to sail, you better never let me lay eyes on you again for I will have you hanged."

The sailors retreated sullenly, but Stouvall knew the discussion wasn't over. The captain turned back to Scarsdon.

"I don't see the deed to your plantation on the table in front of me. How do I know it's worth anything at all?"

Scarsdon smiled. He presumed the captain was trying to find a way out of his predicament. "My place is fifty miles from here. I will provide the horses and we can leave right now. If you do not agree that my land, crops, mansion, and slaves are worth at least $100,000, I'll call off the wager."

Stouvall appeared to shift uncomfortably in his chair before replying. "If you are so sure of your stallion, you must be willing to give odds."

"I will give you three to one odds on the condition, that if I produce my deed to the property before the race, you will seal the bet now."

Stouvall rubbed his palms against his thighs as if drying sweat from them. He looked at his first mate. Mr. Shepherd blurted, "Don't do it, captain! It's a fool bet!"

Stouvall responded, "I would advise you to listen closely to what I am about to say, Mr. Shepherd. Go back to the ship and wait for my return. Do it now!"

Standing abruptly, Shepherd bumped into the table, spilling Stouvall's drink. The first mate jumped back, barely escaping the captain's thick arm as it lashed out at him. Appearing frightened, Shepherd hurried to the sea and the shelter of the *Ocean Breeze*. The captain's voice followed him. "We will finish this later!"

Shepherd hoped Stouvall knew what he was doing.

Scarsdon believed that the captain felt trapped in a situation from which his manhood would not permit him to withdraw. Certain that he had Stouvall cornered, Scarsdon loudly pressed his offer. "Do we have a wager, captain, or is your story of slaves outrunning horses just a fantasy born in a bottle of liquor?"

The crowd laughed and jeered. One loud heckler behind the crowd mocked the captain in a simulated female voice. "Oh captain, you're so big and strong. Please don't back out now." The voice changed to a deep baritone. "I need some of that easy money, too."

"These Northerners are all talk and no show," bellowed another agitator.

Knowing it was time to lock his wager in place, Stouvall lurched to his feet and thundered, "If any man here questions my courage, let him step forward now!" A long silence followed, broken only by the shifting of onlookers.

"Do we have a wager or not?" Scarsdon demanded.

Stouvall glared at the sneering faces, turned his eyes downward and mumbled, "We have a wager if..." His voice trailed off.

Thinking the captain was completely buffaloed and anxious to close the deal, Scarsdon prodded. "If what?"

The captain slowly raised his eyes to meet Scarsdon, feigning hesitant fear. "If you do the riding and I set the conditions of the race, it's a bet."

Scarsdon had intended to ride in the race anyway. He could think of no course his stallion could not travel more easily than any man, replied, "here is my hand on it"? "Let all these men be my witnesses."

With the meeting of palms and a quick, painful withdrawal of Scarsdon's numb hand, the race was set. For the rest of the night and most of the next day, the two men rode toward Scarsdon's plantation. Stouvall's heart raced with the excitement a man feels when examining a property he is about to acquire.

CHAPTER ELEVEN

During the 50 mile journey, the only sounds were the rhythm of hooves striking the earth and the exhalation of air from the horses' nostrils as their bodies labored under the weight of their human burdens and the relentless strain of maintaining a full gallop. Stouvall struggled to adapt to the gait of his horse, cursing his sea legs and a sense of balance best adapted to a shifting deck on a rolling sea.

Gradually his childhood riding skills returned, allowing the captain to find a comfort zone and present a passable level of horsemanship to the scrutiny of his greedy companion. He carefully evaluated his opponent's riding ability, attempting to ascertain if Scarsdon knew when to spare his horse and when to urge him on, if he sat easily in the saddle or if his weight fought against the powerful stallion's stride. Finally, the sea captain turned his critical eye to the great stallion. He saw no flaws in the animal, just a magnificent living machine honed by perfect breeding and professional conditioning into a formidable competitor.

The confident plantation owner had made two major blunders: he had agreed to let the captain set the time and conditions of the race, and he had offered to show Stouvall his plantation. The captain knew that the long ride would both tax and tire Scarsdon and his stallion. The sea captain's strategy was simple. He would give the plantation a cursory examination, and then insist that they return immediately so the race could begin shortly after their arrival at the *Ocean Breeze's* anchorage.

Unaware of the captain's plans, Scarsdon looked forward to spending the night on his goosedown mattress in the master suite of his plantation house. He intended to begin the return journey the next day, riding one of his many horses with the racing stallion in tow. He savored the prospect of breaking Stouvall and owning the captain's ship. He envisioned himself standing on the *Ocean Breeze's* deck as he gave orders to the financially ruined captain to sail back to Africa where black gold could be harvested for the auction block.

Arriving at Scarsdon Manor, the plantation owner took great pride in explaining every detail of his home and the surrounding lands. He hoped to lure the captain into a side bet—the *Ocean Breeze* against a tract of land that he had paid for, but not received the title. Scarsdon's pleasure in describing his vast wealth was suddenly replaced by irritation.

Dismounting by the stables, Scarsdon handed Irish Whiskey's reins to a slave who had been rubbing down a mare that was about to foal. Behind him, Stouvall blared, "I have seen enough. Your plantation is easily worth $100,000. Show me the deed of ownership so we can start back."

Scarsdon stood, dumbfounded.

"I intend to start the race tomorrow at noon," Stouvall informed him, "with or without you."

Scarsdon balked. "But my horse is tired and I must eat and rest before we return."

Stouvall smiled slightly, countering, "Are you forfeiting the race?"

"Never!" Scarsdon's face turned red with anger. He wanted to ask for at least a few hours of rest, but the expression on Stouvall's face silenced him.

Calling to the slave who was walking Irish Whiskey away, Scarsdon ordered that the stallion be unsaddled and another of his favorite horses readied for a long ride. Turning to the captain, Scarsdon inquired sarcastically, "Do you mind if I water my horses, including the one you're riding, and give them some grain before we start back?"

Stouvall answered in an affectedly friendly voice. "Certainly not! I admire men who care for their stock."

Those were the last words exchanged between the two men for a very long time. Within minutes, the two silent men and three horses were moving east toward the sea.

Repressed anger deafened the men to the creaking saddle leather and the voices of nature around them. Each mind was filled with turmoil, plotting, and the race to come. Scarsdon had an additional worry—he suddenly feared that Stouvall really did own a slave who could outrun a horse.

Always speculating and imagining the worst, Stouvall assumed that Scarsdon was planning to ambush his race entrant if it looked like Irish Whiskey might lose. He had ordered Shepherd to position the *Ocean Breeze's* crew along the 50-mile course that would test man against beast. Using the word "man" in relation to Kuntamba was distasteful to Stouvall, causing him to change the word to African.

Although the two men were separated by less than twenty yards, the distance was made larger by their enmity. It was this growing rage that would give Kuntamba a stake in the wager.

Riding his powerful stallion, Irish Whiskey, Scarsdon neared the starting line just before the sun reached its zenith. A boisterous group of locals gathered to make their final wagers and to see the slave that dared to challenge a white man and the best horse in the Carolinas. Irish Whiskey had raced many times before. The steed loved to run. It was in his blood. He knew when a race was near. Irish Whiskey snorted, sniffing the air in search of the scent that horses release in their nervousness before a race begins. The air was void of the odor that set his heart pounding and his body taut in anticipation.

A hush settled over the gathering at the appearance of Captain Stouvall and the slightly built slave that he had refused to sell. "If my slave wins," the captain began, "you will give me the deed to your plantation and all of its stored grains and fibers, as well as ownership papers on all the slaves who reside there."

Scarsdon's reply rang with bluff authority. "After I win, you will transfer all the receipts from the slave auction to me, as well as your title to the *Ocean Breeze*, after which the ship will be physically released to me."

Stouvall caught Scarsdon's ploy to alter the bet. "No! The odds are three to one. I will give you an amount equal to one-third the value of your total wager, which was set by you at $100,000."

Scarsdon grimaced and turned his horse to the starting line. To his right, the dark runner stepped back from the same line and approached his legal owner. At that very moment, a pistol was fired into the air. The great gray horse broke into a gallop, disappearing into a wooded area with his dark-souled owner on his back.

Stouvall bellowed, "Go! He's getting away from you!" The captain was enraged. Only the knowledge that his wealth was now dependent on the strange African restrained his hand and silenced his tongue.

Kuntamba would not move—he had a request. He knew that many thousands of his African countrymen had been brought to this land of lush vegetation. He knew their African language, and even the memory of their homeland, would soon be lost in the graveyards of America. He accepted the fact that few, if any, slaves would ever return to the land of their forefathers. But, in his wisdom, the dark runner had found a path. It was a path that he knew all of mankind must someday travel.

Although his feet were forever exploring new ground and his eyes always seeing a changing landscape, his real journey was an inward quest for the world's wisdom, his place in that wisdom, and his purpose in life's continuum. He realized that presently few men could follow him in this world. He accepted his role as guide and preserver of truth. He knew his brothers and sisters of all skin hues must first begin their quest in the field of the mind, beginning with learning and ending in unity with all existence.

Kuntamba addressed the captain as the sound of Irish Whiskey's hooves receded in the distance. "I will win your race if you will promise to educate those who work your fields and bring you wealth."

Stouvall was trapped. Everything he owned was at stake. He had no time to think; by now, Scarsdon could be miles ahead. The captain angrily nodded his head in agreement.

Kuntamba turned and began to run. Stouvall watched the slim legs and smooth black skin of the African's back as the distance between them widened. In a half dozen contractions of the big captain's heart, the almost mystical grace of Kuntamba's stride carried him beyond the sight of those in the crowd who were staring after him in fascination.

The captain drew a long, deep breath. His wealth was now dependent upon this unusual person. Stouvall acknowledged that no part of his mind objected to use of "person" anymore. He could not explain why it pleased him. He wondered who was in charge: himself or Kuntamba. The answer no longer seemed to matter. He considered his anger when Kuntamba had bargained with him and tried to trace its source.

He replayed the image of the dark runner's form disappearing from sight. Stouvall was an observant man by nature, but there was something wrong with his mental picture. He forced his mind to replay Scarsdon's stallion charging up the slope that led into the dense woods. He saw the animal's unbridled energy and eagerness to serve its master. He watched as the great hooves cut into the ground, throwing the loose soil behind his muscular hind quarters. But when he probed his memory for Kuntamba's running form, he saw only grace and a stride that seemed to glide over the earth.

The captain suddenly realized what was troubling him: the horse's shod feet attacked the earth as if challenging it to resist the strength and exuberance of its 1200 pounds of muscle and bone. Kuntamba's stride barely left an impression in the dirt. He moved as if weightless, in perfect harmony with his surroundings. No clouds of dust rose to fill the air around his feet to provide physical evidence of his motion. Captain Stouvall smiled. He knew that Kuntamba would win.

Miles away, Scarsdon eased Irish Whiskey to a trot. He wanted to pace the stallion, conserve his energy while still getting far enough ahead to maintain a clear lead. He knew he was in a 200 mile race. He planned to rest and feed his stallion every fifty miles. He calculated that he would have at least a three-hour lead at the beginning of each interval and planned to begin each leg of the race just as the dark runner approached. He believed that his strategy would force the African to run when he should be resting. Scarsdon was sure that victory would fall into his grasp when the slave who could supposedly outrun a horse collapsed from exhaustion.

Scarsdon arrived back at Scarsdon Manor for the second time in 24 hours, dismounted and handed Irish Whiskey's reins to a slave, ordering that the horse be fed and rubbed down. Moments later, Scarsdon was consuming a cold meal and a glass of wine. It occurred to him that the dark runner carried no food or water. A sense of exhilaration washed over him. "Give no food or water to the running slave," he commanded his overseer. "Make sure none of my darkies help him in any way." Scarsdon felt better, even confident. No living creature could run 200 miles without rest, food, or water.

The plantation owner relaxed as he lay back on his great bed and slept. After 2-1/2 hours, he felt the thick hand of the overseer shaking him awake. "Master Scarsdon, I'm sorry to awaken you, but the dark runner is less than a mile away and coming fast."

Scarsdon immediately ordered Irish Whiskey saddled, then dressed and washed the sleep from his eyes. Hurrying outside, he mounted his horse and looked down the trail at the dark runner's back. Angry, he jabbed his spurs into the stallion's tender belly, forcing the animal into a run before its muscles had warmed to the task. The valiant horse bravely attempted to answer his master's demands with a burst of speed that carried him toward Kuntamba.

Scarsdon held the reins firmly, urging Irish Whiskey to a hard gallop. The gray stallion responded, driving his iron clad hooves into the ground at an ever increasing speed. His nostrils flared as he tried to shy to the left of the running African, but Scarsdon jerked the reins to the right, forcing the animal's head and eyes to lock on the man who ran just ahead of him.

A contest of wills was born. Scarsdon wanted his mighty stallion to trample the dark runner and Irish Whiskey had an instinctual aversion to stepping on any living creature. The contest ended as quickly as it had begun. Refusing his master's commands, the horse twisted his powerful neck to the left, jerking the reins free from Scarsdon's grip and causing Irish Whiskey's hindquarters to sweep around Kuntamba's back. When the gray stallion regained his balance, he and his master were facing in the wrong direction. Kuntamba's silent steps widened the gulf between them. Scarsdon cursed. He couldn't believe that the African had avoided being struck, yet he was running onward as if nothing had happened.

Once again, Scarsdon urged the pride of the Carolinas into a gallop. Once again, they took the lead. But Scarsdon's confidence was fading. The African showed no sign of fatigue. The plantation owner began to reevaluate the situation; he was winning, but would barely have time to feed and water his horse at the 100 mile marker.

Scarsdon decided to gamble. He knew that there was no quit in his mount. Exhausted, lame, or near death, Irish Whiskey would continue until his master reined him in. This splendid reserve, which the big captain and his African runner could not anticipate, was his ace in the hole. If the race was close, Scarsdon was confident that Irish Whiskey could respond with one last burst of speed. Leaning forward, he patted Irish Whiskey's neck. "Let's go, boy," he said.

At the 100 mile mark, Scarsdon had a one hour lead. He spent fifteen minutes feeding and watering his horse before returning to the course. He studied the trail as he rode, anticipating the approach of the African as he rounded each turn. He did not have long to wait.

He soon saw the dark runner's effortless motion flowing toward him. He studied Kuntamba's face for signs of fatigue, hoping to see the slave's mouth gasping for air as his tired legs strained to sustain the impossible pace. Instead, Scarsdon saw an expression of pleasure that approximated his stallion's eagerness to run. The African seemed relaxed, almost as if running was more natural than walking. Making the involuntary connection between his horse's love of running and the slave's tireless grace, Scarsdon briefly sensed a harmony that erased fatigue, greed, and wagering. The feeling extended beyond him, temporarily energizing the gray stallion with new vigor.

The intangible encounter bothered the plantation owner. He didn't know he was in a race with a holy man, a man whose mere presence evoked positive changes in those around him. Scarsdon's moment of revelation was short-lived. An hour later, when he looked over his shoulder and saw the slave's dark form gliding through the shadows toward him, he was infused with a frustrated anger.

Scarsdon heard his horse beginning to blow. He had to listen carefully, but it was there. Time and miles were wearing his steed down. Scarsdon had to slow the pace and allow his horse to recover, but the dark runner was behind him and closing in fast. Turning his attention to the rhythm of Irish Whiskey's hooves, Scarsdon heard an imperfection. The cadence was there, but it was marred by a sound that whispered of limits and a heart that did not know how to quit.

Kuntamba was also listening. He too heard the first sounds of the horse's forced breathing and the slight irregularity in his stride. Beyond signs of fatigue, the dark runner observed the swirling aura of anger and frustration that engulfed Scarsdon. It caused the man to sit rigidly in the saddle, his body stiff in its response to the rhythm of his mount's pace. The combination of anger and rigidity slowly wore down Irish Whiskey's natural balance and timing.

The dark runner knew the stallion's soul lay in the field of potential, waiting to be born in the throes of pain that guards the door to physical existence and self-awareness. Still, hints of what great epochs of time would forge into a center of light were reflected in the great horse's heart and its obedience to a tainted and spiritually disfigured master.

Kuntamba compassionately searched for a way to spare the animal whose love of motion paralleled his own. He tried to project the force that filled his being into his four-legged rival, but it was useless. The African lived on the external energy of the universe while the horse lived only by intake of food sprung from the land. Kuntamba withdrew from the fruitless effort, realizing that the magnificent creature ran because he was bred to run.

The dark runner increased his pace. He had a plan. He would make an all-out effort to win the race in the shortest possible time and then ask the captain to send a rider back to Scarsdon with the news that the race was over. He hoped that his competitor would slow his pace and allow the noble beast to finish the competition alive.

The African, Scarsdon, and the splendid gray stallion ran side by side. Turning his head, the African fixed his eyes on Scarsdon's drawn face. Kuntamba tried to pass his compassion for the great horse across the space that separated them, but the windows of the gambler's soul were dark with anger and fear.

Kuntamba accelerated effortlessly. Behind him, he heard the black horse straining to answer the call of its god. Within the hour, Kuntamba was out of Scarsdon's sight. Ninety miles and fourteen hours later, Captain Stouvall claimed victory and waited for the gambler's arrival.

CHAPTER TWELVE

The sun was setting when Scarsdon and his exhausted mount walked side by side into view. The loser claimed a stone bruise had caused him to dismount and lead his horse. Everyone present knew that Scarsdon and his horse had been badly beaten by the slender slave owned by Captain Stouvall, master of the *Ocean Breeze*.

The local bettors protested, claiming the sea captain had lured them into a wager they could not win. But when Stouvall's heavily armed crew threatened bloodshed, the banker holding the wagers distributed the winnings, completing his commissioned task.

Scarsdon promptly paid his debt. He had won the plantation on the turn of a card and although he enjoyed the great house and lands, had never acquired a strong attachment to the property. Only his pride was truly wounded, and that would soon heal.

When Captain Stouvall stepped aboard ship, he had the title to a large plantation, $25,000 in cash, plus the revenue received from the sale of his shipload of slaves, but he wasn't happy. He should have been jubilant with victory, but there was a bad taste in his mouth.

Stouvall looked around for Kuntamba. When he couldn't readily locate the African, he became agitated. Unable to find the dark runner, the captain called, "Kuntamba!" All heads turned. The summons had a plaintive, lonely quality to it, and none of Stouvall's usual fierceness. It sounded as if the captain were asking, not demanding.

Kuntamba walked up to the captain from the far side of the ship and waited expectantly.

"What do you want, Kuntamba?" asked the captain.

"Captain Stouvall, it was you who called me," Kuntamba said gently. "But there is the matter of an unpaid debt."

The larger man cast his gaze down, which he hadn't consciously ever done before. "I will keep my promise," he said, "Even though you extorted it from me at a time when I had no choice but to agree."

The lean African stared at him without speaking. The ship's captain continued. "Once I'm back in New England, I will hire two teachers—one white and one African. I will personally deliver them to Scarsdon Manor and instruct them to teach all that show a willingness to learn. No slaves will be sold. None will be chained or whipped. Each shall be paid according to their effort. If they run, they will not be pursued."

Stouvall paused. Still, the African stared. "If and when," Stouvall said haltingly, "The time comes when Africans can walk free and hold title to property, those who are still alive or the descendants of those who died on the plantation will be given title to the land of their labor and birth by myself or my descendants."

The captain paused, surprised at his use of the word "descendants." He had none and had no expectations of having any. It bothered him, but when he looked into the African's smiling eyes, he felt suddenly at ease.

The dark runner had two reasons to smile: the faint stirring of the captain's hungry soul had borne its first fruit and Kuntamba knew that, just steps away, a beautiful woman of means smiled and waited. Matilda Jones had booked passage on the *Ocean Breeze*, traveling north for her own purposes.

She witnessed the captain's treatment of Kuntamba and overheard Stouvall honoring an agreement with a slave who had no recourse under law. She heard Stouvall agree to teach and free slaves, actions that could cost him his life in the South. These demonstrated acts of honor told Matilda that the captain had become a man in the truest sense. His wealth was of no consequence to her. What was important was that the captain's heart had awakened to the beckoning of its concealed essence. She knew this because, long ago in her youth, she had awakened the same voice in her own heart.

Matilda was aware that once the inner voice was heard, its call would be impossible to resist. She had traveled the path that enlivens and brings forth the power that is at one with eternity. She knew it was an energy that patiently waited for each person to step away from the cloak of spiritual ignorance that blocked the internal light of wisdom. Matilda decided she would wait calmly for the dark runner's dynamism to uplift the captain's spirit and enable him to see the world through eyes that were not clouded by passion, fear, or materialism. Only then would she allow her eyes to meet the captain's because only at that moment in their parallel journey could recognition take place. Only then would the captain be able to recognize his own image in the eyes of another.

Captain Stouvall ordered Mr. Shepherd to set sail, looking about as the rustling of a skirt and the shadow of a woman disappeared into the passenger quarters. It was only a glimpse, but something indescribable about her held his attention, locking the fleeting image of her graceful movements into the recesses of his mind. There it remained, like a seed waiting for Spring and the right conditions for germination.

CHAPTER THIRTEEN

The *Ocean Breeze* headed north by northeast. Stouvall planned to follow the coastline to Norfolk, Virginia, where he hoped to engage the townsmen into a wager. Their purses would be flush from the proceeds of a recent sale of a large tobacco harvest.

It was the time of year when the Summer's stifling humidity became a memory. Fall was arriving, bringing with it rest for tired bodies, moments of rare leisure, and cause for celebration. Food and game were plentiful, as was the precious inebriating liquid that flowed from stills. Slavery thrived in Virginia, whose borders extended to the Ohio River, but was only profitable on the coastal plains.

Guided by a full moon, the *Ocean Breeze* with Stouvall at the helm eased into port just after midnight. His holds empty, Stouvall hoped to purchase tobacco, salt pork, and whiskey for resale in his home state. His first thought had been to purchase whiskey and tobacco, which he could trade for rum. The rum could then be traded for gold and human beings.

The word "human" did not bring repugnance. Stouvall did not reject its implications. In that edifying instant, the captain realized he would never again traffic in human suffering. He shook his head, asking himself what had happened to him in the last few months that changed him from a slaver to a man who considered slavery to be evil. Sensing Kuntamba behind him, Stouvall turned and looked into the gaze of his silent, unsolicited teacher, realizing the impact that the dark runner had made in his life.

Kuntamba asked, "How many Africans are in this land, and are they all slaves?"

Stouvall paused and turned, staring at the rolling sea before answering. "There are tens, maybe hundreds of thousands of slaves spread across many hundreds of thousands of square miles. Almost all are African. Some are red, many are white, and a few are yellow."

Because Kuntamba looked puzzled, the captain explained how men of so many colors and races became slaves. It gave him pleasure to be able to instruct his "teacher," but the enjoyment soon turned to concern. As Stouvall's words fell on Kuntamba's ears, he noticed that the dark runner exhibited a strange reaction.

The African's shoulders sagged slightly, his eyes filling with a sadness that seemed to drain the vitality from his lean body. His chest heaved as his lungs filled with air. In that moment, the pain that filled Kuntamba's being became visible to the captain's searching gaze.

All of his life, Stouvall had considered pain a necessary element of existence. His childhood had been filled with misery. During his adult life, he accepted and dispensed grief without a second thought. He carried the burden of his parents' rejection as a child and he had experienced the pain of unrequited love, but never the crushing onus of compassion. The captain wondered how his words had injured Kuntamba. He sincerely regretted having been an unknowing instrument in causing the dark-skinned man's sorrow. Stouvall did not know it, but in bearing some of the dark runner's pain, a pain he was unable to understand, he had begun the process of purifying his soul.

Kuntamba wanted to explain why he felt the pain that the powerless endure, pain that is spawned in ignorance and suffering. He desperately wanted to convey to the captain the magnitude of a singular truth—do unto others as you would have them do unto you. Kuntamba knew the captain would not understand that he suffered because of the enormity of the inescapable retribution of dark minds imprinting on innocent souls.

Leaving the captain on deck, the dark runner retreated, seeking a place of solitude where he could contemplate the immensity of the slave trade. He needed to find and adjust his inner balance so that he could continue his spiritual journey in a world surrounded by insensitivity and greed.

In his quarters, Stouvall was plotting another wager, his greed for money not yet satiated. If he were going to lure the locals into a race with Kuntamba, he needed to decide on a course of action. He considered the flat, low-lying coastal plain, but changed his mind when he remembered how it merged with the great dismal swamp, a place where disease was as common as the vast swarms of mosquitoes that thrived in its dampness.

He contemplated sailing up the James River toward Richmond and the fall line where the tidal plain area rose up to meet the foothills of the Allegheny Mountains. He wanted Kuntamba to run free in the forests and on mountain paths surrounded by white and red oaks, poplars, ash, walnut, cherry, and tulip trees. He wanted the dark runner to see the beauty of the American landscape, to marvel at the plant life, and be amazed by the elk, bison, and bears, matching strides with the wolves whose territory he would be trespassing. He wasn't completely sure of his motives in sharing these experiences with Kuntamba.

Stouvall remembered mountain men who inhabited the area; their love of privacy and their willingness to discourage interlopers. He knew they would use the same reasoning on the dark runner as they used when sighting along their rifle barrels to kill wild game. Instead of skinning a carcass for salting or smoking, they might drag the slave's torn body into town, hoping to claim a reward for a runaway slave. If none were forthcoming, Kuntamba's body would be left to rot by the roadside as a warning to those that lived and died under the whip.

Returning to thoughts of vast sums of money, Stouvall recalled that much of the Virginia coast in the south eastern corner of the state consisted of long, sandy beaches. He could post men along the course to protect Kuntamba, and even watch the race himself with a telescope from the deck of the *Ocean Breeze*. A great idea occurred to the captain: he would invite those interested in the race to join him on the deck of his ship. A keg of rum could be opened for their pleasure. As the liquor flowed, fogging minds and inflating courage, he would subtly encourage the revelers to engage in additional wagers.

The flapping sound of a loose sail caught Stouvall's attention. Looking seaward through a porthole in his cabin, he saw the silhouette of a ship he knew to be a slaver. It was the *Orion*. He knew its captain and crew, who were little more than murderers and thieves.

Stouvall and Captain Masoc had tangled before. Masoc had taken both a physical and financial beating. Stouvall knew that Masoc yearned for a chance to get even. But what bothered the big captain more was that he was sure that the *Orion's* captain had stopped in South Carolina to auction his slave harvest. It would mean the ship's skipper would have heard of Kuntamba's race against the gray stallion.

If Masoc and his men retold the story, as Stouvall was sure they would, his chances of luring the Virginia gentry into a race were almost nil. Still, the captain was not easily discouraged. He would go ashore to watch and listen. If an opportunity arose to make some extra cash, he would be ready. Stouvall intended to tell the Virginians a story about the Carolina race that emphasized Kuntamba's winning by default because of injury to Scarsdon's mount. Masoc and his men could surely not deny such a story.

Shortly after reaching dry land, Stouvall watched as Masoc and his crew tied their skiff to the pier. Looking seaward, the master of the *Ocean Breeze* noticed that his ship was shifting with the changing tide. He thought of Kuntamba. The dark runner must be warned about the men who sailed the *Orion* and the danger that they represented.

Although he considered that Kuntamba should not run at all, avarice won the day. If only he knew the dark runner's physical limits and how fast he was truly capable of running. If he knew these things, he could design a course that would make the African unbeatable.

Wading out into the shallow water where his rowboats were tethered, Stouvall selected one and rowed to the *Ocean Breeze*. He wanted to talk to Kuntamba. When he was still several boat lengths from his ship, Stouvall called out the African's name. When there was no reply, his mind filled with suspicion. Had the African reneged on his promise, slipped overboard and swam ashore? Stouvall felt the old anger returning.

He climbed hastily up the rope rigging to the deck. "Kuntamba, where are you," he roared. His tone bordered on the violent. After making a quick circuit of the ship's deck, he paused, his anger becoming irrepressible.

"Kuntamba, I will find you and I will kill you!" he said, but the sound of his voice and the senseless pain it promised carried regret in it. Before his words had faded, the tide of his emotions ebbed, bringing the realization that he could not, would not, raise his hand against the unusual and tireless runner. Lowering his head, Stouvall accepted Kuntamba's disappearance and decided to head home at dawn. As he walked back to his quarters, he stopped and inexplicably looked up at the crow's nest. He saw nothing at first, then gradually his eyes adjusted to the starry background and he was able to discern the outline of the dark runner's body.

Within seconds, Stouvall was looking directly into Kuntamba's dark eyes. In that instant, regret doused his anger. "I'm sorry," he muttered involuntarily.

Kuntamba nodded, his face turned skyward. The captain swung back down towards the deck, checking the ship's rigging before heading back to his quarters. On his way, he passed the silent form of Matilda

Jones. Their glances met. It was a moment that neither would ever forget.

Early the next morning, the receding tide attempted to carry the *Ocean Breeze* out to sea. Stouvall rose from his cot, dressed, and went up on deck. He felt good. The trip had been extremely profitable and the nearness of home beckoned him. He called out for Mr. Shepherd, but instead of a reply, heard the muffled voices of his seamen coming from the bow of the ship. Looking over the rail, Stouvall found the crew watching a commotion on shore. Putting his spy glass to his eye, he saw riders racing back and forth on the beach. Long, lanky mountain men with wide hats and smooth bore rifles stared in his direction. A boat full of men headed straight for the *Ocean Breeze*, pulling hard on the oars.

His immediate concern was that they were coming for Kuntamba. Finding the dark runner, he told him to wait in the captain's quarters.

Kuntamba smiled. "There is no need," he told the captain. "They only come to bet." The dark runner was pleased. The captain had put someone else's safety ahead of his own. His world was expanding beyond his self-centered desires.

Stouvall welcomed the visitors begrudgingly and inquired what their purpose was. The leader of the uninvited guests responded. "We hear you have a slave who can outrun horses and that you're willing bet your nigger can outrun any of our animals." Before Stouvall could reply, the spokesman demanded in a loud, irritating voice, "Is it true?"

The captain took his time formulating a response. He suspected that Captain Masoc had informed the ragtag collection of men about Kuntamba and that it was actually Masoc who had issued the challenge that would pit the dark runner against the mountain men's horses.

With his glare fixed on the men who had dared invade his ship and confront him, Stouvall replied by slowly shaking his head from side to side before he spoke. "My runner is tired from his last race. Perhaps on my next trip through this area we can discuss the terms and conditions of a match race between my African and your best animals."

The spokesman for the mountain men, McLean, was a tall, angular man with sloping yet wide shoulders and a long, thin neck. He had a small head and an ample mouth, and was missing several teeth. He stank of whiskey, and the sour odor that emanated from him was the stench of a body that is no longer able to break down intoxicants. The pungent sourness flowed from his body, swamping everyone who stood downwind of him.

Trying to put some distance between McLean and himself, Captain Stouvall hesitated. He recognized the essence of the short-tempered irritability that he struggled to contain in the foul-smelling man. Shrugging as if to say there was nothing he could do, the captain turned away.

Seeing the shrug as a sign of weakness, McLean pressed on. "Your nigger will run or he will die!"

The remark caught Stouvall off-guard. His great muscles tensed, and the instinct to protect another person flooded through him.

Only Kuntamba's soft utterance of "I will run" had the power to suppress the captain's rage.

Thinking he had forced the captain to race his slave, McLean pushed his point. "In his last race, your darkie ran against a lame horse. Our horses can run in swamps and mud up to their bellies. In the mountains, they are sure-footed as a mountain goat. You pick the course and the distance, and our horses will run your slave to death. All you need to do is settle the bets and hope you have a ship to sail home on!"

In a deliberate show of contempt, Stouvall turned his back on the mountain men and looked at Kuntamba. The dark runner nodded almost imperceptibly. The captain knew Kuntamba would win. Spinning back to McLean, Stouvall stepped forward aggressively until his huge index finger was only inches from the man's face.

"Today we bet," the captain declared loudly. "Only those with cash in hand will be able to wager. Select your best horse and rider and meet me on shore at daybreak tomorrow."

McLean grinned, showing his gap-toothed smile. "What? Your darkie can only run against one horse?"

The mountain man's intent was simple. Many horses meant much jostling about and an inevitable, or intentional, injury to the slave. McLean had heard stories of Indians running wild mustangs to the ground. Now that the captain had agreed to race, the bettor wanted to protect his wager by flooding the field with horses. He knew that if the race carried the contestants beyond the captain's sight, fresh horses could replace exhausted ones. If only one or two horses competed, the switched animals would quickly be spotted.

The crafty mountain man waited expectantly for the captain's response. When the captain agreed to the entry of several horses, McLean's mouth opened in a lusty cheer that was echoed by his companions and celebrated with the passing of a jug.

Their elation faded when Stouvall added, "If you give me odds of three to one." Seeing their hesitation, Stouvall knew it was time to attack. "You wanted this race. You claim your horses are unbeatable. Is it just the whiskey talking? If so, I will sail in the morning."

McLean was clearly agitated. He paced back and forth, looking for support from his friends. "Odds don't win races," he stated finally, "Horses do."

Stouvall closed the negotiation, repeating the terms. "We bet today and run tomorrow."

Satisfied, the mountain men climbed back into their boat and headed for the shore. Some were singing and toasting the agreement. Others sat quietly in the craft, thinking.

CHAPTER FOURTEEN

Early the next morning, just an hour before dawn, a crowd gathered on shore. They quieted in the darkness as they listened to the lap of the waves and the sounds that would signal the arrival of the first contestants. Just as the morning sun broke the horizon, two medium-sized horses were eased by their riders from the cover of a clump of trees. They were lean, hungry-looking creatures whose gauntness signified endurance rather than starvation.

The animals were poorly groomed, their hides scarred from whip lashes and racing through thick underbrush. The leathery hands holding taut reins disputed the vision of men and animals working in harmony. The men were professional riders who knew horse flesh better than they knew their own. They controlled their mounts, driving the animals to victory with the use of a whip.

Approaching the crowd, one of the riders dismounted and tethered his horse nearby. The group was restless, looking seaward to guarantee that the *Ocean Breeze* remained anchored offshore. A few threatened to row out to the ship an drag the African from his bed, but their impatience was wasted. As the sun reached its midpoint on the horizon, Captain Stouvall, his first mate, and Kuntamba stepped ashore several hundred yards away.

Their approach was quiet and without fanfare. When the crowd saw the lean, slight African, laughter rippled through their ranks.

"Do you really expect that bony slave to outrun our best horses? He'll be lucky to survive the first climb up to the fault line," shouted an anonymous voice.

Stouvall studied the loud assembly. The voice was familiar to him. He answered, "Mr. Masoc, would you be interested in making a side wager? Let's say the title to the *Ocean Breeze* against the title to the *Orion.*"

Masoc didn't answer.

The crowd was suddenly quiet, turning its attention to Masoc as it waited for his response.

Masoc's voice wavered, barely audible. "I don't own the *Orion.* My creditors do."

Stouvall knew he had Masoc cornered. "Then perhaps you can wager the proceeds from the sale of your slaves in South Carolina."

Once again, Masoc was forced to respond. "That money also belongs to my creditors."

Stouvall closed the conversation. "What a pity. Such a big mouth and nothing to back it up."

The crowd hooted raucously before turning its attention to the approach of several riders. Stouvall raised both hands above his head indicating that he wanted to speak. Slowly the group settled into a semblance of quiet. "There will be no race to the fault line," the captain said. "This race will be run on the sandy beach so that all can see."

Recollecting how easily Kuntamba glided over the thick dust of the West African road, barely leaving an impression in the dirt, Stouvall was positive that the runner's light steps would lead him to victory over the heavy horses. "As long as at least one horse and rider remain in the race, and as long as Kuntamba runs, is how long the race will be."

He added, almost as an afterthought, "If anyone here or out on the course interferes with my runner, Kuntamba will be declared winner and I will collect on all bets."

There was a moment of confusion as everyone considered the captain's conditions. Before the crowd could protest, a large rawboned mountain man moved toward Stouvall. McLean's eyes were hard and his weathered face twisted with defiance and contempt. He was feared even among the mountain people because he reveled in bloody knife fights and anything-goes brawls where ears were bitten off and limbs twisted from their sockets.

The mountain man stopped directly in front of the captain, and both men stared at each other unflinchingly. McLean's animalistic anger weighed against Stouvall's calm intelligence, but behind the captain's composure lay a wealth of violence that began in his youth. McLean lacked both composure and refinement, preferring to settle any difference of opinions with his fists. He sucked in his breath, rocked his weight back on his right foot and twisted counterclockwise, driving his right hand into the space that had held Captain Stouvall just a fraction of a second earlier.

The big sea captain shifted his weight instantaneously onto his left foot, moving his body out of harm's way and allowing him to counter with a left hook and straight right combination. When his opponent didn't go down, Stouvall followed with an elbow smash to the face and a left to McLean's nose with the heel of his hand. The mountain man collapsed to the ground, unconscious. Stouvall lunged forward to finish him off, his blood boiling with rage.

Once again, Kuntamba's calm voice penetrated the captain's rage. The African's voice rang out clearly, calling to the faint light that struggled to survive in the captain's heart. "The sun is rising," whispered Kuntamba deep into the captain's mind, "And your soul is crying out for truth."

The fragile sound pierced through Stouvall's awareness, awaking a deep sense of regret. A miserable feeling of failure washed over him. Stouvall knew he had a right to self-defense and if he had not defended himself, he would have been the one laying bloody in the dirt. It was the realization he had willingly surrendered to an uncontrollable anger that disturbed Stouvall the most. As he looked into Kuntamba's eyes, he slowly understood. He was the captain and controller of men's lives, yet he was a captive to his own greed, anger and passions. In that instant, he crossed the line that divides those who are ruled by circumstances and those who battle to control their own destinies. Stouvall mentally promised that anger would never again be his master.

He had much to learn.

Watching from a distance, Matilda saw the fight and intuitively recognized Stouvall's moment of remorse. The captain's decision lifted her spirits like the first soft breeze of spring. She knew, however, that the captain still had many long and trying winters of self-discovery in his future.

Matilda knew the captain's relatively sudden move from self-centered insensitivity to someone who could no longer deal in the evils of slavery, someone who felt remorse and cared about other people, had begun with the arrival of the unique African. She also knew that if Stouvall had not been ready to accept the first touch of wisdom, Kuntamba's presence would have had no impact on the ship master whatsoever.

She was aware the captain, her eventual life partner, had entered a place of learning. He was about to defy the demons of his lower nature. He had begun his inner quest and she intended to be by his side to guide him, and offer insight and unconditional love. Captain Stouvall didn't know it, but his life path had altered.

Several scruffy, angry mountain men approached. Stouvall glanced around, searching for his men, but the crew was already stationed along the course. Turning toward the sea, he saw that the sun had cleared the horizon. Stouvall nodded to Kuntamba, and the dark runner broke into an unhurried stride. "The sun is up. The race has begun!" Captain Stouvall shouted to the onlookers.

"Where is Scotty?" yelled someone in the crowd. But Scotty had already pointed his horse northward and was leaning forward in the saddle as his crop descended on his mount's rump. The animal's ears and tail came up simultaneously as its powerful hindquarters drove him forward into the sand, answering Kuntamba's effort with a burst of speed. The crowd cheered. Within minutes, more than fifty riders were testing their mountain-bred stock against each other and the dark runner.

Before the sun had climbed ten degrees, the horses and riders had faded into a distant mass. Only the image of the African's distant silhouette against the clear blue sky was proof of the morning events.

Stouvall believed that the man called Scotty was Kuntamba's most formidable opponent. He watched the horseman carefully as he raced into the lead. The man was not only an excellent rider, but he had adapted his racing style to the thick underbrush and forests of the mountains. Scotty sat a little too far back from his horse's center of gravity, forcing him to lean forward more than he normally would. In short races, or even contests that lasted a couple of hours, the one or two inches involved in his riding technique would not have mattered. But in a competition that could last for days, every flaw was magnified.

The captain sensed Scotty's courage and determination, but knew those qualities must be balanced with energy and strength. Stouvall wondered who would falter first—man or beast?

Ten hours later, Scotty completed the circuit, bringing him back to the starting line. He started to alight in order to feed and water his horse, but Stouvall interrupted him. "This is a non-stop competition. If you want to stay in the race, turn around and head back up the beach."

"My horse needs water and I haven't eaten," Scotty protested.

Stouvall merely smiled. "Neither has my runner."

The horseman was a proud man. If the darkie could race without food and water, so could he. He swung up on his horse and turned around, heading back up the beach. He had begun to understand that speed was less important than stamina.

Four hours and sixty-five miles later, the rider watched the shadowy form of the dark runner as it moved toward him. The African glided along the damp sand left by the retreating tide. Kuntamba's effortless grace fascinated the horseman. He studied the runner's motion, not by looking directly at him, but by staring at the reflection cast by the full moon on the tide pools and wet sand.

The mountain man didn't see fatigue in the runner. What he saw was a seemingly mystical creature that had a oneness with the forces of nature. Scotty was unable to define his experience but something deep inside of him, possibly the tiny spark of the eternal that dwells in all mankind, recognized a kinship with the passing African. The spark awakened the start of a new reverence for life, a reverence that had lain dormant since Scotty's birth. With an expression of concern, the horseman reached down and stroked his mount's neck, whispering, "I will not run you to death."

Thirty hours later, and still maintaining a lead of more than twenty miles, Scotty dismounted and led his faltering horse back to the starting line. On the way, he stopped by a clearing where a cool stream of fresh water flowed. Using his hat, he served his horse a measured amount of water. Rubbing the loyal animal down, he washed the dried sweat and salt from his body.

The gestures were small rewards, but to anyone who knew Scotty, his actions were a complete reversal of character. The tired horseman knew that the race was over for him and a sizable amount of money was lost. It didn't matter. Scotty's partner, Coursdon, was still out on the course and Scotty hoped he would fare well. Coursdon was acknowledged to be the best rider in all of Virginia.

CHAPTER FIFTEEN

The race against the slave had fired Coursdons' competitive energy. Early in the contest, he had decided he would rather die than let a subhuman slave defeat him. Coursdon believed that winning was just a matter of taking a long, leisurely ride up the beach and back a couple of times. He hadn't witnessed the ease with which Kuntamba moved over the ground. Coursdon had not encountered the African's charged aura as he ran by with a chorus of splashing waves and squawking sea gulls heralding his passing.

Coursdon didn't know that the dark runner was only truly at ease when his feet were caressing Mother Earth as his lungs filled with the power that sustained the universe. When he did pass through Kuntamba's advancing and retreating energy field, Coursdon realized that he had engaged in a competition that could not be won.

Rounding a finger of water that reached inland in search of the lowlands, Coursdon noted that his horse was moving erratically. He looked for signs of wolves or bears, but saw none. He slowed the pace slightly, allowing the mare to settle down and ease into an energy-saving trot. He cleared the inlet and looked northward. What he saw disturbed him.

A small whirlwind appeared to be coming toward him, but the air was still and the ocean was quiet. Coursdon studied the strange phenomena with unblinking eyes, then urged his mare into a steady lope. Gradually he and the strange windless concentration of energy drew closer together until the rider was able to make out the outline of the running slave.

The African's mouth and eyes were closed and his feet seemed to barely skim the ground. Logic told Coursdon to shy away from the strange vision, but his curiosity overruled. The rider knew nothing of religious ecstasy or those rare moments when true holy men purified by the blood of self-conquest stepped beyond the reach of the physical world and touched the eternal.

Coursdon had grown up on a Southern plantation. He was the last and smallest of seven children. His childhood had been full of work and fights. One contrary word would send his small fists flying. Because of his compact size, he was frequently asked to ride other men's horses in local competitions. Everyone who knew him concluded he was fearless. But Coursdon had one fear that haunted his dreams and taunted his manhood.

Every dark face and every pair of black eyes reminded him of a terror-filled night long ago. His curse began during his seventh year. Young Coursdon was sleeping in an upstairs bedroom on a warm, fall evening. The moon was full. The surrounding forests, orchards, buildings, and fields were shadows in the moonlight. The boy was restless, aching from muscles taxed beyond the limits of their immature strength. He rolled over and over, listening to the soft sound of the rhythmic stroking of a solitary drum. Soon he lay still, caught in the drum's mesmerizing tattoo.

He listened to the monotonous tempo, which steadily increased, for over an hour. Finally, its lure pulled the youngster from his bed, guiding his steps to a secluded place where he crouched unnoticed beneath a small bush. He stared with fascination at the drummer and several slaves as they moved methodically, gracefully around a small fire. Nearby, he saw a wooden coffin. He knew it contained the remains of a young adult slave who had been shot as he attempted to flee to freedom.

Coursdon watched as the dead man's mother moved slowly around the coffin, side stepping, spinning, and walking backwards as she went.

The boy was spellbound by the motion of her hands and the way they moved as if they were possessed by an intelligence of their own. He couldn't turn his eyes away when the old one leaned down, chanting at the head of the dead body. In her hands she held two long bones. Coursdon knew they were not animal bones. The youngster had seen many butchered animals and the bones did not resemble any he had seen before.

The seven-year-old was captivated as the old woman rolled the bones between her clasped hands and drew first one, then the other, downward against her thighs. As the heads of the long bones touched her knees, she threw back her head and screamed as if she were in the pains of childbirth. Gradually her screams turned to whimpers as the bones crept up the inner portion of her thighs and touched her womanhood. At that instant, the corpse sat up, and mother and son said a final goodbye. After the dead man returned to his final rest, the old woman fell to the ground and rolled over and over as if trying to shake an unseen demon from her back.

The beat of the pulsing drums stopped abruptly. The silence signified the end of the bizarre service and sent everyone back to their quarters. It was over except for the young boy who refused to move until the sun lit his path and revealed each shadow for what it really was. His impressionable young mind had captured every detail of the ritual that brought the dead back to life. The incident fired his imagination with a fear of the dead and the haunting belief that all Africans possessed the ability to commune with those who were no longer contained in corporeal bodies.

Decades later, when he saw the dark runner who seemed to float just above the ground, his mind flooded with visions of beating drums, dancing slaves, chanting women, and the piercing eyes of a corpse who sat bolt upright. With the sudden return of the long suppressed memories came a panic that could only be purged in flight.

Coursdon reached high and to his right, driving his arm and the short braided leather crop down on his mount's rump. The seasoned horse responded with a burst of speed that propelled the animal and its terrified master on a ride that would only end when the horse could go no further. The terror-filled images seemed unending, but the breathless ride was actually less than three minutes in length.

At first, his mare just seemed to stumble, then quickly recover. Before long, Coursdon felt the animal's body quiver as she staggered to her left. Something broke through his fear: it was his love for the gray mare that had served him well for many years. Fond remembrances of the day he won the spindle-legged foal with the turn of a card filled his mind. He recalled bottle feeding her and spending his last dollar to buy grain when he himself was hungry. He smiled, recollecting the short, choppy stride she used when she ran around and around her corral. That distinctive stride had resulted in her name—Quicksteps. Coursdon relished riding the small mare in the wind as his hair blew in unison with her mane. It was those memories and his feelings for the gray mare that vanquished his demons, allowing both him and his mount to slow down, pause, and rest.

Coursdon had wrongly linked the African practitioners of witchcraft from his father's plantation with Stouvall's slave. He didn't know that Kuntamba abhorred sorcery. It was impossible for Coursdon to understand Kuntamba's motives or to grasp the concept of seeking personal perfection while being immersed in the demands, needs, and hungers of material life. But Coursdon knew that Quicksteps, his gray mare, was in trouble. Reining her in, he eased his companion to a stop, dismounted, and began to walk. He knew she needed to cool down slowly before being given a measured amount of water.

For almost an hour, Coursdon and Quicksteps walked down the dusty road toward home. Finally the man permitted his horse to stop and graze on some new grass near the roadside. He stroked her neck, putting his ear against her throat. He heard a sound that pulled at his heart.

It was a rasping sound that invariably meant permanent damage had been done. When he listened again, hoping that the additional time had eased her body's demand for oxygen, he once again heard the sound of air being forced through a damaged windpipe. Placing his head to her chest, he heard the gurgling sound of a heart in distress. The rider began to weep. What had he done, and why? Only two words came to him—fear and greed.

Dropping to his knees, remorse filled his heart and soul. There they remained; a man and his horse beside the road, motionless. For Coursdon, lost in his grief and regret, the passing of time had no meaning. He did not see the setting sun or the gradual arrival of darkness, nor did he hear or feel the returning African's swirl of energy. But Quicksteps did. The sudden shifting of her bulk and the way her ears tipped to attention jarred Coursdon from his pain. He looked up at his horse. Once again, he listened to her breathing, but only heard the unimpaired flow of air moving in and out of her lungs. He placed the side of his face to Quicksteps' chest and listened. To his surprise and elation, he heard only the rhythmic sound of a perfect heart's healthy contractions.

Looking in the direction of Quicksteps' focused attention, the rider saw the dark runner approaching fast. In that moment, Coursdon vowed to never again run from his fears. Raising his eyes, he forced himself to look into the African's face. He expected to find the mystery and power of witchcraft reflected in the dark runner's eyes, but instead experienced a sense of benevolence that invigorated his body and mind.

Within minutes the dark runner was gone, leaving Coursdon to question whether his experiences were real or imagined. Had Quicksteps really been unable to breathe, and were the sounds of her damaged heart an aural illusion? Had the strange African healed the mare without even touching her? Why did he feel so good? He did know one thing. Witchcraft and the undead would never again strike blind fear into his heart.

A few hours later, Captain Stouvall received word that Coursdon had left the course and would not be returning. All the other amateur riders had long since been exhausted in a heated competition that tested speed and manhood rather than stamina and intelligence. The race was over. The captain had won, but there was no excitement in his victory. The opposition just seemed to fade away, leaving Kuntamba's indefatigable steps traversing the course alone.

Stouvall collected most of what was owed him, but a few bettors refused to pay until the African slave crossed the finish line. The captain reminded them that the dark runner still ran while all of the opposition had quit the course. Two men argued strongly that Coursdon had been several hours ahead of the captain's slave when he dropped out. They persisted, stating that until the African passed the point where Coursdon quit, the captain's slave would not be declared the winner.

The sea captain's first impulse was to smash the welchers' heads together, but he knew that it was only a matter of time before Kuntamba would stride across the finish line. Turning away, he said gruffly, "I will wait, and you will pay."

Meanwhile, Kuntamba moved along the beach, savoring the onshore wind and running with a carefree abandon that carried him along the constantly changing water line left by the retreating waves on the moist sand. He was as comfortable in the motion of running as the great whales that swam offshore and basked on the ocean's surface before diving to the depths of their liquid home.

The dark runner turned toward the finish line, passing the place where Coursdon had defeated his fear and discovered how much he loved Quicksteps. Those who viewed his approach knew they were witnessing a superhuman demonstration of speed and stamina. Some of them were filled with a transitory sense of uplifting joy, followed by a soothing quietude that stirred recollections of wrongs committed long ago. The feelings were fleeting as a passing flock of geese. For some that watched the slave pass, the flash of inner serenity would create a hunger that time and conditions would call to life.

When the *Ocean Breeze* set sail, most of those watching from shore were confused. Their pockets were empty, but it somehow didn't seem to matter. Even the losers were strangely without outrage or a need for revenge.

CHAPTER SIXTEEN

Kuntamba stood on deck, facing North. He was eager to know the land that Stouvall called home. He wanted to observe the captain's manner and study how he used his newly acquired wealth. Kuntamba was not alone in his observations. He knew that Matilda, the beautiful woman whose lineage stretched back to Africa, also regarded the ship's master with a calm sense of expectancy.

The dark runner recognized a kindred soul in Matilda. He saw someone who had engaged in the battle of self-conquest and stood victorious after every skirmish. Only time and a continued toil stood between her and a transcendence that approached perfection. Kuntamba knew she had a debt to pay.

In her youth, Matilda had been guided in her spiritual journey by an advanced soul. With Captain Stouvall, she would become the teacher. Her labor would evolve into a pleasure that would encompass the captain, who would be her eventual husband. They would grow and unfold spiritually until, as co-sojourners, they would tread the eternal path that expands exponentially into infinity.

Kuntamba psychically saw Matilda's fate. She, however, sensed her future in a very different way. She saw the captain's inner growth much like that of a flower bud. It was full of potential, promise, and unseen beauty still confined by immaturity. She sensed that Kuntamba's uplifting presence was preparing the bud of Captain Stouvall's nascent soul for a lifetime of service to humankind.

The *Ocean Breeze* docked at Portsmouth, New Hampshire, just before winter's arrival. Captain William Bernard Stouvall paid his seamen well for their services and gave each a share of his winnings. He did not forget the families of the men who had died under his command.

Kuntamba watched and was pleased. The captain turned to Kuntamba. "You are a man of few words. Your presence enabled me to see the wrong of slavery. Your running has made me wealthier than I ever dreamed, and yet you ask nothing in return. I once thought you were subhuman. Now I know otherwise. I owe you a debt that is beyond my ability to repay."

Stouvall pondered how he could have thought of Kuntamba, or any other person regardless of status, as less than a man. He continued speaking. "I have brought you to a strange land that will soon become very cold. I now know that slavery is wrong, and I ask you to forgive me. I am giving you your freedom. You can stay with me, or you can leave."

Kuntamba smiled. The captain had begun his own journey. "No forgiveness is necessary," said the dark runner. "When your personal growth lifted the darkness of greed and ambition from your soul, you stepped beyond the need for forgiveness."

The captain started to speak, but Kuntamba silenced him with a raised hand. "My future lies here in this land. I would like to stay with you until my path becomes clear, then I will leave. For now, I am content to watch as you discover a new life."

As the months faded into the time of snow and blizzards, the dark runner quietly watched the courtship of Stouvall and Matilda, two souls that were meant to be together. Their relationship started slowly, maturing into an inseparable bonding. Each recognized in the other a hunger that could only be satisfied in a mutual embrace. Before the arrival of spring, the captain and Matilda were married. In time, they would pass to their children the lessons that gave life purpose and direction. Matilda was content, and her happiness greatly pleased the captain, lighting his path and guiding his steps.

Soon the first blush of spring was on the land. William Stouvall searched for Kuntamba. He had news that he wanted to share. The captain looked everywhere to no avail. Finally, he checked the *Ocean Breeze*. He did not find Kuntamba, but he found his own telescope on the ship's rail. It was pointed in a southwesterly direction. It was a simple message from the captain's first encounter with Kuntamba via the spyglass. Now the telescope's position told the captain where the dark runner was going. Stouvall called to him silently, telling the dark runner how his life had changed. Stouvall sent Kuntamba a silent message telling of his love for Matilda and the child who was conceived two months earlier. Mostly, the words stemmed from a gratitude that sprang from a growing sense of time, purpose and place.

Kuntamba, a day's run away, felt his friend's heart-sent message. The dark runner had left the ship and stepped into the unknown with nothing to protect him but his quality of harmlessness. The African's nature could only participate in the positive. He knew all actions and thoughts were bound to their source. That knowledge was the keystone of his existence. It allowed him to observe and experience the gamut of life objectively.

Kuntamba ran inland, consuming the miles as easily as a breeze moves from the ocean to the land. When he passed a small band of Indians, alert guides only sensed a crosscurrent of shifting winds that seemed to rise out of nowhere.

A day later he swept by the whiskey-sodden, sleeping bodies of a gang of bandits. Their foul body odor was saturated with vibrations of violence that warned Kuntamba of their presence. He moved on, following curious rivulets that grew into streams, eventually swelling into rivers. He saw bear, deer, and mountain lions. He saw rabbits and small, unidentifiable creatures whose names he had not yet learned. Occasionally, when the timing and mood were right, he slowed his steps and walked along the way, humming a monosyllabic tune. He paused to reach out and touch one of the less guarded creatures. Sometimes small animals scampered away only to stop a few feet away, turning to look back at him.

Other creatures stood exposed and vulnerable as the dark runner extended harmless fingers to them. After a few poignant moments, Kuntamba continued on his journey, drawn by an insistent urge into the unknown. He tried to understand the compulsion that drove him, feeling an odd force guiding his steps in a southwesterly direction. Kuntamba had learned early in his spiritual quest to follow the soundless urgings that spoke to his heart. Invariably they led to greater understanding and opportunities to serve those less fortunate than himself.

His mind drifted back through time, reviewing the events of the past ten months. He recalled the brutal enslavement of his African countrymen and his beloved sister's last questioning glance. He recalled the great ocean wave that had bonded him to the captain and the look in the captain's eyes when he realized that his life rested in the grip of his most prized slave. He thought of the races where he had matched strides with horses and men. In all of his mental wanderings, he saw only images of actions past. They aroused no sense of bravado within him. He was without pride, viewing past events with the same impartiality he extended to the terrain that surrounded him.

It was Kuntamba's ability to stand apart from his previous actions and thoughts that enabled him to learn without emotion or self-involvement obscuring his vision. He summoned mental images of the captain and his wife seeing each other through the eyes of love. For an instant, his stride faltered and his objectivity clouded as he recognized an inner hunger for the love of a woman whose spiritual maturity paralleled his own.

For the first time in his adult life, the dark runner's unerring feet failed to avoid an obstacle. He stumbled, almost falling, before recovering his balance in the next stride. In that moment of vulnerability, it occurred to him that the chance of meeting a female counterpart was almost impossible. Still, some as yet undiscovered force was pulling him westward. Perhaps the future held more promise than he dared hope for.

Whatever the future concealed in the convolutions of time, he was willing to let it unfold with the gentleness of dawn following the rhythm of the earth's rotation. He knew his fate could not be avoided or altered. Long ago, he had learned the immutable law that guides the universe cannot be hurried.

The dark runner's reverie was broken by the sound of rushing water. He turned his inner gaze out upon a mighty river that overflowed its banks and flooded the lowlands. He had arrived at the Mississippi River just as the melt water from the spring thaw was breaching its banks and racing outward in a futile hunt for confining walls. Kuntamba stared out across the vast wetness, searching for land. There were low hills far in the distance.

PART TWO

1803: The Making of an Adversary

CHAPTER ONE

Many years before Kuntamba had set foot on the *Ocean Breeze*, a continent and an ocean away the American sailing ship, *Philadelphia*, slipped quietly through the Strait of Gibraltar on a dark, moonless night. The sailing ship hugged the North African coast, avoiding juts of land. Its dark sails and the shadowless night concealed its approach. The *Philadelphia* fought the shifting currents up the Mediterranean Sea and eased past the island of Sicily.

High above the sea on the coastline of North Africa, a dozen cannons sat mute, enveloped in a low fog. The sentinels, who should have been on the alert, were lost in an alcoholic slumber on the damp earth. A drunken lookout shifted in his sleep as the creaking of a sailing ship's rigging caught in a crosscurrent of air while, below the rampart, the crew of the *Philadelphia* prayed they would make port unmolested.

At that time, the fledgling government of the United States of America willingly submitted to the extortion and blackmail of the Barbary pirates. The United States government paid the illegal ransom, hoping that ships flying the American flag would be permitted to pass unharmed. But the Barbary pirates, sensing America's vulnerability and her unwillingness to engage in warfare far from home, became greedy. They began capturing American cargo ships and holding them for what they referred to as a "finder's fee."

Onboard the *Philadelphia* was a young seaman of moderate means. Most of his life had been spent seeking the ultimate source of his own existence and laboring at the creation of wisdom and the perfection of goodness within himself. His name was John Feriluc. He was not interested in wealth, power, or the other physical trappings of his era. Only the discovery of truth and wisdom interested him. He defined truth as universal knowledge. He associated wisdom with the unseen eternal forces that guide the world and its inhabitants.

Feriluc was tall and fair-skinned with deep blue expressive eyes and long light brown hair. He walked with his head held high and his eyes on the horizon. John had hired on the *Philadelphia* because he wanted to see the world. Until then, his wisdom and understanding of life had been gained through introspection, books, and discussions. What he had learned was soon to be tried in the spheres of pain and fear.

Following the *Philadelphia* as it eased past Sicily and began its sprint for Athens, Greece, two unladen pirate ships rigged for speed raced from near the port at Palermo on the Tyrrhenian Sea. The pirate ships closed in behind the American ship, blocking her retreat. From the deep water just outside the harbor of Tripoli, a third pirate vessel pulled up anchor and moved out into the channel between the islands of Crete and Tubruq.

When the captain of the Philadelphia tried to escape northward to the Ionia Sea, he was met by a fourth ship flying the skull and crossbones flag. The captain was sure the pirates wanted to capture his ship and its contents without a fight. He couldn't outrun them, and knew it was futile to fight. Still, he wanted to test the pirates' resolve. Unleashing the full wind-catching capacity of his sails, he tried to sprint past the only pirate ship that stood between him and his port of call. A volley of cannon balls across his bow convinced him, however, that the pirates were deadly serious.

Within a short time, the Philadelphia sat dead in the water as pirates swarmed on board from both the starboard and port sides in search of rich cargo. The Philadelphia was carrying large amounts of rum, gold, and tobacco. Just after daylight, the Philadelphia sailed into the port of Tripoli, guided by a pirate captain.

On the forward port bow of the ship stood the captain of the Philadelphia, his crew, several male passengers, and two women dressed as men. All were bound together by a long coil of braided rope that was connected to several large iron links looped through the anchor chain. The captives had heard stories of drunken pirates dropping or weighing anchor, watching with glee as their hostages were pulled overboard by the heavy anchor chain. The wait seemed interminable, but no one was in a hurry to discover his or her fate. The captives knew their lives depended upon the whims of the pirates.

Well past midnight, two shots rang out. To the man, each pirate stopped what he was doing and stood at attention facing the gangplank. Out of the darkness appeared a large, thickly built man with a pockmarked face and slightly bulging eyes. He held a torch in his right hand, brandishing it over his head as he announced, "Captain Francisco Baptiste is coming aboard!"

Baptiste was tall and lean. His loose clothing concealed a surprisingly muscular body that was endowed with grace and perfect balance. In his veins ran the blood of French, Spanish, and Moroccan ancestors. His features were fine yet masculine, and everything about his physical appearance was dimmed by dark eyes that burned with the maniacal fires of hell. Baptiste possessed a characteristic that he would never discover: his profile was very similar to that of Kuntamba, the dark runner.

The buccaneer's authority had been contested in the past, but Baptiste's merciless method of disemboweling his rivals dissuaded all threats to his leadership. Baptiste's command was accepted without question.

"Untie the hostages and line them up in front of me," he ordered. "And be quick about it." Turning to the man with the pockmarked face,

Baptiste demanded, "Bring more torches so that I might examine the prisoners more closely."

The raiders looked at each other fearfully. Baptiste was in one of his moods. If he didn't find someone among the captives who appealed to his appetites, there would be no rest. There would be no drinking or division of spoils and the air would be filled with the hostages' screams as the captain sought relief for his lust through sadism.

As the prisoners stood silently in front of Baptiste, all eyes looked down on deck except for the master of the Philadelphia. His stare was locked on the pirate's face. Baptiste slowly drew his sword. He would sacrifice the insolent American pig that dared to look at him. He hesitated as it occurred to him that the United States government would pay handsomely for the return of the captain of the Philadelphia. What a shame the skipper would not be the same man who guided the Philadelphia from its home waters to the Mediterranean.

To humiliate the American captain and unveil those who were in disguises, Baptiste shouted a command. "Strip them all naked so that those who try to conceal their gender are exposed to my eyes." The prisoner's clothes were ripped and torn from their bodies. Within minutes, the humbled captives' bare flesh was displayed for all to see. Only the captain of the Philadelphia enjoyed a degree of privacy that was provided by his extended stomach casting a shadow across his private parts.

Baptiste stood motionless except for his head which rotated from side to side as if it wasn't connected to his body. His eyes fixed on a middle-aged seaman whose arms and chest were tattooed with images of busty women. The pirate captain was reminded of his mother, a denizen of a brothel and a practitioner of the world's oldest profession. His eyes narrowed as he remembered watching and listening from his hiding place under her bed, the only place where he was safe from the men who preferred children. During his short residency in the house of ill repute, he saw blood and death, naked men and women, and an endless stream of tattooed sailors.

The captain's mood swung suddenly from sexuality to violence. Three quick steps and a downward swing of his sword collapsed the waiting seaman into a writhing heap of blood and pain. Baptiste paced back and forth in front of the terrified spectators. The drawing of blood seemed to incense and energize him. His stare fell on the two naked women. The older one was past her prime. The younger one, her daughter, was full-bodied and angelically beautiful. Baptiste's eyes followed the curve of her ankles and upward past her thighs. His corrupted look rested on her womanhood, visually caressing her breasts, then looking into her calm, emotionless face.

The youthful woman's expression awakened images of his mother's passionless voice fabricating ardor as she stared vacantly at the grime-covered ceiling. For a reason that Baptiste, the progeny of a prostitute and an unknown customer, couldn't explain, the memory made him feel worthless and tainted. He wanted to speak, but couldn't. So, he waited, as did everyone aboard ship.

Finally, he spoke gruffly to the female. "You are part of the spoils of war. As such, you may be used by anyone who desires to partake of your flesh." Baptiste suddenly felt better. After a night with his men, she would be just as dirty as his mother was. A short while later, her space in line was filled by the closing of the captives' ranks. Left behind was the image of a woman whose clear eyes and inner courage had temporarily silenced the pirate's voice of command.

Because Baptiste's mind and body craved the pleasures depraved sexuality brings, the ethics of right and wrong did not plague him. His lower nature was unchallenged and in full control of his appetites. In the beautiful young woman he had unconsciously recognized a purity that his mother had never possessed. Unable to reconcile the young woman's courage with his mother's open acceptance of a prostitute's life, he became agitated and began to spin in furious circles. Holding his head back, eyes closed, his long hair flowed behind him. As quickly as the strange gyrations began, they ended. His outstretched killing sword was pointed directly at John Feriluc.

John felt the tight grip of panic spread from his stomach to his knees, metastasizing his weakness to helplessness. He tried to force his concentration deep inside where he stored the written and spoken wisdom of ages, but his spiritual immaturity was unable to open the inner vaults that guarded the teachings he prized so highly. He strained to recall the words of the ancients who told why physical life should be treasured and when, when it was prized, it lost its value.

Baptiste's rapidly approaching steps accelerated Feriluc's panic. All that stood between him and Baptiste's desire was an animal nature that demanded survival at all costs.

The frenzied pirate stopped in front of him. His expression, the bloody sword, and the nude, lolling corpse of the seaman destroyed Feriluc's resistance. Lowering his eyes, he acquiesced to Baptiste's superiority without knowing or caring what lay in store for him. His only concern was that he might live.

With the cunning of a wild beast over its prey, Baptiste exulted that his special needs would be satisfied before the sun cast light on the evidence of his crimes. However, before they retired to his quarters, the pirate captain wanted to be sure Feriluc's will to resist was completely destroyed.

He stopped in front of Feriluc and an older male hostage. "One of you is about to die," Baptiste announced. "You, my fearful companion to be," He swung his sword at Feriluc, "Or you, old man."

Baptiste's cold, sadistic words chilled Feriluc, but the old man had beheld death in dark images of battle, starvation, and disease. He knew the angel of death had slipped by him many times in the past, and he did not expect her to leave empty-handed this time.

The old man looked directly at Baptiste and smiled before answering. "I would gladly die to save the life of the young man next to me. What bothers me most is that I must die at the hands of a coward not fit to lick my boots."

Baptiste's expression swiftly changed from playful to deadly. He noted the old man's bulging waist and the sag of muscles no longer resisting gravity's relentless pull. The malicious abductor decided to have a bit of twisted amusement. The suggestion of a confrontation offered him a perfect opportunity to display his prowess in front of his men while ripping the last shred of resistance from John Feriluc's mind and will.

Pivoting, the pirate called to his men, "Give me a fighter's circle and hand my unworthy opponent a sword."

The old man's name was Calvin Williams. He had held a sword in battle while defending his country and, as a young man, had learned the art of the rapier. He knew how the match would end, but was determined to fight until he could no longer lift his foil in defense or attack. His only goal was to draw blood and show that the pirate was not invincible.

Calvin's fingers locked around the sword's handle. He looked at the blade. It was dull and notched from colliding with harder steel. It was a poor weapon, badly designed for his purposes. The knowledge forced him to make a decision. He chose to spend the major portion of his energy in a sudden all-out attack.

He lunged forward but his legs, motionless and rigid for hours, refused to follow. One stumbling step, and he was down on the deck, rolling over and looking up into the eyes of death. In the glare of the torches, he saw a sadistic viciousness that told him death would wait a few minutes longer to claim his soul. Pulling himself up to his feet, Calvin moved to his left until the circle of pointing swords forced him to turn into the advancing attack of the buccaneer captain.

Williams met each slashing sword stroke with a perfect counter, but the relentless clashing and pounding of steel on steel slowly ebbed his strength. Calvin's breathing took on a rasping sound as he labored to pull the life-giving oxygen into his lungs. Slowly time, old injuries, and the tireless press of the pirate's assault drained the old man's reserves, leaving only his helpless, flailing arms and an unshakable determination to fight to the end.

With a twist of his wrist, Baptiste disarmed his prey. After a long, agonizing pause, Baptiste spoke. "If you wish to live, drop down on your hands and knees and lick every inch of my boots."

Williams wanted nothing more than to sit down on the deck and stretch out his exhausted body. His lungs labored to restore his strength. His unyielding stare signified his refusal to surrender to the pirate captain. Baptiste may have defeated his prisoner physically, but Williams' will and pride remained unscathed.

Baptiste repeated his demand. Williams refused to answer.

The buccaneer turned to his men. "Shall I spare him or shall I kill him?"

Before the gathered seamen could respond, Baptiste swung his body in a semicircle with his right arm and saber held out at a rigid right angle from his shoulders. The tip of his blade caught Williams' chest several inches above his nipples. Blood gushed from the deep horizontal slash.

Baptiste listened for a roar of approval from his men. When he did not hear any calls for more blood, his unbalanced mind came up with a reason for their lack of involvement. "They think I should have played with him, cut off fingers, or nicked his body with a hundred pricks of my sword." Believing he had shown Calvin Williams too much mercy, he plunged the weapon through his opponent's heart and body and into the wooden mast that Williams had fallen against. His body would remain there until it either rotted or was pulled down by unseen hands. It would, as others had, move with the pitch of the vessel and the throes of rigor mortis.

Without a sound, the sailors turned and walked away. They would steal, rape, and kill in self-defense, but the sacrificial murder of the old man unsettled them.

Excited and anticipating a night of pleasure, the pirate pointed at John Feriluc. "Follow me!"

John shuffled after the captain as if in a trance. His steps were short, eyes lowered. He stumbled down the stairs into the pirate's private quarters, then watched with morbid curiosity as Baptiste laid out several small knives and a pair of iron bracelets. No thought of escape or grabbing one of Baptiste's knives entered John's mind. He just stared. With certainty, he knew that the hellish night of torment and degradation would change his life. He would find temporary relief in moments of pain-induced unconsciousness, but each awakening would bring more intense suffering and greater debasement.

Feriluc survived the night of torture, but days would turn to weeks before his body began to recover and his wounds began to close. It would take years for his mind to find a balance that would enable him to look into men's faces. He would never speak of the horrors he had endured at Baptiste's hands. In his heart, an undying hate grew, consuming his every thought in a desire for revenge, a revenge that would repay his tormentor with a slow and insufferable death.

CHAPTER TWO

Thousands of miles away, the President of the United States learned of the Philadelphia's capture. He had been pushing the concept of a strong central government. The ever-increasing demands of the rulers of the Barbary states of North Africa-Morocco, Algiers, Tunis, and Tripoli were exhausting his patience. The seizing of Christian nations' ships and holding their crews for ransom was intolerable. It galled President Jefferson to be forced into paying pirates for the right of passage on the Mediterranean Sea. When President Jefferson learned how much the ruler of Tripoli was demanding for the return of the Philadelphia, he made a decision.

The American Navy was dispatched to the Mediterranean with orders to restore free passage on the Mediterranean Sea by using whatever means necessary. Not even the daring exploits of John Paul Jones during the Revolutionary War were more courageous than the deeds of one lieutenant Stephen Decatur.

On a foggy night in February 1804, Decatur rowed into the harbor at Tripoli with a handful of men and boarded the Philadelphia. He and his men surprised the pirate crew, set the ship on fire, and rescued the hostages before rowing back to their own ship. Captain Baptiste was shot dead during the rescue.

Baptiste's death did not bring closure for John Feriluc. Instead it created a fermenting vat of anger and self-disgust. When his rescuers learned of his defilement, instead of expressing sympathy and support, they spat at him and kicked him. Feriluc was studiously avoided by fellow hostages.

The War with the Barbary Pirates ended in 1805. President Jefferson made his point regarding a strong central government, and the Mediterranean Sea was opened to the commerce of the world.

Returning to America, Feriluc went into seclusion. On occasion, like most recluses, he needed to be among people and listen to the sound of other human voices. When John was passed on the street by strangers, he imagined he saw disgust on their faces instead of the actual harmless curiosity. His only reprieve from self-hatred was the bowed heads of African slaves who tried to pass unnoticed. The slaves' forced submission and their seeming inability to raise their eyes above his waist gave John a feeling of power. This enabled him to presume he was not the lowest of the low. He began to go out of his way to pass or address slaves. Each time a slave stepped aside so he could pass, or answered with a mumbled "Yas, sir," Feriluc's ego recovered a little more.

Feriluc was rebuilding his self-respect on the abuse and belittlement of those who could not defend themselves. His behavior was a poison that, when mixed with the vitriol of his inner consciousness, spawned outbursts of violence. The moments of imagined superiority enabled him to stand with raised eyes in the presence of his countrymen. It temporarily eased his feelings of self-loathing while, at the same time, internally compressing his self-directed anger and disgust. His new sense of worth was fragile. A head turned to look in his direction or someone spitting on the ground cracked the brittle veneer, releasing volcanic eruptions of anger.

Feriluc's rage was vented on the same dark-skinned slaves whose presence was the foundation of his self-esteem. The explosive displays of viciousness and violence invoked the ire and retribution of men who owned the slaves. Feriluc was often forced to move. He usually fled in fear of his life.

Sometimes he slipped away in the early morning hours, erroneously believing his shame had been exposed. It was his fear of being identified as the only American captive on the Philadelphia who lacked the courage to face death, who chose personal defilement over self-respect, which ate away at his manhood and drove him from place to place. Accompanying his persistent fear of discovery during Feriluc's transient period was a growing need to express his self-disgust. He started fights. He stabbed men and was stabbed in return.

It wasn't long until the last vestiges of civilization lay behind him. He explored the great American frontier. His travels toughened him. He learned to ride, and handle a six-shooter and a rifle. To those who knew him superficially, he was all man, someone to avoid if one was looking for trouble. The few who saw beneath his acquired veneer saw a disturbed and unpredictable man who trusted no one.

Feriluc didn't realize it, but he had become like Captain Baptiste, thief and murderer. The only evil ornament that did not adorn his soul was sexual depravity. In fact, he had lost all interest in sex. He believed himself unfit, too vile to even entertain thoughts of female companionship.

When he read that the United States Cavalry was recruiting men to serve on far-flung outposts in the American West, Feriluc enlisted with the intention of becoming an Indian fighter. In this new adventure he saw himself as a killer of the enemy. If he had looked inward, he would have discovered his motives were nothing more than a hunger to appease his own inner demons with the blood of others. If Feriluc could have seen his future, he would have known he was entering a time when his repression of the past was causing him to become insatiably violent.

His effectiveness in killing and driving Indian tribes of the southwest from land claimed by the United States government earned him promotions and, eventually, the command of a garrison. It was only his rank that commanded the respect of his men. Otherwise he was despised and feared. Feriluc's men had seen the carnage left behind the flash of his sword. They had been ordered to slaughter women, children, and every animal that crossed their path. The few soldiers who hesitated were lashed. Only one soldier dared to refuse Feriluc's orders to slaughter the innocent, and he was promptly hanged without ceremony or trial.

One evening in midsummer 1811 after his command had returned to camp, Feriluc suddenly felt disoriented as he walked across the clearing. The feeling did not arise from within—its source lay in the hills behind the camp. He turned slowly and searched the surrounding landscape then, like a compass aligning itself due north, fixed his eyes on a long, steep slope.

Feriluc felt ill. Stumbling into his tent, he fell heavily onto his cot. He had no way of connecting his sudden nausea and vomiting with a conflict between good and evil. He didn't understand that he was about to be given one last chance to repent and change his life.

PART III
1811: The Crossing

CHAPTER ONE

In the early spring of 1811, Kuntamba stood and looked down over the mighty Mississippi River. An urge to continue in a southwesterly direction filled his being. The feeling was akin to what some birds felt when winter threatened and the southern region called with a promise of warmth. It wasn't an irresistible impulse, but was always present just behind his thoughts and meditations.

A swirling, rushing body of water was directly in front of him, seemingly uncrossable. Kuntamba considered running upstream toward the mighty river's source, but something deep inside demanded that he cross the river as soon as possible. In the past, the passing of time had been of little importance. He wondered what had awakened his new awareness of time.

He spotted an inviting mound that would give him a better view of his surroundings. He climbed to the top, searching for a way to cross the turbulent river that blocked his path. Sitting down, he began to meditate. In a semi-trance, he accepted universal law as his guide to the future. He offered himself physically and spiritually to his destiny, praying that only his highest understanding of right would guide his thoughts and actions.

The African knew he was one of a very few embodied souls who through effort and circumstance was able to understand life's purpose and direction. He was aware his death would close one of the doors to knowledge that his wisdom and virtue held open. During his lifetime, Kuntamba always looked for a qualified and willing student to share his wisdom, but he had found none. A few were qualified, but their destinies lay elsewhere.

Much of his spiritual power had been acquired as his feet flowed over the ground and his lungs filled with air. The act of running enabled his mind to explore the ethereal regions of truth. Any student who followed his path would need to travel with him. He or she must have already acquired a level of self-mastery and transcendence of the material world that approached his own. The ability to do so would make them equals in many ways. In his life, he had seen many aspirants, and a few who approached mastery, but none of them could follow his particular path.

Kuntamba thought of fathering and raising a child with a woman who truly understood him. The concept seemed so implausible that he immediately rejected the idea. He had never met a woman who stirred such feelings in him.

As his reflections progressed, he was aware of a new thought entering his consciousness. Maybe he had been brought to this new land to find the only woman who walked the earth that could awaken his passion and join him in his spiritual odyssey. The thought gave him hope and strengthened his sense of purpose. The universal law would work through its positive and negative aspects and guide him to his fate, whatever that might be. Long ago, Kuntamba learned that each trial was a test to measure his worthiness to continue his inner journey.

A slight sound recalled him to the physical world. Rising to his feet, Kuntamba called, "Come forward, friend. I mean you no harm."

When his invitation went unanswered, he repeated his words in his native tongue.

The roar of the river and rustling wind muted his words, but their meaning was heard by listening ears. A moment later, a tall, dark form stepped out from the cover of thick brush. The stranger smiled. It had been many years since he had heard his native tongue. The newcomer walked toward Kuntamba with his arms extended in a hungry search for the feel of another person's warm skin.

Kuntamba instantly recognized that the approaching man was a fellow countryman. Their brief hug disclosed the man's loneliness. The men spoke to each other with tongues that had been rendered silent through lack of contact with others. At first their words were labored and difficult to understand. As the day slipped into night, they achieved clarity.

Magwamsa told how he had been captured as he slept by his wife. Her violent protestations of the inescapable net were met by a blow to the head that silenced her voice forever and released her spirit. Magwamsa was bound and carried to the ocean by dark-skinned enemies of his tribe. A long pole that was carried on the shoulders of other Africans separated his tied hands and feet. After a long sea journey, he was brought to the eastern shores of America. He feigned his own death and was thrown overboard with the other corpses. After swimming ashore, he dragged himself inland. He rested until enough strength returned to forage for roots and the dried fruit that still clung to the trees after a hard winter.

The local Indians accepted his presence and offered him food. Magwamsa preferred to live alone. He quickly learned that the color of his skin would bring white men and their long rifles. If they could take him alive, he would be sold. If he were killed, a bounty would be paid for his scalp. Over the past ten years, he had wandered the dense forests, praying to find a way home. When Kuntamba told him the only path that led to Africa was across the vast ocean, Magwamsa's shoulders drooped and the light of hope left his eyes.

Kuntamba immediately regretted his careless words. He of all people should have known the power of speech. His thoughts turned to Captain Stouvall, his wife, and the child she would have birthed by now. He envisioned the *Ocean Breeze* waiting in the harbor to once again defy the mountainous swells of the ocean. Kuntamba studied Magwamsa's face. The African looked tired and old beyond his years.

"I have friends," Kuntamba said. "They live in a place called Portsmouth, New Hampshire. You will need to travel northeast, halfway between the rising sun and the north star."

The African's expression grew tense. To have lost all hope, then to recover it in a matter of minutes caused an almost unbearable swing of emotions. He leaned closer as Kuntamba continued. The dark runner spoke of Captain Stouvall and his woman, who had a trace of African ancestry. Kuntamba told him of his journey on the *Ocean Breeze* and the captain's capture of fellow Africans. He related the captain's slow emergence into the world of morality and compassion.

When the dark runner paused, he saw that Magwamsa was smiling. Kuntamba concluded, "Tell the captain and his wife that Kuntamba the dark runner is well. Those words should bring smiles to their faces. They will accept your presence in their home. When the time is right, the captain will take you back to Africa if you still wish to go." Magwamsa's expression turned pensive. The mythology of his homeland traversed the generations by spoken word. One myth told of a holy man, a runner whose running steps never tired. It was said that his presence was a blessing that could heal those who crossed his path. Most believed the story of the dark runner had its origins in the spirit world. Only a few individuals knew he possessed a human form, but all were aware his appearance represented a change that would gradually lift human experience out of the mire of ignorance.

Magwamsa fell to his knees, prostrate, and tried to kiss Kuntamba's feet. The dark runner simply reached down and placed his hand softly on the top of his countryman's head. "We are equal. Only time and experience separate us. In the unknown stretches of the future, I may be kneeling before you."

Not understanding, Magwamsa nevertheless obeyed the dark runner's unspoken command to stand. He looked into Kuntamba's face and realized why the dark runner had seated himself near the river. He needed to cross. The realization made Magwamsa very happy. He could now repay the holy man's gift of hope.

"May I help you?" Magwamsa asked. "You have traveled far and now find your way blocked by the flooding river. Two times I have watched the river over flow it's bank. If the clouds continue to carry their moisture from the west and north, it could be months before the river's main channel will be able to contain the southern flow of water."

"The Indians who live along the river's banks seldom contest the currents. Only when necessary, when they are driven by hunger, will they brave the river when it is flooding. First they select a place where the river has spread its waters over the greatest area. They know the wide places are usually the most shallow, with fewer undercurrents. Using their canoes, they enter the water above their intended crossing point and let the river carry them through the narrowest channels, driving them south at high speeds."

"At just the right moment, they use a large paddle to guide their craft across the main body of water with very little work on their part. Once they are beyond the river's main flow, they paddle till they reach dry land." When Magwamsa saw that Kuntamba was interested, he added, "I know where there is a canoe. Would you like to try the Indian method of crossing?"

Kuntamba nodded. Magwamsa hurried away, disappearing into the brush. The dark runner remembered the African war dugouts in his native land and the way they charged upstream against surging currents. He had watched their boats crashing through wind whipped waves, marveling at the power of the muscular men as they propelled their hand-hewn craft.

Kuntamba had never seen an Indian canoe. He waited expectantly. Within minutes, Magwamsa returned, stumbling, partially blinded by a burden that only allowed him to see the ground directly in front of him. Setting the craft down next to Kuntamba, he turned and went back to retrieve the paddles. Kuntamba studied the slender object. Its two sides met at the front, back, and bottom. Its weight was minimal, and it had a sparse frame. The dugout was covered with the skins of two large animals that were sewn together with long, thin strips of hide. He wondered if the small boat could carry two men down and across the tumbling waters.

When Magwamsa returned, Kuntamba stated, "I will cross alone. It is not right that I should permit you to risk your life helping me."

"Why would you deny me the opportunity to be of service to someone other than myself?" Magwamsa replied. "If I die before my home shores welcome me, I will know I have helped a friend who carries within his mind and soul the wisdom that can set men free. Besides, I must travel with you so that I can bring the canoe back to its owner."

Kuntamba nodded. "Let us begin."

The dark runner watched as Magwamsa dropped the light craft into the shifting water. He grinned as Magwamsa stepped awkwardly into the dugout, tipping it onto its side and spilling Magwamsa into the water. Inadvertently, the larger African had forced the canoe away from the bank and out into a swirling eddy that had formed on the downstream side of a large rock. Magwamsa's arms flailed industriously. After pulling himself into the vessel, the big African sat upright and immediately began bailing water with his cupped hands.

Unable to resist commenting on his friend's predicament, Kuntamba said, "Magwamsa, how will you paddle, throw water from this craft, and steer at the same time? Is this the way Indians get into their canoes?"

"No. I learned this in Africa," Magwamsa said as he shook the water from his hair.

"It must be a skill used only by the best boatmen," Kuntamba joked. "By the way, let me congratulate you. You have washed yourself and the inside and outside of the craft in one motion."

Pulling the canoe up against the bank, Magwamsa asked, "Would you like to show me how a holy man climbs into an untethered vessel that bobs and twists at the slightest touch?"

As much as he loved the land and the feel of solid earth under his feet, Kuntamba knew he had to cross the swirling water. He studied the dugout and Magwamsa's gleeful expression. Noticing that Magwamsa, the heavier man, was sitting at one end of the craft, the dark runner waited for a wave to catch the craft and press it up and against the bank. Just as it crested, he stepped into the canoe and sat down.

"How did you do that?" Magwamsa asked.

"It is quite simple, my friend. Your weight steadied the vessel while a wave moved it closer to me. Let us only hope that our crossing is as easy."

Soon the two men who had spent less than twenty-four hours together would part forever. But each would carry the memory of the other in his heart and mind for as long as both drew breath. That connection would enable Kuntamba to guide the runaway slave who had helped him cross the mighty Mississippi towards Captain Stovall and freedom.

In the years to follow, Magwamsa would not know it was Kuntamba's mental impressions that guided him. It didn't matter. As long as Magwamsa sought truth, Kuntamba would know. In his early years, Kuntamba had been guided by an unseen protector. Now, through Magwamsa, he could repay the debt.

CHAPTER TWO

They steered the craft out into the current. Both men were confident that the surprisingly lethargic body of water could be crossed. Within seconds, the pull of the river's unseen undercurrent caught the flimsy canoe and sent it rushing down the river's central channel. Magwamsa tried to kneel in the stern of the dugout so that he could use his oar as a rudder, but the craft was bobbing like a leaf in a rushing stream.

Turning around, Magwamsa saw Kuntamba using his paddle to keep the canoe pointed downstream. His motions were relaxed and steady. Magwamsa watched as the dark runner moved the oar to the opposite side of the dugout where he reached far out over the water before plunging the paddle into the river, pulling back toward himself.

The holy man's motion had a rhythm and confidence that captured Magwamsa's attention, lessening his fear and enabling him to release his death grip on the sides of the canoe. Downstream, Kuntamba saw where the river jumped its east bank and flowed outward in a great glistening sheet of wetness across the lowlands.

In the center was an island. The main flow curved around the sodden hill then widened out onto a flood plain before rejoining its westerly half in a weak confluence. Kuntamba felt the current's pull softening. Mistakenly, the dark runner concluded it was just a matter of time until they were out on the plain where the water would be more navigable. There was one problem he had not anticipated. They had to navigate the bend in the river where the flow of water accelerated around a curve and created a wide area of turbulence.

Taking advantage of the short reprieve, Magwamsa steadied himself in the canoe's stern. He waited with his paddle poised for the instant when the fragile craft met the churning waters of the river's bend. He glanced back over his shoulder just as the canoe was spun in the river's chaotic and shifting currents.

Magwamsa stabbed his oar into the water, turning the blade until it was in line with the canoe's length. When the vessel's bow pulled to the port side, he turned the paddle's blade in the same direction. He felt the twisting currents tearing at his oar, trying to pull it from his grip. At the worst possible moment, he withdrew the paddle to reposition it. Just ahead lay a whirlpool. The eddy caught the craft in its churning spiral and tried to pull it down into the center of its vortex.

Perhaps it was Kuntamba's power or perhaps their separate destinies would not let them die. Or possibly it was Magwamsa's wild paddling. Perhaps it was the fickle river adjusting to an increased flow of water generated by a thunderstorm hundreds of miles away. Whatever the reason, the whirlpool shifted downstream, leaving Kuntamba and Magwamsa floating slowly out onto the flooded plain.

The sun was high when the two countrymen reached dry land and looked back over the watery course they had just traversed. They both agreed they had picked one of the worst possible places to cross.

Aware the time for parting had come, Kuntamba said, "Know, my friend, that distance cannot separate minds. If you are an arm's length or a continent away, and you call out my name using the voice of honesty and selflessness, I will hear you and respond. You of necessity live alone. Your loneliness will end and happiness will be yours, but something will always be missing. Embrace this feeling. If you endure its emptiness, you will find the spiritual source of all that is."

"I can tell you no more. Your journey, which is both physical and spiritual, is your only true teacher. Living is an endless series of tests that measure growth and determines the lessons we must master or transcend. Now the river and your trials wait. If you cross down there, where the river widens and the water surrenders its restlessness, the eastern shore will welcome your safe return."

Magwamsa did not want to part from the only person who had interrupted his solitude since he was ship-bound, reluctantly stepped into the canoe and slowly paddled out onto the river. With him he carried the demons of isolation and a promise for the future. In his mind lived hope and fear.

From the shore Kuntamba watched the distance between them grow. He reached out with psychic hands and the power of thought, guiding Magwamsa across the treacherous currents. Finally there were two forms--one on each side of the river, with extended arms waving goodbye and expressions lost in the separating distance.

Magwamsa turned and hurried toward his future, his mind filled with thoughts of the slave trading captain and the woman whose ancestry reached across oceans, joining continents and people. Kuntamba's was consumed by a question. Why would the fates permit two men from the same area of Africa to meet in a desolate uninhabited land half way around the world, then send them to fulfill destines which lay in opposite directions?

Abruptly, with the suddenness of a flash of lighting, he comprehended. The understanding he sought could not be put into words. It arrived silently, waiting to grow into a wider appreciation. The understanding also carried a realization that whatever is, has been, or ever will be, is connected in a oneness that transcends time and place.

Kuntamba's searching gaze moved up and down the great river's sprawling length and across its dangerous waters. It filled him with premonitions and visions of farms and vast cities teeming with people. He wondered why the people of the future would pick such a precarious place to settle. He didn't know about barges and trade, the movements of goods, or the vast arable tracts of land that lay all around him. Nevertheless, he believed his vision.

He had no way of knowing that a few years earlier the Lewis and Clark expedition had passed his present position on an adventure that would open up the northwest. Kuntamba knew the land he traversed, and much of the world's population, was on the cusp of change, change that would move mountains, free men's bodies from toil, and teach their minds, offering them eternity while blinding them with materialism.

These thoughts consumed him as he ran across a seemingly endless flat land that reached to the horizon and beyond. The images inexplicably added purpose to his undefined mission. He felt displaced. The sky was overcast and the air was damp. The ground beneath his feet was sodden from weeks of rain. His steps left shallow imprints in the rich soil that slowly filled with a liquid brown ooze, marking his trail with a long line of tiny reflecting pools.

The dark runner increased his pace, wanting to leave the land of wetness behind. But his rhythm was poor and he was unable to find the center of relaxation that would allow his mind, body, and soul to commune in harmony. He slowed to a walk and raised his head so that if his eyelids had been open, he would have been looking up at nature's dark promise of rain.

He began to meditate. Using eyes that saw without light, a vision of Magwamsa in hurried flight came to him. Extending his vision over the land and surrounding hills, Kuntamba looked on emptiness and places where the red man no longer thrived. He saw a pale sun setting in the Southwest, felt its warmth and a guiding influence that he could not resist.

He left his contemplation and broke into a long effortless stride. The motion carried his steps southward. The landscape was drier, making it possible for him to run more easily. Gradually Kuntamba increased his leg speed, finding the tempo that made the trance-like state possible. Over the next hours, his body and mind would be recharged with the omnipresence energy of creation. His steps softened, causing the faint indentations his weight left on the grass-covered earth to fade into nothingness. Indians would follow his trail and wonder if the man they pursued could fly.

Returning to the world of change, Kuntamba followed a path that in a hundred and fifty years would become an interstate highway. But he did not see asphalt or white lines. For him it was a prairie alive with large shaggy animals that snorted and pawed the earth. Enormous bulls battled each other with curved horns, pushing giant heads together as their hind legs fought for traction and the right to claim territory and breeding privileges. Kuntamba's form glided through the ranks of the American bison almost unnoticed. Some animals raised their heads as he passed, stared at him dolefully then returned to their grazing.

Looking out over the gentle roll of the land, Kuntamba saw vast colonies of creatures that decorated the earth's surface with small mounds. Closer examination revealed that the mounds had been created by excavation and the forming of tunnels. He watched the furry little creatures darting in and out of their underground homes. The dark runner marveled at a family organization that always positioned one animal on the highest ground available. The sentry usually sat on the mound in front of the tunnels and watched while the rest of the colony foraged.

He noticed the lookouts were constantly scanning the sky with heads that almost rotated in a full circle. When a strange sound or the call of a distant colony member caught their attention, noses sniffed the air as they hurriedly searched for the approach of the ever-present coyotes or the undulating movements of a hungry snake.

The wind shifted as dark clouds seemingly materialized out of nowhere. The prairie dogs disappeared underground while off in the distance bison broke into a run as lightening crackled across sky. Even the birds seemed to vanish from sight. The dark runner watched as a strange phenomenon of nature fought its way into existence from afar. It reached down from an enormous churning thunderhead with a great swirling arm. Soon a huge spinning mass of dust, rocks, and plant material was captured in the tornado's embrace as it revolved outward in ever widening circles.

The whirling air mass recoiled upward, losing its grip on the earth before it charged down into a small lake. The winds churned up a watery froth as it drained the pond's basin. Moments later, it disgorged its liquid meal in a centrifugally-spinning horizontal rainstorm. On both of its flanks, grey clouds discharged torrential rains. Through the clouds and across the vortex of the tornado, a constant series of electrical discharges exploded in a web-like series of lightening strikes that stretched to the ground.

Nature added the chaotic rumble of distant thunder and a sound that resembled the reverberations of war drums. Kuntamba ran through sheets of rain and gale force winds. He was a man whose life was undisturbed by fear, anger, or desire. The rainstorm, the high winds, and the twisting monster that consumed everything in its path before spitting it out to make room for its next spiraling mouthful, were exciting and exhilarating.

The storm's power filled his senses, awakening primordial feelings whose source could only be touched at the moment of creation. Kuntamba ran on, savoring the immense field of nature's might that engulfed him. As he passed beyond the sound and fury of the tornado, the howling winds and the driving rain, for a brief instant he regretted the temporary nature of the experience.

CHAPTER THREE

He was not prepared for the stifling, windless humidity that followed in the storm's wake. The air was hot and heavy with moisture. Kuntamba's body was unable to release the internal heat his muscles were generating. He began to perspire. Seeking respite, the dark runner slowed his pace and adjusted his direction toward the clear blue sky that filled the southern horizon.

Dusk found him running with the effortless grace that is born when mind, body, and spirit harmonize. Behind him, copper hued natives on horseback followed and watched. Soon they were openly paralleling Kuntamba's path. Dusk settled into night. The strange black human continued to run. The Indians moved in closer, driven by curiosity and restrained by fear of the unknown.

They had seen the black skinned humans before. A neighboring tribe had permitted a runaway slave to join their community. But this black man who ran without tiring was different. He didn't seem to need rest and was not slowed by darkness. And strangely, he carried no food or weapons. He had been seen sipping water from his cupped hands, but other than this occasional need, he appeared to the Indians to be more like a spirit than a man. The native Americans' first sighting of Kuntamba occurred just as the tornado and its torrential rains eased, revealing the dark runner's striding silhouette framed in the background by a twisting maze of churned earth and forking lightning.

At first the dark-skinned man, whom they believed was born from nature's awesome power, frightened them. They were positive he was the human incarnation of the god of storms, but their god had two facets. The first was the destructive bringing of wind, rain, floods, and tornadoes. The second was the replenishing of the land, the spreading of seeds, and the harvest of the weak and dead.

The Indians wondered which facet the dark runner would bring into existence. They pushed their sturdy ponies, trying to move nearer to the running image that seemed unconcerned with their presence. Each foray carried them closer to the dark god that had visited them. One brave warrior raced to within a few feet of Kuntamba, hoping to count coup by touching the embodied power of nature with a tentative hand. A glance from the dark runner's black eyes filled the warrior's heart with fear and an urgent need to escape.

That evening as Fighting Buffalo sat in the dancing light of a campfire, he embellished his story about his close encounter with the god of storms. The children, the squaws, and the young men who were impatient to become warriors, insisted that the story of the god of storms be retold throughout the night. They loved the part of his birth from the womb of nature and his running in the protective embrace of his parents, Wind and Rain. The day's raid on a small wagon train, the short furious fight, the taking of scalps and their duty to protect the land from all intruders was all but forgotten.

The morning light found the young warriors still thinking and talking about the dark running god, but the story telling soon ended. The tribe was on the move. They were going to their summer campground. The Kiowa would spend the long, hot summer months near the shady banks of the Canadian River.

White men and marauders from the south knew the Kiowa to be fiercely independent, predatory, and ruthless in battle. For hundreds of years their reputation of courage and a willingness to fight to the death had preserved their way of life from outsiders. Unknowingly, they had engaged an enemy, the *white man*, whose numbers were endless and whose weapons had a power Kiowa imaginations could not grasp. The ancient Kiowa way of life had entered its twilight.

The Kiowa had fought and defeated the Apache, Mexican bandits, and members of neighboring tribes that were constantly testing the Kiowa's courage and vigilance. The tribe believed as their ancestors had that the Kiowa would always roam free. They had a oneness with the land, the mountains, and the rivers. The vast blue sky gave their spirits a sense of expansiveness that most white men could not understand. The Kiowa people were curious and eager to learn. They were developing a written language and a calendar. The wise elders studied the stars, experienced visions of the future, and contemplated the meaning of life.

Surely the gods would not permit the unholy white man to defeat the Kiowa. Indians knew their place in the worlds of body and spirit. Their balance was not upset by physical possessions, or a hunger for more than they needed. The white soldiers appeared weak. They rode on horses and carried extra water and food. Kiowa braves could run for days, subsisting only on the contents of a small pouch carried at their waists. Most Kiowas believed the appearance of the dark runner was an omen that predicted their ultimate victory over the white soldiers. A few elders, remembering the dual nature of all things including the storm god, were not so sure.

The chief sent warriors to find and meet with the dark runner. The Kiowa leader hoped the offspring of Wind and Rain would use his power to defend the Kiowa against the growing strength of the white man's mounted soldiers and the long killing rifles. His messengers returned empty-handed. They told of fading footsteps and wondered if the storm god had returned to the clouds. The chief, uncertain whether the dark runner was really a god, decided to talk with the tribe's shaman.

Miles away, Kuntamba paused in a pine forest. He lay looking east toward the rising sun and the clouds that threatened to block out the dawning light. He saw the great circumference of the horizon. He knew his homeland was an ocean and a continent away. He recalled the twinkle of distant stars. He wondered how vast creation was. The dark runner believed that the world, the stars, and the space they moved in were limitless. He knew everything that existed was caught on the wheel of change. He also understood that all of mankind, white, black, or Indian, existed because of, and within an omnipresent field of immutable law.

He began to understand. God is absolute and unlimited, and all that exists is endowed with the eternality needed to forever explore and grow into the innumerable fields of experience that the infinite aspect of God provides. He became intensely aware of his own existence, his state of being. With awareness came an undeniable belief in his indestructibility. He knew he would never cease to be. His growing spiritual essence would always continue. It was a particle of wisdom that he could not pass on, try as he might. It gave him power over death. He knew with certitude that dying was an illusion.

His life had always been an adventure. This new understanding of life's continuity added another dimension. No matter how much he experienced or how great his spiritual acumen, he would always be just beginning.

Kuntamba studied the rising sun's bright hemisphere. Far to the west where the dawn had not yet filled space with light, a solitary shooting star breached the horizon then fell from view. Behind it raced a swarm of faint streaks. They followed the first tiny meteors as if in pursuit before colliding and generating a burst of light.

The African stood erect, closing his eyes in meditation as he took several long slow breaths and waited. He was searching for the meaning of the racing star fragments. Before long his mental screen cleared. It was soon filled with white men in blue uniforms riding great horses across the plains in pursuit of a band of Indians. He focused and recognized the copper-hued natives who had followed him the day before. The soldiers killed their prey without coming close to them. One solitary soldier knelt on the ground, his weapon spewing fire and delivering death.

Without checking to see if the warriors they had just shot were dead, the soldiers turned southeast toward the summer campsite of the Kiowa. Kuntamba saw the senseless massacre of the entire encampment. He strained to make out the countenance of the man who had ordered the slaughter, but his face was shrouded by a dark blood-red aura. Kuntamba shifted his focus and was surprised to see himself fleeing from the mounted soldiers.

The dark runner broke his trance. He knew his visions dealt with the future. What he did not know was when these events would come to pass. He believed that if the fates gave him a view of what was to come, he had the right to attempt to alter the actual outcomes.

He had an impulse to run, but where, back to the warriors who had followed him or toward an unknown location where the tribe camped? Should he try to warn both groups? 'No,' he thought. 'I may not have enough time.'

The image of the brave who had dared to approach within a few feet of his running form filled Kuntamba's mind. He remembered the Indian's steady but frightened gaze. He saw him push his horse to a gallop, then turn back so their eyes could meet in the safety of distance.

He recalled seeing a warrior who nature and time had fashioned into a perfect instrument of survival; a brave who would not surrender to fatigue, pain, or sorrow. He saw a man who would soon die in a victorious effort to save his followers. The dark runner hoped that the connection made when their eyes met would enable him to invade his courageous visitor's dreams with images of blue coated soldiers killing Kiowa braves.

CHAPTER FOUR

That night and not too far away, Fighting Buffalo stirred in his sleep. His dreams disturbed him. He was restless and agitated, but the dreams would not let him return to wakefulness. He saw the ground rise up and rush his warriors. He stared without fear or emotion, as the mountain of soil became an oncoming wave of charging horses. He looked into the animals' fiery red eyes and inhaled the smoke that belched from their nostrils. On the backs of the apparitions from hell, rode the pale skinned blue coats. Their right hands held swords that dripped with blood, while their left hands fired pistols that never seemed to run out of ammunition.

In the horror of his nightmare, Fighting Buffalo thrashed his arms and legs as if trying to fight off demons. The earth in his dreams shook from the meeting of hooves and land. Almost as quickly as it had begun, the shaking eased into the thundering sound of hooves racing south toward the Canadian River.

Fighting Buffalo did not want to look at the carnage left in their wake, but he could not resist. He saw himself mortally wounded and dying. All around him lay the twisted remains of his hunting party. His dream filled with tears and the voices of his ancestors calling for revenge. Behind every fallen tribe member, he saw the face of the dark runner. At that moment he was released from the tortures of his dream into a wakeful state of ominous dread.

Fighting Bull tried to shake the pictures left in his memory by the nightmare, but they were too powerful. He ran to the lookout point and searched the surrounding land for signs of soldiers. Seeing none, he sat down to think. Soon the rest of his hunting party joined him. He told them of his dream and asked for their opinion. To the man, each agreed the vision was a prophetic gift from their forefathers, but none knew what action should be taken.

"I will meditate on it, and then I will decide what must be done," Fighting Buffalo stated. He sat perfectly still except for his breathing, without food or water through the heat of day and the chill of night. Just as the sun was warning of its approach with the first light of dawn, he stood up and with one blood curdling yell summoned his braves to battle.

They awoke reaching for bows and stone axes, looking for a nonexistent enemy. They did not question Fighting Buffalo's authority. Hurried feet and silent voices rounded up hobbled horses and smothered the last sparks from dying campfires. Once mounted, they waited patiently for direction.

Nearby, their leader sat astride his mount. His eyes were closed as he concentrated. He was recalling his vision, trying to determine from which direction his enemy would come, but the details of the nightmare had faded, leaving only impressions of death. Slowly he urged his horse in a great circle that enclosed the campsite. He was looking for a place where the ground dropped away, forming a hollow large enough to conceal a hundred horses.

After several long tense moments, he pivoted his mount around and galloped about three hundred yards due east. He had found a large mound of earth behind an arroyo that angled back between two rounded hills.

Whistling, he called his warriors. When they had gathered, he began to speak. "We will dig holes and set snares and traps along the near edge of the arroyo. They must be so perfectly concealed that even you will be unable to find them. We do not seek to capture buffalo or any animal that hunts or grazes this land. We seek to injure and slow down the blue coats who will attack from the concealment of the gully."

No voices of dissension were raised. No instructions were needed. The Kiowa, like most native Americans, believed in the power of dreams. If Fighting Buffalo had been guided to a specific interpretation of his sleeping vision by disembodied spirits of the past, then it was their duty to follow his instructions. After all, not only was Fighting Buffalo their leader, he was the son of Kiowa's greatest living holy man.

The next night, Fighting Buffalo's party built a large campfire. They did not sleep beside it. They waited concealed behind rocky outcroppings in narrow gullies and within clumps of bushes. Nearby but still out of sight, their tethered horses grazed. The rising sun slowly spread its light across the camouflaged positions of the hunting party. Gradually the long shadows of morning faded, leaving only a longed for return of the shade's transient coolness. In its place, a white-hot sun baked the earth. At first the ground and the sparse vegetation absorbed the sun's warmth but as the day wore on, even the land and plants began to reflect the sun's radiant energy.

Up from the ground and down from the yellow sky the radiant heat moved. It collected just above the earth's surface and seemed to flow, seeking the concealed braves of Fighting Buffalo's war party. Through the heat of day and the chill of night, the warriors of the plains, mountains, and desert refused to move. To the tribe, the war party was a living unit. After the call to battle had been issued, attitudes changed, causing the collective defense and survival of the war party to become more important than individual pain, hunger, or thirst. They would remain immobile and transfixed until death, if necessary.

The fates had other plans. Coming events would test their courage and survival instincts. At first, all they heard was a strange creaking sound. A soft breeze out of the west confused the direction from which it came. The wind rolled fine grains of sand across the ground and whistled as it pushed through dried brush, forcing long dead branches to speak the sounds of friction and agitation.

The voice of the wind carried overtones of creaking leather, telling the Kiowa that Fighting Buffalo had anticipated the blue coats' actions accurately. They were thankful for his leadership, and they were positive that victory would be theirs.

In his position closest to the arroyo, Fighting Buffalo pressed his ear to the ground. He was listening for the sounds of brush being crushed, feeling for the vibrations caused by a host of hooves as they compress the soil before releasing it back to its original state.

Behind him, each warrior resolved to fight with courage and, if necessary, to die with honor. Each knew his spirit guide would lead him to a place where the water flowed pure and sweet and their ancestors waited to greet them. Each brave was aware that only those who fought courageously would tread the straight path to the heaven world. All silently vowed to never dishonor their parents or tribal ancestors.

Hundreds of yards away, where nature's flash floods had cut a long deep furrow into the ground, a single column of cavalrymen entered the arroyo. A branch on a creosote bush snapped as the razor thin leather strap that held the plants' bent form in place gave way to the drag of a passing horse. The release of its stored energy against the horse's flank sent the animal sidestepping into a camouflaged pit.

The horse neighed loudly as its forequarters dropped down into the narrow shaft. The panic-stricken beast fell nose first onto the ground, breaking its legs and sending a startled cavalryman tumbling, head over heels. The gray stallion lay on the ground, its eyes wide and rolling in pain. Terrified, the animal tried to lurch to its feet, but fell pathetically to the ground. The horse lay on its side; eyes fixed on the god it was about to die for.

Sergeant Riley reached for his revolver, intent on ending his horse's misery. Behind him, the chilling voice of Major Feriluc commanded, "Wait!" Looking over his shoulder Riley saw Feriluc walking toward him. His face was dark as he stared at the stallion. He cursed the Kiowa before pointing at the hunting knife on Riley's belt.

The sergeant nodded. The major was right. The sound of a gunshot could carry over a mile. In the back of his mind, Riley recalled his horse's neighing scream of fright. He wondered if his animal's final sound would carry as far as a gunshot, but it didn't matter because he had his orders. The column of soldiers moved around Sergeant Riley as he knelt beside his steed. He waited patiently for the last man to pass before beginning his farewell.

When Riley joined the army, he had requested to bring his own horse. He was told if his animal could pass all the tests of stamina, speed, and obedience, it would be accepted into the corps. He remembered breaking the stallion. Others had tried and failed. But when he settled into the saddle, the horse bucked a few times then looked back at him like an old friend.

The sergeant ran his hand over the creature's twisted front legs and said goodbye. He knelt down, and with a razor sharp knife, parted the jugular vein on the right side of the animal's neck. The horse's blood pumped out onto the ground. Its eyes lost their fright, closing slowly as his master eased its head to the ground. High above, the carrion eaters were already circling. Riley remained, waiting until the beat of his horse's heart no longer vibrated in its chest.

After heaving the saddle onto his shoulder, Sergeant Riley slung his canteen around his neck and locked his rifle in a bloody hand. Without looking back, he began to walk. If Feriluc didn't push too hard, the sergeant figured he would catch up after the company made camp for the night.

Unknown to Riley, Feriluc, fearing other traps, or possibly an ambush, circled back to their last campground. The prior night using his spyglass, the major had spotted the flickering flame of the Indians' campfire. The observation told him where he needed to go, but not the exact location of the Kiowa. The incident with Riley's stallion helped him devise a strategy. He assumed that somewhere ahead of him the Kiowa were planning an ambush. To counter the threat, Feriluc decided to divide his forces into two columns that would move beyond the arroyo then merge into a long skirmish line that would sweep back over the arroyo, flushing the Indians out in the open.

At midmorning the next day as the mounted blue coats passed on both his right and left sides, Fighting Buffalo began to worry that he had led his men to their death. He knew if the soldiers formed a line and swept back toward his position, he and his warriors would be helpless against the white man's weapons.

He looked up at the sky hoping to see his spirit guide. He chanted low, calling to the hawk that glides on the wind and dives with the speed of a lightening bolt. He searched the horizon for the tiny speck that would tell him his prayers had been heard. He remembered how the hawk had visited him in his youth, feeding his hunger with a rabbit before leaving a feather as a sign of brotherhood.

Far in distance, with the sun as a background, a small black dot grew until it became fluttering wings. Finally as Fighting Buffalo continued to chant, the bird circled above his crouching form, riding the thermals and staring down. Fighting Buffalo cupped his hands around his mouth and called in one solitary scream, "Eeeeii."

Over a half a mile away, Feriluc looked back. He thought he heard something. He looked at his men, but they appeared to be unconcerned. Returning to his task, Feriluc shook his head. He was very jittery.

To the Kiowa warriors the sound of the hawk was a summons to assemble. But the appearance of the bird of prey with the hooked beak, the red tail, and sharp talons confused them. They were not sure of the source of the call so they remained stationary.

Fighting Buffalo whispered, "The blue coat leader has an object that can shrink distance and tell him where we wait. Meet me where Mother Earth has washed out a place for us with her summer storms. Move when the wind blows so that nature's breath conceals your movements, but don't delay."

Fighting Buffalo watched and waited. His eyes followed the distant blue spot that marked the last cavalrymen's disappearance into the distance. He winced when the blue spot turned north before fading from sight.

The war party had tethered the horses in a small valley near his last sighted position of the blue coats. Fighting Buffalo was certain the party's mounts had been discovered. He looked up. The red tail hawk was once again circling above. The bird gave Fighting Buffalo confidence and an enhanced sense of protection; from his confidence flowed a plan.

He would lead the blue coats away from the children and elders who waited at the summer encampment. He knew death was near, yet he did not fear the spirit that separates bodies from souls. His only regret was that his family would never know what happened to him.

CHAPTER FIVE

Miles away, Feriluc was elated. He had the Kiowa's horses. The Indians were on foot. In a short while, their scalps would be in his saddlebag. The scalps would prove he was a great Indian fighter, capable of outmaneuvering the enemy in their own land. He was anxious to catch and slaughter the horse-killing enemy. He wanted to finish the braves quickly, and then head south to the place where his Indian scout had told him the Kiowa spent their summers.

But Fighting Buffalo and his young warriors would not die so easily. Fighting Buffalo began to run. As he moved, the entire war party followed. At first, the pace was slow but as the flexibility returned to joints that minutes earlier had been locked in a trance-like immobility, the pace accelerated. As the miles surrendered to the rhythmic foot falls of the war party, hearts, lungs, and muscles labored before finding the balance that would sustain a day-long run.

Fighting Buffalo always talked as he ran. He told the young men who depended on him that they were becoming full-fledged warriors. He explained that in running from the battle, they were leading the blue coats away from their families. Finally he detailed his plans. "After dusk, at the place of many streams, we will run on different paths. Those who survive will turn south to warn our people."

A dozen miles away, Feriluc's men were beating the brush trying to flush out Kiowa warriors. It was slow tedious work that infuriated

Feriluc with the inherent delay. When the chore stretched into hours, Feriluc's patience snapped. He could not believe that he had been outsmarted by a band of heathens.

He sent his scouts out in search of the Kiowa's trail. An hour later, they returned and reported that seven warriors ran northwest. Feriluc was infuriated. His pursuit would carry him away from the Kiowa's summer campground then he calmed. "What did it matter?" he thought. "They will be there all summer."

Far ahead of Feriluc's advancing platoon, Fighting Buffalo was guiding the war party through a narrow canyon. He visually searched the precipitous walls, looking for ancient paths left by deer and small game. He looked for the shadows that might conceal caves. He studied the exposed rocks for damp streaks that indicated water seepage. He was keenly interested in the places where the vegetation was lush and unseasonably green.

In his pouch he carried enough dried meats, berries, and nuts to sustain him for days. On his vision quest he had fasted for seven days and nights. If he could find water and a good location to attack from, Fighting Buffalo was positive he could delay the blue coats long enough to give his warriors and his people a chance at survival.

The war party ran on with Fighting Buffalo always searching to find a place where precarious boulders waited to be sent tumbling down against his enemy, blocking the canyon. Most of what he sought, he found in one nearly perfect location. All that was lacking was a place where the land and rocks could be set in motion, clogging the passage and forcing his pursuers to take a long detour. He knew that his life would end in the narrow channel.

Darkness followed the setting sun, surrendering its shadowless blanket to a full rising moon. Only the Kiowa's running figures, moving through moonlight, darkness, and shadows, remained unchanged. Fatigue had come and gone, leaving in its wake a mystical trance-like state that was beyond pain. A damp chill settled on the land. It brought with it precipitate moisture that soaked frayed leather moccasins and cooled perspiring heads.

Far ahead of him, Fighting Buffalo saw what he had been looking for. He slowed to a walk. Behind him, the warriors became suddenly aware of their intense thirst and the hunger in their bellies. Long ragged breaths pulled at their lungs, causing their chests to heave. They looked around. The ground fell away and the sound of gurgling water called to them. They were at a place where several streams merged. The braves grew restless. They had satisfied their thirst and hunger and the moment that would divide their collective strength had arrived.

Fighting Buffalo stared intently at the expectant faces that awaited his instruction. He saw no fear or doubt, only determination and the need for guidance. Fighting Buffalo spoke slowly. "The lives of our people depend on our actions and courage. Our families may never know how we fought or died, but our ancestors, whose wisdom lives within us, will know, and they will be proud of their Kiowa descendants."

"From this point on, one band will become three. Two of you will follow the stream that flows out of the northwest. You will run in the water against the current until mountains and steep valleys slow your path, then you will head south to the valley where our young ones play in the hot sun. Two warriors will follow the stream that runs south and east. After three days, if the rifles of the blue coats have not sent you home to your ancestors, run with the wind in your face or at your back till you reach our families and warn them of the coming attack. The third team will run with the morning sun on your left side and the setting sun on your right. Yours will be the first words of warning our families will receive, if you survive. Because you will be running toward our summer hunting grounds, the blue coats will follow you first."

"Leave now! Enter the water and ride the current whenever you can. Run where the buffalo will cover your trail. Stick to the gullies and the thick brush. Never think of failure and never admit you are tired or hungry. If the enemy draws close, separate so that those who follow will be forced to divide their numbers."

"If you must die, choose the place and take at least one of the blue coats with you. If we inflict enough casualties on our enemy, or divide his forces and spread his supply lines, he will have to retreat to the fort to regroup. If only one of us survives to warn our people, we will have won and our lives will not have been wasted."

Without a smile or even the embrace that war comrades share, Fighting Buffalo placed the backs of his hands together, looked skyward, closed his eyes extending his arms out horizontally from his sides. A moment later, as his arms relaxed, his eyes opened and he was alone.

Three teams of warriors ran in separate directions. No one spoke. Each knew their leader was planning to return to the place where the hills parted and only shadows touched the ground. They had watched as Fighting Buffalo's head turned, searching the gorge's slopes. In the recesses of each warrior's mind, a resolve was forming. Each swore that if he survived, he would return to the canyon where Fighting Buffalo fought and died to save his people.

All six warriors were aware that once their leader took a defensive position, he was trapped. When he attacked the blue coats, his location would become obvious. The soldiers manning the long rifles would perform their dishonorable duty by killing from a safe distance.

Fighting Buffalo looked to the sky where the hawk circled. He felt calm, almost detached. In his youth, it had been foretold that he would die honorably while looking down on his enemy. He rightfully believed that day had come. Those he had promised to protect had slipped away on silent feet. Turning, he ran toward the canyon, the blue coats who approached from the narrow valley's far side, and his own destiny.

From above, Fighting Buffalo heard the cry of the hawk, the red-tailed bird of prey that had been his guide since his youth. He believed the bird could bridge the intangible distance that separates those who live in the physical world and those who had slipped or been torn from their bodies. He was pleased when the fleeting shadow of the hawk flew straight toward the gorge and his time of prophetic fulfillment. He was confident there was enough time to locate the cave where the cool water dripped and the vegetation grew lush and green.

Fighting Buffalo's running body cast a shadow equal to his height as he entered the ravine just above a shale deposit. A few hundred yards more and he was climbing a path so narrow that only one foot at a time could gain traction. Seventy-five feet above the canyon floor, he slipped into the concave depression left by a large boulder that had crashed to the arroyo's floor a hundred years earlier. Within its depths he was shielded from the sun and Feriluc's prying eyes.

Below, the path through the gorge twisted in serpentine convolutions. Fighting Buffalo was sure the column of mounted soldiers would be forced into a single slow-moving queue. It would be his signal to attack with arrows and rocks. He took a long slow drink from nature's filtered seepage. Soon he was busying himself collecting rounded rocks. He selected stones that required two hands to hold above his head, to hurl their dead weight out from his place of concealment. Where they fell and who they struck was up to gravity and circumstance. Fighting Buffalo lined his arrows up neatly in front of him before settling back to wait. As the hours passed, he took out his pouch and ate some dried meat and nuts.

Several miles away, Major Feriluc brought his command to a halt. He had considered riding around the canyon but decided against it. The extra miles traveled would allow the Kiowa time to escape. He knew the narrow valley was perfect for an ambush. He also believed the Kiowa were hiding in its recesses, waiting for him to pass so they could escape southward and warn their people of the cavalry's approach.

Feriluc was not stupid. He had what he believed to be a foolproof plan. He sent several riflemen out to assess and guard the high ground on the rim of the arroyo. He divided his company into four platoons that would enter the gulch at five-minute intervals. He hoped to limit the Kiowa's targets while providing firepower from several locations. He expected to lose a few men, but that was part of war. Feriluc believed the Kiowa were exhausted from their long, hard run. He felt certain they had stopped to rest and recuperate. It was one of several mistakes.

The blue coat major had been through the canyon before. He knew the going would be slow. Careful to a fault, he sent marksmen ahead to provide cover and gain positions of advantage. If they were attacked, his riflemen on the ridge would enter the fray.

With the wave of his hand, the first platoon led by Feriluc moved forward at the alert. The horses' steps were a little crisper while the soldiers sat unusually straight in the saddle, their heads up, eyes shifting over every rock. Every bush that swayed in the breeze and each pebble that rolled down the cliff's face was studied over the barrel of a long rifle.

Twice the platoon passed through narrow passages that were perfect ambush locations. Concentration became so intense that only the sounds of the horses' exhaled respiration could be heard. Finally everyone entered a stretch where they could ride two abreast. A few hundred yards more and the men could see the open flat land just beyond the last narrowing of the gorge.

Feriluc's scout told him seven warriors had entered the canyon and seven had exited. The scout didn't know Fighting Buffalo had returned on a path that carried him north over a shale deposit and into the arroyo. The soldiers began to relax. Even Feriluc seemed at ease. The men had held their rifles at the ready for over an hour. Fatigue and tension caused arms to sag and rifles too lower.

When the first boulder came crashing down, hitting loose shale just above the moving column, it dislodged a wide sheet to rock and debris that cascaded down burying three horses and their riders in its rush. Feriluc and his men were unsure whether Mother Nature or the Kiowa was to blame.

When a steady rain of hat-sized rocks continued to pour on his men with an accuracy Mother Nature was incapable of, Feriluc knew the Kiowa had decided to stand and fight. He ordered his men to dismount and take cover against the gorge's walls. The tactic had merits and weakness.

The men, who took cover immediately below Fighting Buffalo's position, were out of his line of sight. Those on the opposite wall were exposed to his view and the reach of his long bow. With deadly precision, Fighting Buffalo began to pick off the exposed blue coats. He was so concentrated on not wasting a single arrow that he did not see the glint of a rifle barrel from across the canyon. Even the puff of smoke from the long rifle did not capture his attention. He did not feel the lead ball that entered his forehead, releasing him to join the company of his ancestors.

For hours the blue coats waited for the assault to continue. Fearing retreat back through the pass would only invite more attacks, Feriluc decided to order a broken ranks charge to the open flat land a few hundred yards to the west. After the dead and those unable to ride were tied to horses, the major directed the bugler to sound the charge. Within minutes, the clatter of horses' hooves no longer echoed through the twisting confines of the parted rock. Beyond the boulders and places of elevated concealment, Feriluc counted his losses: six dead men and eight severely injured. He assigned Sergeant Riley's decimated platoon the task of escorting the dead and wounded back to the fort.

CHAPTER SIX

O nce again Feriluc sent his men out in search of the Kiowa's trail. From behind, he heard the screech of a hawk. Spinning his horse around, he watched as the bird perched on a rock just in front of the cave that housed the dead Kiowa brave. The bird's eerie call and the way it perched near the body of the Kiowa disturbed Feriluc.

Did the warrior who fought so wisely possess spiritual powers, or was the hawk's presence coincidental? It did not matter. The major was determined to follow orders, destroy the Indians, and kill the game they survived on. Because the Indians he pursued were exhausted and on foot, the major believed the pursuit would be short-lived. As he took up the Kiowa trail, some of his bravado faded and was replaced with respect.

Even with their stone-age weapons, the Kiowa were not helpless against his well-disciplined, well-armed force. He realized he was in the middle of a tactical war. Because he was negative and sour-minded, he was unable to understand the power of visions and the intuitive wisdom achieved by living in harmony with nature.

For years Feriluc had been slowly burying the remaining remnants of his higher nature. He intentionally embraced the dark side of existence. As the years passed, he left behind the internal conflict that arises when right and wrong struggle on the battlefield of the mind.

Consequently, his soul was a reverse mirror image of the saints and holy men who had transmuted their own lower natures with wisdom's bright power. His innate spirituality was entombed in a self-created world of spiritual darkness, a place where fear and anger dominated.

Feriluc tried to search the dark venues open to him but found no guidance. It did not disturb him. He was a rational man who always relied on deliberate examination of facts. Because he lived in the primitive world of violence, he was unable to seek or recognize any spiritual qualities in the Kiowa.

To Feriluc, the hawk was simply a creature that happened to occupy a certain area at a specific time. The almost inexhaustible flight of the Kiowa was attributed to fear. He could not conceive of an indefatigable state induced by minds refusing to surrender to fatigue, tapping the infinite energy of the universe. The possibility that the Kiowa would surrender their own lives to protect tribal members was illogical to Feriluc. After all, the Indians were heathens, unschooled in religion and civilized behavior. The sound of a galloping horse interrupted Feriluc's ruminations.

His lead scout, out of breath, gasped his news. "There is a place where three streams converge about an hour's ride from here. The six Kiowa warriors divided into three groups of two braves. Two of the groups left unmistakable trails. The third group must have taken to the water for they left no impressions. The braves that ran north and east entered lands where the Kiowa and white men are equally disliked."

In an explosive display of frustration and anger, Feriluc pulled his hat from his head and slammed it hard against his leg. A horse standing nearby bolted at the sound of leather crashing against flesh. Reacting to the major's rage, the Indian scout retreated several steps. Unable to speak, the blue coat major nodded his head and turned away.

Mounting quickly, the scout spurred his horse and cleared the area. Feriluc began pacing back and forth. His mind was racing, but he could find no plausible way of dealing with three widespread teams of Kiowa warriors.

Four of the six Kiowa braves were running toward areas that if his forces followed, would invite attack by hostile Indians. Feriluc wanted to divide what remained of his company into three squads of twenty men each, but if the Kiowa divided their forces again, he could end up with ten men chasing one brave. Supplies, food, ammunition, and protection of forces held in reserve would all be lost.

If Feriluc turned and made a run for the Kiowa's summer encampment, it was likely that at least one of the fleeing warriors would succeed in warning his people. The blue coats would lose the advantage of surprise. The major's experience with the warrior in the canyon had taught him to respect an enemy that fought without modern weapons and still won the day against a much larger and more mobile force.

He had been out maneuvered and he did not like it. Reluctantly he changed directions, leading his men back to the protection of the garrison. He was anxious to re-supply his troops and prepare for a new search. In writing his report, Feriluc realized that the only evidence of the pursuit of the Kiowa warriors was dead and injured soldiers and footprints in the sand.

Ten days later, the major left the outpost leading two companies of cavalrymen. His mission was to escort a wagon train west as far as the Rio Grande River in the central New Mexico territory. After assuring the immigrants' safe passage, he was to turn back toward Missouri, searching for and destroying every Indian village, pueblo, and encampment he could find. He was ordered to erase the buffalo herds and any other game that might provide the Indian tribes with meat. The order that he most relished was the charge to find the Kiowa and destroy their ability to make war.

Feriluc was in a hurry to arrive at the painted cave. The cave a landmark that indicated the first leg of his journey was ending. It was near the place where the Rio Grande began to fill its banks with the drainage from several tributaries, a place where the sun's heat was repulsed by tall trees and precious water did not have to be rationed.

Looking forward to crossing the mountain range of blood-red rocks, he knew that once the mountains were behind him, he would turn northwest in search of the high plateau that nature had surrounded on three sides with tree-covered mountains. This was the place where he would turn from the tedious duty of protecting the wagon train and become the hunter of Indians and buffalo. But that time and place were hundreds of miles away, therefore he would be patient and plan well.

CHAPTER SEVEN

Not far from the Canadian River, Kuntamba stood on a ridge overlooking the Kiowa's summer camp. He saw women, children, elders, and young men who were not yet warriors. The dark runner's eyes searched for the old ones. He wanted to see the wise counsel givers who taught the art of living and the purpose of life. He knew no race of people could find happiness and purpose in their lives without spiritual guidance and the ability to merge each individual life into the harmony that makes existence possible. He hoped to find someone among the Kiowa who saw the objects and physical pleasures of this world as nothing more than the playthings of children. Kuntamba believed that if he could find such a person, language barriers and cultural differences would fall away.

He watched the Kiowa children at play and the women at work from afar. He noticed an old man who stood straight and walked on light feet. Wherever the old man went, people paused what they were doing before stepping aside politely. Even the young children quieted their boisterous play when he drew near. For an entire day and night, Kuntamba waited, observing the elder whose presence commanded respect.

The dark runner noted that the elder, whom Kuntamba considered to be a Kiowa shaman, ate little and slept on the ground facing the sky. He saw that even birds in nearby bushes were undisturbed by the shaman's passing. It was then that Kuntamba knew his quest had been blessed with the gift of mutual understanding. Soon he would meet with a kindred soul, a man who had in circumstances far different from his own, transcended the veil of physical pleasures and found the wisdom that waited beyond the desires of the moment.

Kuntamba experienced a moment of anxiety. The apprehension arose from a deep hunger to meet and converse with another person who understood what it was to stand alone, isolated from others not by distance but by spiritual maturity. He was eager to meet with this kindred soul, who for his own reasons had entered the pilgrimage for spiritual perfection.

As the dark runner watched, the Kiowa holy man walked into a clearing where he stood stationary for a minute before slowly turning until he had completed more than a full circle. When he finally stopped, he was looking straight at Kuntamba's concealed position. He barely nodded before walking a short distance to sit in the shade of a large pine tree.

Kuntamba smiled knowing that his host was aware of his presence and waited for him under the tall tree. Afraid that his sudden and unexpected appearance would disturb the tribe, the African decided to let the sun fade from sight, letting the Kiowa people seek sleep before meeting the shaman. The Kiowa holy man, Shining Sun, sat alone with his eyes closed. According to legend, when he was born, his body emanated a soft illumination that warmed all those nearby. For this reason, his mother called him Shining Sun.

Long after the moon had crested and the campfires had reduced themselves to hot coals, Kuntamba walked quietly past two lookouts before noiselessly seating himself across from the old man. Shining Sun had never seen an African, although he had heard stories of black men escaping bondage and the whip of the white man. Even before he laid eyes on Kuntamba, Shining Sun knew his visitor was a man who possessed great spiritual power and wisdom.

The shaman had become aware of his visitor's presence through the same awakened senses mothers call forth when a child is in danger. What speaks to mothers is the voice of love. Shining Sun's ability to reach out to Kuntamba was gained through the labor of self-conquest. His victory over his lower nature enabled him to consciously touch those around him. Kuntamba was his equal as a projector and receiver of this harmless force.

As a young man, Shining Sun had met a man and woman who lived far to the south during his journeys. They were brown-skinned and exhibited a natural spirituality that entranced him. They fed his hunger to find a oneness with truth.

The unusual couple lived in the mountains and could traverse great distances in short periods of time. They were always available to heal the injured and cure the sick. Shining Sun wondered if the holy ones who had tutored him in his youth had come to visit. But the unseen holy man who had waited for darkness to conceal his coming was different. It had to do with motion. His guest had an energy that preceded him, almost like a wolf's tireless pursuit of its prey but without the intent to injure.

Shining Sun's questions were answered as his eyes opened and the shadows in front of him shifted and materialized into the form of a lean black man whose stare seemed to close the distance between them and touch the essence of Shining Sun's being. In reaching out to Shining Sun, Kuntamba opened his senses, permitting the outflow of a spiritual energy that could only be received by an equal. Shining Sun accepted Kuntamba's gift, allowing his own purified force to extend to his guest.

For several moments two men from different continents, foreign to each other in every way but one, basked silently in each other's presence. Kuntamba did not speak the language of the Kiowa and Shining Sun was unable to communicate in the words of the African or the strange sounds of the pale invaders, but between their minds flowed a series of mental pictures that could not be misunderstood.

Shining Sun saw for a second time the death of his son, Fighting Buffalo, and the tireless courage of the Kiowa braves who led the cavalry away from the summer encampment of their people. He saw the cloud of blue coated men on horses charging toward his present home and knew death waited in the soldiers' holsters and scabbards.

The dark runner saw Shining Sun's grief and realized the news of Fighting Buffalo's death had preceded him along the same channels of the mind that connect children to parents and husbands to wives. He saw the history of a people who had become one with the land, the seasons, and the cycles of nature. Without letting Shining Sun see, Kuntamba saw the rise and fall of the Kiowa nation. He saw that they survived as a people, but the distant future was unclear and did not reveal the Kiowa's final destiny.

He learned long ago that the physical world was a place of change, suffering, and experience. He was aware that these elements were teachers that stirred and refined intelligence while making growth possible. He knew all growth must eventually lead to questions of eternal life and the why of existence. He also learned that when these questions filled men's minds, the quest for spiritual perfection was about to begin.

Kuntamba was not positive Shining Sun understood the necessity for change, especially when it was forced by violence. The dark runner saw the universe as nothing more than energy, a force that could take an almost infinite variety of forms. For him, life was a harnessing of this energy because once it entered the field of action and interaction, it acquired dimensions of right and wrong. Thus the wheel or cycle of life was born and life itself sent spiraling ever so slowly away from the darkness of spiritual ignorance.

The dark runner did not communicate to Shining Sun the inevitability of change or his sense of the force that was carrying not only the Kiowa people into a new age, but also those who lived in Africa and other nations of the world. Kuntamba blinked, realizing Shining Sun had sensed an ominous swing in his thoughts. Reaching out, Kuntamba extended his arms with his palms facing his new friend.

The old Indian responded by pressing his palms against those of a man he had just met, but had known for an eternity. Without moving, the Kiowa holy man began his silent communication. "The hot summer is approaching. The land will dry. The white men kill the buffalo, forcing us to fight against other tribes for the right to hunt what little game remains.

"There has been little snow this past winter and the river runs low. To the south the land is arid and water is scarce. Out of the northeast the blue coats come, intent on our destruction. Other tribes raid our villages and steal our horses. If we stay in this valley, many Kiowa will die. If we flee, no matter which direction, many of my people will perish."

Kuntamba looked into Shining Sun's face and replied voicelessly. "In a thousand years of living on the plains, in the mountains, and valleys of this land, the Kiowa have faced and survived many difficult challenges. What do the stories of your ancestors tell you? In the distant past were there places your people once migrated, but are now forgotten? Where did you, as a young man, venture in search of truth? In any of your travels did you not find at least one place where your people will be safe?"

Shining Sun sat quietly lost in thought. His arms relaxed, settling at his side. In the distance, the yipping of a dog warning its master of the new day's approach, returned Shining Sun to the present. Without looking at anything in particular, he began to communicate in a barely audible voice. "There is a place many days ride from here. Because we do not have enough horses to carry our people and our belongings, most will need to walk."

"This valley is entered through a narrow mountain pass. A dozen warriors could prevent the mounted soldiers from entering. Long ago I spent a summer in the valley of lush but slow growing grasses. I camped and meditated by a meandering stream that flows around the meadow's eastern perimeter. It was there that I had my first vision, but that is another story."

"To get to this valley, thirst must become our friend. For three days no water will be available except what we carry. My people will be forced to take a long circuitous route that will confuse the blue coats and their scouts. We will need to cross the lands of hostile tribes. Some of our warriors will die in battle, and our elderly and sick will lie dead on the ground of our enemies."

"If we can make it to this valley and if I can find it again, my people will thrive in the summer and fall. When winter comes, the cold will drive us down to the lowlands where the white man rules."

Shining Sun's head lowered in defeat. Kuntamba waited. He knew the wise man that guided the Kiowa was being tested in an internal struggle. The conflict was brief. It ended with Shining Sun's body taking on a new energy.

He raised his head. His eyes fixed on Kuntamba. "We will survive," he declared in his own language. "I pray we may meet later. Now I must go." Kuntamba did not understand the words, but he understood the intended meaning.

The sun was up and the Kiowa community was well into the work of the day when the children discovered the African sitting quietly in the shade of a tree. They did not scream or call for help but they ran to tell their elders of the strange dark-skinned man who had taken up residence under a tree. The children said he neither spoke nor moved. The elders smiled and promised they would walk with the children to the far side of the village to see what the visitor wanted as soon as they could.

Shining Sun positioned himself outside the tepee of his grandchildren and Fighting Buffalo's woman. The chirping birds called her out to the warm sun where she looked into the penetrating eyes of her father-in-law, the tribe's holy man. When he lowered his gaze and turned away, she knew that the father of her children was dead.

Instantly she looked up, hoping the great hawk's image would not cross her field of sight, but there it was--flying just above the horizon, straight toward her. As the bird dropped silently to the ground and folded its powerful wings back, a low wail began to build in the throat of Fighting Buffalo's woman. The sound constricted as it struggled to give voice to Woman Who Walks With Crooked Foot's sorrow. Finally in an effort that was equal to parturition itself, her expression of pain found freedom.

Her sorrow escaped into the air on a mournful wail, transforming the movements of busy people into a sorrow-filled dirge. Other women, especially the older ones who had met death many times before, echoed the wail of sadness. The children ran for shelter, and the chiefs hurriedly gathered to hear Shining Sun tell the story of Fighting Buffalo's death.

Before the holy man would speak, he insisted on sitting in the middle of camp where all could see him. His wait was short. Soon the women and children and parents of the six warriors who traveled with Fighting Buffalo began their slow procession passed his seated form. As each family member walked by, Shining Sun nodded his head ever so slightly. Without words, he was telling his people their sons still lived. His good news was met with sighs of relief and expressions of gratitude.

Rising to his feet, Shining Sun called out to Kuntamba. Many of the parents and adults had not believed the young ones' story of a black man in their camp. When the dark runner approached, eyes stared in disbelief, and even the wails of loss were caught on the inhaling breath of surprise. The tribe had never seen an African before.

Where had this strange dark man come from? How had he entered their camp unseen? Was his presence a good or bad omen? Gradually the crowd's noisy questioning gave way to curiosity.

Shining Sun spoke of Kuntamba's wisdom and identified him as the bearer of the news that six Kiowa warriors still lived. When asked how the dark runner had come to be among them and what his purpose was, Shining Sun fell silent. Looking at Kuntamba, the Kiowa holy man motioned him to come forward. Calling for silence, Shining Sun sat down and closed his eyes, extending his arms outward, palms facing his guest.

Kuntamba responded to the request. The two men sat, palms barely touching, their breathing synchronized. For the time it takes a shadow to shrink by half, the curious ritual continued. The communication ended abruptly with arms gently returning to positions of rest.

Shining Sun spoke. "Our visitor is called Kuntamba. He comes from a land that lies beyond the great body of water described in our legends. He travels on foot, much the way our forefathers moved and hunted before the time of the horse. He visits us because a vision told him of our plight. He travels south because an unknown compulsion pulls him in that direction."

Those gathered nearby nodded their heads. They understood the dark runner's need to follow the urging of his inner self. They did not question how he had crossed the great body of water. Their holy man believed the dark one's words and they had no reason to doubt. They would all remember this day and the black visitor. The story would be told and retold until truth blended with myth. The stories waited to be recited in the future. For now, there were other problems that had to be dealt with.

The tribal members were caught in a dilemma. The announcement of Fighting Buffalo's death ushered in a period of grieving. The appearance of the dark one called for celebration. Shining Sun made the decision when he declared, "For now we grieve and we plan. The blue coats are coming to destroy us and a long trial of pain and death is about to test our courage and will."

At midday, Shining Sun and Kuntamba met with the tribal leaders and told them of the mounted cavalry, wagon trains, and the tribe's need to move to the mountain plateau where the creek became a waterfall. When asked where this place was, Shining Sun pointed to the west.

The Kiowa holy man stressed to all the need to gather food, dry meat, and the tiny seeds that fell to the ground. He discussed hunger, thirst, and the long trail they needed to travel to confuse the white man's Indian scouts, braves from a rival tribe.

Shining Sun's voice stilled and he stood silent in front of his leaders.

The tribal chiefs asked, "How do you know these things?"

"I know them to be true because I have seen them," replied Shining Sun. "I also know the event my vision has foretold can be changed if we act wisely and work hard. If we are as brave as our ancestors who conquered this land, we will survive."

Shining Sun had spent many hours considering what needed to be done, but he could not offer his detailed suggestions unless he was asked. The chief who had not had time to comprehend the magnitude of the threat to his people did not hesitate to call for ideas. "Do you have a plan for us to consider?" he asked Shining Sun.

The old shaman spoke with quiet authority. "If the Kiowa nation is to survive, our young men, maidens, and the wisdom of our elders must precede us to our place of concealment. They will work hard to ready the land for the eventual arrival of the tribe. They must catch fish, pick berries, and gather firewood to prepare for the coming winter."

"Those, who remain behind in this camp will sleep little and work hard. Every seed and root should be gleaned from the land. There will be no more feasting or wasting of food. When darkness settles on our camp, our warriors will hone their weapons, fill their quivers and help the women with the work of garment and moccasin making. No one shall eat till they are full. We are Kiowa! Pain must become our friend, and hunger a welcome guest."

"Our scouts must follow the blue coats, attack when they can, and when possible, lead them away from the encampment. When the white soldiers approach within two nights and one day's ride of our present location, we must flee to the north, south, east and west. Then we will be tested for our worthiness to bear the name of our Kiowa ancestors."

Shining Sun took a step back and sat down. He studied the faces of the tribal leaders and those who had come to listen, before he added, "I have said what the gods have told me. Now the survival of our people is in your hands."

The dark runner stayed for ten days helping his friends prepare for the coming ordeal. Late one night as the exhausted camp slept, Shining Sun and the dark runner sat in the muted light of a half moon. Their arms were extended with palms touching. Kuntamba told the Kiowa holy man that his people would survive their coming trials. He also disclosed to Shining Sun that the tide of white men would rise and expand in numbers for hundreds of years.

He spoke of Kiowa tribal beliefs as the hope of the world. He implied that any species that is blind to the right of all other life forms to exist sets the stage for its own demise. Finally Kuntamba said goodbye and promised to reach out across the physical space that is populated by deserts, forests, and mountains. Both he and Shining Sun knew that minds in spiritual harmony can dissolve the miles as easily as a glance at the sky.

Shining Sun stared up as a large cloud blotted out the moon. He studied the clouds' slow drifting pattern and knew that when he looked down, his friend, Kuntamba the African, the only person with whom he could share his fragments of wisdom, would be gone. He heard no footsteps, not even the rustle of leaves caught in the back draft of a passing body. He looked around, then back up at the half moon and felt somehow diminished. It was as if Kuntamba's return would fill the moon to its full circular brightness and quench his soul's need for spiritual companionship.

CHAPTER EIGHT

More than a mile away, the dark runner was satisfying another hunger. His mind and body were savoring the motion of running. He enjoyed the press for air followed by the endless second wind that charged his stride with eternal energy. Even the discomfort of retraining muscles too long trapped in other labors was welcomed with ecstatic zeal. Hours later, after the cobwebs of inactivity had given way to the harmony of total physical and mental balance, the dark runner's mind began to drift. It sought and found the transcendent state which always allowed him to commune with his omnipresent source.

Kuntamba ran south across New Mexico. He was soon climbing up the dwindling vestiges of the Rocky Mountains. The ground was uneven and littered with rock fragments, which nature had lain down on a base of shifting sand. Kuntamba's feet unerringly slipped between the sharp edged shards of broken shale, but could not avoid the sand that shifted under his weight and destroyed the rhythm of his breathing and meditation.

He slowed to a walk, eyes searching the horizon and the low cliffs that shadowed his path. He listened with intensity that extended his hearing, beyond the sounds of wind-blown sand and the caress of a breeze that followed the contour of the land. He called on senses that civilization, with its eternally competitive drive for supremacy, had long ago discarded as an illusion.

Clarity of mind and purity of Kuntamba's purpose honed extrasensory antennae. They told Kuntamba that a powerful presence had left its imprint on the land and the brown sandstone cliffs that loomed ever larger before him. Even the air had a quality of history about it.

The dark runner stopped and sat down. He relaxed and waited. Slowly, the residual energy of a long gone people whose history was both violent and desperate filled him. The gentle blowing of sand across his bare feet whispered of love, death, labor, and spiritual blindness. Looking around, Kuntamba felt the confusing energy of a civilization's rise and fall move through the hollow canyons, forlornly echoing a nation's death.

An overwhelming impression permeated his being. The people who had long ago lived and thrived in this arid land had not surrendered their ownership, but intended to return. He felt that he was both trespassing and violating a confidence, but the feeling was tainted by a disturbing uneasiness.

His inner consciousness urged him to continue his journey. It was this unusual prompting that caused Kuntamba to question what in this arid land aroused such urgency for him to hasten his steps? He wondered if in the far reaches of the southern landscape, events were being set in motion that would void his long journey.

"No! My impulse to travel south grows stronger not weaker," he whispered.

His mental questioning shifted. Was it possible that the *Ancient Ones* who called this land home long ago were displeased with his sensory interpretation of who they were?

Once again he vocalized his answer. "No. Since leaving this land, the spirits of the ancient ones' have matured and moved on to new experiences. All that remains in this land of rock and sand is the imprint all races leave on the earth after they have settled, flourished, and finally died out."

A tiny pale yellow butterfly fluttered erratically across his path. Kuntamba held out his hand trying to touch his elusive visitor. "Thank you, little brother, for your gift of beauty," he said quietly.

His steps carried him over the land. Behind him lay the intangible whisperings of an ancient civilization. Just ahead was the campsite of those that hunted Indians and killed animals because they had been ordered to. Out of the silence came the faint sounds of metal on metal. Soon, the garble of many voices blending together added their information to Kuntamba's questioning mind. The smell of horses, dried sweat, and the acrid odor of a shallow latrine wafted on the wind. Abruptly the dark runner shifted his path from one that was wide and easily traversed to the rough terrain that wove through thick brush and up nearly impassable slopes.

Kuntamba was aware that the cavalry, like the Indian tribes, posted scouts. He would have to be careful. Soon he was looking down on the blue coats' encampment. Only a small contingent of men could be seen. Some lounged while others tended the chores of cooking. Looking at the camp, Kuntamba saw that the makeshift corrals were almost empty. The dark runner hoped no Indians or buffalo would be caught in the cavalry's great sweeping net of horses and men. He believed their catch would be meager.

The Kiowa's summer camp was several days run away. At least for now, the Kiowa were safe from the calvary's rifles and drawn sabers. The land was dry. Deer, antelope, prairie dogs and rabbits had already consumed what little vegetation the sparse winter rains had provided for grazing. The blue coats would return hungry and thirsty. Kuntamba would wait. He wanted to look upon the man who commanded men to kill helpless women and children.

The sun was low as Feriluc led his troops back to the camp. He was angry because no Indians had been found. His scout claimed to have picked up the trail of a solitary runner, but the footprints provided no evidence of tribal identity.

Kuntamba wanted to know how the soldiers regarded the blue coat leader. It would tell him if the blue coats killed because they were compelled to or because they enjoyed the letting of blood.

Normally the dark runner would have slipped past the military encampment. He would have eased around the low hills and down the canyons like the flow of the Rio Grande tumbling south, yet something within held him fast. Perhaps it was inquisitiveness or maybe it was fate.

In his long journey he had met and survived many difficult situations. Each encounter was part of his destiny. Kuntamba wondered if the tall man with the wide shoulders and thick neck, the leader of the blue coats, was about to enter his life.

PART FOUR
The Fateful Meeting: Midsummer 1811

CHAPTER ONE

Kuntamba watched the blue coat leader walk across the clearing. The white man's body seemed too long for his legs. The African suddenly realized he was unable to move. He felt an odd sensation of connection with the blue coat chief, one that held and repulsed him at the same time. Kuntamba suddenly understood that his positive energy was being equaled or neutralized by the negative force of the soldiers' commander.

The dark runner was surprised when the man he had been watching turned and stared intently in his direction. Numbness crept over the African's body as the major's fixed gaze locked on his position of concealment. Kuntamba was positive he was hidden from sight, still the white man who killed without just cause continued to stare in his direction. By the dark runner's estimate, the distance between him and the white man exceeded three hundred yards. Kuntamba wondered what extrasensory perception the man possessed since he could feel from afar energy contrary to his own.

Not for the first time in his life, Kuntamba questioned the workings of the universal law. He knew the world, the planets, and the stars in the sky all existed because of an omniscient force. He knew that this force was perfect, otherwise all that is would collapse on itself. If universal law guided the planets, the seasons, and the workings of his own body then it must have omniscience. This made the universal law, and man's invoking of it through wisdom or ignorance, possible. In his visions, Kuntamba had come to know universal law as the great benefactor, teacher, guide, and adjuster of all spiritual claims and debts.

Kuntamba wondered why, when he had an aversion to violence and evil, the law had permitted him to cross paths with the blue coat major, a man with the darkest soul his senses had ever touched on. As the dark runner's thoughts returned to the present, he realized he was inhaling deeply. His entire body was involuntarily reacting to the dense negative energy that the major projected. In the past, Kuntamba had used a deep breathing technique to gather his physical and spiritual energy before entering populated areas. The practice enabled him to keep an inner focus while being bombarded by the scattered energies of a thriving community. His focused spiritual energy always recharged his being, shielding him from the negative forces of others.

This time the dark runner wasn't confronted with the scattered dark influences of ignorant men. The blue coat's power was concentrated. It caught Kuntamba while his mind and soul were open, receptive, and flowing outward in search of truths concealed by the sands of history. After minutes of tortured breathing and the forcing his mental energies outward in an enclosing envelope, Kuntamba recovered his inner balance and laid back to rest.

Not far away, Major Feriluc suddenly feeling sick stumbled into his tent, falling heavily onto his cot. A sudden feebleness gripped his body. He had trouble directing his vision. When he tried to sit up, a wave of dizziness forced him down to the security of his bed.

Gradually the ordeal passed. In its wake, it left an energy that demanded relief. His head was clear and his senses were more acute than they had ever been. He wanted to challenge the upsetting force that lay hidden in the brush several hundred yards away, but before he could move, his head filled with the horrors of the night long ago with Baptiste.

He tried to force the unrelenting images from his mind, but time and repetition had given his shame more strength than his willpower possessed. Lying back, he let the horrors of the past flow unimpeded across his mental screen. When a moment of peace finally settled over his mind, fearing his memories of Baptiste might return, Feriluc ran outside scanned the distant slope. When no wave of repulsion or anxiety gripped him, he began to fear the unseen power that had made him physically sick had slipped away.

Drawing his pistol, he fired one shot into the air. Within seconds his men were running toward him. Feriluc boomed a command. "Mount up and form a large circle around that hill!"

He pointed to the hill where Kuntamba lay concealed in brush. The circular formation quickly moved into place. With a wave of his hand and an order to kill anything that moved, Feriluc began tightening the circle, advancing toward his destiny.

Kuntamba saw the enclosing ring of men and horseflesh crashing through the underbrush toward him. His first instinct was to flee down a shallow gully, but two horses were just entering the narrow wash. He considered burying himself under the loose sand, hoping the fates would protect him. He quickly discarded the idea. He knew the major would be drawn to him like iron filings to a magnet.

The dark runner turned his thoughts inward, beyond logic and fear. He wondered why he was balking at surrendering himself to his own wisdom and intuition, but even Kuntamba had moments of fallibility. For an instant he saw his fallen body gasping its last breath as the blue coat major and his men laughed mercilessly.

Death was inevitable and not to be feared. He knew life, the spark of the infinite that resides in all of mankind, was indestructible and eternal, as it must be if its source was without limits. Only one concept troubled him. For many months he had been traveling southward, guided by nothing more than an impulse. Were all of his efforts and imaginings to die with him on the blood-soaked sand? Would someone else complete what providence had been guiding him toward, or would a vast field of unfilled potential be discarded with his death? He could not help but think that a larger future awaited him than being killed simply because his path accidentally crossed a man who took pleasure in the misery of others.

Once again Kuntamba pulled in a long slow breath, holding it momentarily before exhaling. In that moment, his mind cleared and he knew beyond any possible doubt that death would not visit him on this day. He also realized that the tall leader of the blue coats, around which a malodorous energy flowed, possessed an evil power that he must somehow transmute if his own spiritual journey was to progress. Kuntamba was about to discover how virulent his foe's hate had become.

The dark runner watched and decided on a plan of action. He would place himself directly in the path of the man who was addressed as Major Feriluc. When the major's horse was almost upon him, he would jump up startling the animal and its rider. Kuntamba hoped the major's horse would bolt, opening a path to freedom. He would run up the incline covered with thick dry vegetation. The soldiers at his flanks would, at best, have only brief glimpses to guide their fire.

Slowly the ring of death tightened. Fifty yards east of Kuntamba's position, Lieutenant McCormick called out, "Over here! Something large is moving is the thicket!"

Confident that the kill was at hand, Feriluc drew his sword and spurred his horse into a gallop before pulling his mount up short in front of McCormick.

"Where?" Feriluc commanded.

"In there!" McCormick responded, pointing at a brush-covered gully.

The major wheeled his horse around, slapping his sorrel's rump with the flat side of his saber, charging into the brush with his sword at the ready. As he raced forward, his eyes searching intently for a victim, a coyote broke from cover and raced for open country. It dodged between hooves and used bushes and rocks to cover its flight. While the coyote was drawing the cavalry's attention, Kuntamba slipped through a breach in the circle, and began sprinting up the slope.

159

hooves and used bushes and rocks to cover its flight. While the coyote was drawing the cavalry's attention, Kuntamba slipped through a breach in the circle, and began sprinting up the slope.

CHAPTER TWO

The African was in a full stride and half way up the hill before a cavalryman called out, "It's a negro! The slave runs up the hill!"

Feriluc spun his horse around. His eyes struggling to locate his quarry. His muscular legs drove polished iron spurs into the mare's flanks, causing her to rear in pain before sprinting forward, guided only by the jerking of the reins held in Feriluc's clenched fists.

"Hold your positions! This one's mine!" Blind to the dangers around him, the major forced his steed across gullies and around boulders and onto sandy pits the wind had collected in depressions in the earth. When his mare floundered, her legs driving to find solid ground, Feriluc cursed and almost dismounted to continue the pursuit on foot.

Seeing the black slave widening the distance between them, the blue coat changed his mind. He climbed off his horse and pulled the mare's bridle, guiding her out of the sandy trap. Once again he remounted and began to close the gap between himself and the fleeing slave, but not as fast as he hoped to. Feriluc's mind was racing. Could the skinny slave possess the power to slow the mare or was it all an illusion?

Taking the reins, he whipped the horse's shoulders with the long, thin strips of leather. The mare strained to the limit of her speed and strength. The major could make out the smooth motion of Kuntamba's muscles contracting and relaxing under taut skin. Feriluc noted the ease with which the African ran.

In contrast, he could feel his mare laboring as white lather collected on both sides of her neck, lubricating the constantly moving reins. A snorting exhalation accompanied each stride. A moment later, the sorrel's pounding hooves hit the loose soil that collects on hillsides that are shielded from the prevailing winds. The horse's long stride chopped down to a digging step that sought the firm footing of the hard rocky surface beneath the sand.

Feriluc looked at his intended victim, wondering why the black man's feet seemed to need little or no traction. Was he chasing a phantom? Dismounting, he withdrew his rifle from its scabbard. He knelt down and took aim but his hands were sweaty and he was breathing hard, and the target was elusive and fading.

Feriluc fired one shot just as the dark runner reached the top of the hill. Hurriedly the major removed his telescope from his saddlebag, extended it to its full power, focusing where he had last sighted the slave. To his amazement, surprise, and supreme anger, the black runner stood motionless, outlined against the sky, appearing outwardly unconcerned. Behind him, Feriluc heard his men approaching. Turning, he ordered them to commence firing, then he returned to his telescope.

Incredibly, the African looked straight at Feriluc's telescope before he turned, slowly exposing first the side of his face, then the back of his head. The major blinked, and the dark runner was gone. In that fleeting glance, Feriluc did not see a runaway slave, he saw Baptiste's profile. The blue coat major caught and held his breath as Kuntamba's features were seared onto his brain.

Baptiste's image filled Feriluc with shame and the vile poison of revenge. His muscles tensed, much as they would if he had discovered a large rattlesnake inches away, poised to strike. His heart pounded with the same terror he had experienced while in the pirate's depraved embrace. Total fear gripped his senses, paralyzing his body and mind.

His horse shifted uneasily. The mare's muscles bunched and her eyes flared as the contagion of fear engulfed her in a wave of panic, spooking her in a downhill headlong run. Instinctively Feriluc pulled back on the reins, but the mare had the bit in her teeth. Her powerful neck and head extended forward as fear and momentum pushed her speed to the edge of her physical limits. The blue coat leaned way back in the saddle, trying to shift his center of gravity over his mount's powerful hindquarters, but it did not slow her down.

A moment later, horse and rider reached the level ground. The mare, unable to shake the source of her fear, broke into a flat-out run. She slowed her pace and tried another maneuver—twisting and bucking. When Feriluc could not be dislodged, she lay down; rolling over and forcing her rider to jump clear of her crushing force. With the ordeal over, the animal stood, legs splayed slightly, her great chest heaving.

The blue coat major picked up his hat and the telescope that had fallen from his saddlebag when the mare rolled. He cursed the escaping slave for frightening his mount, wondering if the African possessed supernatural powers. What else could explain the black runner's ability to reach out from more than three hundred yards away and send him and his steed on an unstoppable life and death downhill plunge? Feriluc was convinced that the African, through a supernatural connection to Baptiste, intended to kill him.

Only one other explanation was possible, but it could not be. Feriluc had looked at Baptiste's dead body, and had even kicked at the corpse to be sure no life remained. Yet the near naked African who ran like the wind, at least from the side, looked exactly like Baptiste. Feriluc's first impulse was to organize a pursuit and chase the eerie African until exhaustion left the slave weak and defenseless, but he hesitated, his mind filled with uncertainty. He worried that Baptiste's corrupt heart had somehow taken possession of the African runner. Would he, Feriluc, have to relive the horrors of Baptiste's pirate ship? What if the African runner's magic or trickery subdued him? Could he, the major and commander of hundreds of men, endure another night of forced debauchery? What if his men learned of his cowardice on a sailing ship long ago? Was it even possible to catch the dark-skinned slave whose visage stirred memories buried in his mind by the passing of time and his flight across a continent? What inner power did the black slave possess that he could look down on him, a leader of men, with the same calm a master shows a slave before dispensing punishment?

If he captured the illusive quarry, could he look the replica of Baptiste in the face? Would something, from within, force his vision down in submission? Did he really want to catch a ghost from his past who floated up hills with the same ease an eagle rides the rising hot air currents? Could he hold a force so superior to his own that looking in the African's direction from hundreds of yards away made him tremble with weakness? Could he capture a force that refused to seek cover as bullets buried themselves in the dirt at his feet or flew by his body like blind birds unable to find a roost?

Once again Feriluc questioned the reality of the black man. Immediately his logic replied yes, his men had seen and fired at him repeatedly. It was the last word in his thought, "repeatedly," that created a crack in the veneer of his certainty. It left him wondering if his men were humoring him by firing because they were ordered to, rather than because they saw the African in flight. That would explain the black runner's invincibility. Reason returned when he recalled that it was his lieutenant, not him, who first sighted the source of his turmoil. Doubt still lingered in the major's confounded mind.

Looking up, Feriluc saw two of his men walking by. With a whistle and a gesture of his index finger, the major called them over.

"Corporal Benson reporting, sir," the taller of the two stated.

"May I compliment you on your riding ability. I don't think there is a man in our entire company who could have stuck in the saddle like you did."

Without acknowledging the flattery, Feriluc said, "Corporal Benson, would you relate your observations during the operation just ended?"

Benson hesitated. Was it a trick? Was the major looking for a scapegoat because the slave escaped? Was it not the major who gave the order and led the pursuit? But when Benson looked at his commanding officer's poisonous expression, he responded, "I believe the lieutenant called your attention to some movement in a thicket, sir. When you charged into the brush, a coyote was flushed out. From behind us, someone, I don't know who, called out 'a slave runs toward the west'."

During Benson's explanation, Feriluc relaxed. His expression lost its intensity and the corners of his mouth curved upward ever so slightly. The corporal was unable to tell whether the major wanted to smile or sneer, but he did hear Feriluc say, "There was a slave, it was not an illusion!"

"Excuse me sir," Benson added. "Do you believe the slave was a scout for one of the Indian tribes?"

Feriluc turned away from the impertinent corporal who dared to question him. Instead of replying, the major walked into his tent, dismissing his subordinates with a wave of his hand. Lying down on his cot, Feriluc closed his eyes, trying to visualize the day's events in chronological order but his mind chose to fill his thoughts with old pictures of his ordeal with Baptiste.

Superimposed on the indelible reflection was the profile of the dark runner. Unable to shake the haunting fear and self-revulsion the unwanted recollections forced on him, Feriluc stood up and vowed to capture the African. He had reached a distorted conclusion. The two images, one on top of the other, were proof that Baptiste and the slave were joined. How, he was unsure, but it did not matter.

The major now knew that he had to kill the African. The dark runner's death would amount to a kind of absolution that would cleanse his soul. His actions took on the fervor of a religious zealot. It was a new but defective enthusiasm that enabled Feriluc to consciously confront an adversary whom he believed possessed supernatural powers, powers that enabled the African to run effortlessly, turning bullets away, and startling a horse into full flight.

Feriluc was uncertain why the black man had shown himself. Perhaps Baptiste's evil soul had taken possession of the African's body. Feriluc wondered if the black slave was trying to lure him to his death and hell where Baptiste could dominate him for all of eternity. The longer Feriluc consumed himself with self-created phantoms, the more convinced he became that his survival, manhood, and in a twisted way, his salvation, depended on the annihilation of the African runner.

Feriluc fantasized about trapping, torturing, and subjecting the slave to the same unspeakable horrors he had endured long ago in Baptiste's quarters. With the daydreams came a conviction and determination to track the African that dared to mock him the length of Mexico, if necessary. With his new resolve came relief, as if a massive weight had been lifted from his shoulders.

He did not realize the newly created motivation was born from a need for revenge, or that he was attempting to transfer his past suffering to a third person because of facial similarities. Feriluc did not know he was exchanging the weight of his past crimes for an unshakable and mountainous load of Karmic debt.

Walking outside his tent, Feriluc looked at the sun as it dipped toward the low outline of rounded hills to the west. He stood still as he devised a plan. When he finally moved, it was because his plan was complete. Summoning his scouts, he ordered them to search until they found the trail of the slave. The major made it very clear that failure was unacceptable. As the scouts left the camp, Feriluc called his lieutenants and sergeants together. They were commanded to be ready to travel when the lookouts returned.

In his tent, Feriluc slept poorly. He was anxious to end his recurring nightmares and cleanse his mind with the African's blood, but lurking just beyond his thoughts was a fear that failure might bring him under the spell of Baptiste's reincarnation. Long before the sun gave evidence of its approach, the major was pacing back and forth in front of his tent. Eagerness was turning to anxiety. Where were the scouts? Would he be able to catch the dark runner? What problems had he failed to anticipate? Would the Indian war parties attack his small contingent of soldiers as they trailed the African?

When Feriluc closed his eyes, his imagination filled with the likenesses of Baptiste and the slave. The major resolved to pursue the dark runner until either he or the African breathed no more. His reverie was interrupted as the returning Indian scout approached. A clear trail had been found. Instantly the camp was astir. There would be no coffee or hot food this morning.

Feriluc selected his three best marksmen and the Indian scout to travel with him. He also claimed an additional ten horses as replacement mounts and carriers of reserve food and water. The remainder of his command was directed to heed the original orders. They were to seek and kill the Indians and buffalo.

Directing the scout to lead the way, Feriluc took the reins of two horses loaded with supplies and followed. Behind him, the three marksmen and their pack animals trailed. The major planned to ride from the dim light of dawn until the faint shadows of twilight succumbed to darkness. If the moonlight were sufficient for tracking, they would continue even then. When a horse refused to carry its rider any farther, it would be left behind to die or find its way back to the fort.

He was absolutely positive exhaustion would eventually slow the black slave. The hunter wanted to see his quarry gasping for air as thirst and a skin charring sun drained the last of his energy. Feriluc had no way of knowing Kuntamba was only truly comfortable when he was in motion. Feriluc could not even begin to fathom the forces that energized the African's body, any more than he could grasp the concepts of truth or mercy.

He refused to consider that any man, white, slave, or Indian could survive without rest, food, or water. It was Feriluc's third year in this desert wilderness. He had come across the carcasses of bison turned to a brittle leather from the desiccating heat. The African was barefooted. The midday sun would cook the sand until the thermal waves rising from the earth's surface gave everything a shimmering appearance. Even horses refused to stand still on the superheated sand. The oppressive heat became his ally.

Feriluc knew the slave was an unusual individual. He had seen the black man run effortlessly, ignoring bullets whizzing by his body. But nothing the major had witnessed could tell him how vast the slave's physical prowess really was. He knew the African wore very little clothing and had no pockets for food. He had no way to keep warm when the cold desert nights captured the heat rising from the sand, causing a damp chill to settle on every living creature and exposed surface. The blue coat believed that all of these forces working together made the capture of the African inevitable.

The blue coat had trailed and killed Indians who were born in this dry land of rolling hills and grassy plains. Indians who knew every gorge, stream, and cliff face had succumbed to his relentless chase. Even Baptiste's everlasting power would shrivel into nothingness if a lead ball crashed through his skull. Feriluc believed with utter certainty that the slave would, when the time was right, fall into his grasp as easily as a ripe apple plucked from a tree.

CHAPTER THREE

That night, with the African's trail growing fresher with each passing mile, Feriluc made camp and invited the three marksmen and the scout to join him at the campfire. Because no words were spoken for hours at a time during the day that had just ended, the major suspected that his men were not fully committed to their assignment.

"Gentlemen," he said. "The African you saw escaping up the hill yesterday is far more than just a runaway slave. He is a renowned warrior of the Chiricahua. He won his status by killing women and children. He delights in slow, excruciating deaths that reduce his victims to helpless pleading remnants of humanity." Feriluc's voice rose a full octave above his normal pitch before settling back to its regular heavy cadence. The men looked at each other questioningly, but said nothing. They were well aware of their captain's merciless slaughter of Indians of all ages, regardless of gender.

"We have an opportunity to not only avenge those the Chiricahua killed," Feriluc continued, "But we can also prevent him from murdering hapless settlers who happen to cross his path."

Fifty miles to the south, Kuntamba once again found himself entranced by the landscape and the mystery of a people who long ago relinquished their claim to the land. What remained was an invisible yet indelible imprint on the hills and valleys, a permeating memory of a time lost in the past. Even the wind that moved across the cliff faces, the sandstone, the hills, and the long vacant habitations seemed to whisper of the ancient ones.

Fully aware he was being hunted, Kuntamba intentionally traveled on an indirect route over the most treacherous terrain he could find. He knew the strange and obsessed blue coat leader was relentlessly pursuing him, but didn't quite understand why he was being hunted.

Seemingly without effort, Kuntamba climbed over cliff faces, knowing the major and his men would be forced to swing in a wide circle as they searched for his trail. He sought out the long steep slopes that were covered with loess, the fine -grained fertile loam that collected on the hillsides. This tactic not only made following him extremely difficult, but it carried Kuntamba into the heart of the cliff dwellings left by the Anasazi.

In the ancients' homeland, Kuntamba's senses heightened almost if he were ensnared in dual realms. He was equally at home in physical and nonphysical worlds, but never before had he experienced the sensation of simultaneously occupying two different times. He felt like a visitor in a stranger's home. He worried that his presence might be violating the sanctity of the land.

As he studied the walls, his attention was drawn to some peculiar markings that decorated the flat rock surfaces. He saw handprints in browns, reds, and greens--works of art that recorded the passing of women and children. It raised questions of how one of the artisans had lost a finger, or how one of these long gone warriors reached more than ten feet above ground to leave visible proof of his existence.

Everywhere there were elongated figures of human-like creatures standing with arms extended upward and distorted triangular shaped humanoids with stick-like arms and legs. Halfway up the canyon walls, hundreds of sandstone cliff dwellings still remained, testing the elements and the skill of the dwelling's constructors. The communities and villages located high above the desert floor had been built in the great horizontal gashes nature had carved with wind and water in the perpendicular mountains of sandstone.

The dark runner felt compelled to investigate and explore this land that called out to his spiritual nature and curiosity. He could almost hear the thousands of long since quieted minds, voices, hands, and feet that had labored to build homes out of solid rock. He wondered what force could have driven an entire nation to live like birds clinging to the cliffs for safety, raising their young where they could see forever, but with their feet bound to the limits of the communities' ledges.

He discovered shelters that an advanced people had constructed. He saw level foundations, circular grain storage areas, straight walls, and corners formed at perfect 90-degree angles. Where had they learned the art of building and the use of applied geometry? There was mathematics in everything he saw, but no evidence of writing or numbers. It was a paradox he couldn't fathom.

When he stepped into the shadowed recesses of the cliff dwellings, he felt the heat fall away and the soft caress of cool air engulf him. He stared out over the valley and immediately recognized the cliff dwellings' tactical invulnerability. From these elevated vantage-points, the ancients could see their livestock, planted fields, and the approach of enemies.

Kuntamba wondered how the people in these mountain fortresses interacted with other villages. There must have been a warning system, a way to call the warriors to arms, but the ancient clues escaped the dark runner's notice. He examined the great arching ceiling that the elements had formed in the light brown rock. He was looking for evidence that moisture from the infrequent rains had seeped through the sandstone, providing water for the ancient ones. He found none.

His mind filled with unanswered questions. How was water carried up the steep cliff face? There did not seem to be any paths leading to the dwellings. The dark runner had learned about winches and pulleys on the *Ocean Breeze,* but these people left no proof that they understood leverage, or even the use of ropes, yet they accomplished so much. It was baffling.

The cliff dwellings had round granaries, but no wheels. Kuntamba began to suspect the villages were only used at certain times of the year, but he could find no evidence to support the concept. Too much work and time had been spent in building the cliff dwellings.

He began to search for escape tunnels. Surely a people so masterful in the shaping of rock would have been able to hollow out a tunnel that could carry water and food to the village. Confused, he looked out across the valley at buttes and at the precarious pinnacles that dared gravity to collapse the misshapen forms into rubble. He couldn't help noticing the advantage these wonders of nature would provide as observation posts.

Looking down on the ground, Kuntamba discovered pottery shards. Picking up one of the fragments of an ancient artist's labor, he examined it carefully. His fingers caressed the inner and outer surfaces, seeking to find more than shape and texture. He marveled at the intricate designs and the mastery of complimentary colors.

He questioned why a people so advanced in architecture, and who had at least an instinctual knowledge of mathematics, would select as their habitation a place from which there was no retreat. But what appeared to be most out of place were the intricate designs on what remained of their pottery. It was difficult to believe that ancient artisans could create designs on their vessels that had dimension and proportion, yet demonstrated childish skill in their rock drawings.

Walking back and forth in front of the misshapen triangular bodied figures carved into the rock's patina, Kuntamba sought the meaning of the odd caricatures. Were the drawings guardians of the crops and homes? Were the peculiar markings an address or symbols identifying certain families?

Bending down, the dark runner retrieved a piece of horn that had been shaped into what looked like a digging tool. He rolled it between his fingers and palms. Closing his eyes, Kuntamba began to concentrate.

Instead of centering his mental energy on one point, he forced it outward like mental fingers, tacitly feeling for impressions left by the minds, emotions, and passions of a long gone people, impressions that lay concealed in nature's memory.

He sought the thought patterns that must have preceded the creation of art and a city carved out of stone. He knew traces of a forgotten people still lingered in this land of cliff dwellings. Just being among the dwellings aroused feelings of reverence and respect within him. Kuntamba believed it had taken hundreds of years to build these magnificent fortresses in the sky. In that length of time, the ancient ones would have reinforced their supernatural influence on the land a thousand-fold. It appeared no other group of human inhabitants had moved into the abandoned dwellings, meaning that old influences remained untainted.

Slowly, distorted images drifted across Kuntamba's mental screen. With his mind's eye, he watched with a detachment that belied his interest. Long ago he had learned that when interest, emotion, or desire, entered his meditations, his subjective mind withdrew, leaving his analytical objective mind in control.

He was entering a place that could not bear the weight of logic or questions. The fingers of his consciousness brushed pottery shards, sandstone foundations, and the mud mortar that had locked slabs of rock together for hundreds of years. He touched his core consciousness, the part of his being that was closest to the universal energy that makes existence possible.

Soon he was exploring the part of nature's memory that lived in the sandstone mountains, the cliff dwellings, and in the land that surrounded him. He saw people living without fear, a tribe that had found an almost perfect ecological niche. The ancient culture thrived as it built a vast network of communities. Their wealth grew as the number of trading partners increased.

On his psychic journey, Kuntamba reached out into the past. He followed a river north and south, and explored the wide paths that led east and west, paths that carried goods to tribes hundreds of miles away. He walked through cornfields as a long gone wind rustled the leaves. The sounds filled his ears with the melody of nature. He felt the leaves' gritty surface as if they were in his hand.

His vision permitted him to experience the soft caress of an afternoon breeze carrying a faint hint of humidity. The wind's touch lingered, soothing the tiny abrasions left on his mental body by the corn leaves. Kuntamba was undergoing a rare period when his senses were unfettered by his body. Part of him wanted to stay in this nonexistent world of the past, but he knew that even sublime moments had to end.

He wanted to know the people who had left such an indelible imprint on the land. As the vision changed, Kuntamba watched a man and woman as they dipped a seesaw device into a ditch that drained water from a river. He gazed with special curiosity at the round structures of sticks that were coated with mud the sun had baked rock hard. Looking inside the makeshift enclosures, he discovered corn still on the husk, squash, and beans.

Rising to the aerie high dwelling, he studied square windows and low doorways with perfectly rounded arches. Even in his trance, these observations prompted questions. Kuntamba wondered if the builders understood the principle of load-bearing arches or if they had accidentally formed the arch while searching for aesthetics or ease of entry.

On the ground, he discovered what appeared to be footwear. It was made from a tough plant material that had been woven in an intricate crossing and interlocking pattern. The edges were protected with a bead-like binding. On its sides, flashes of color told of skilled craftsman of another time who had toiled over the remnant. Touching the footwear with non-physical fingers, Kuntamba watched as it came to life on the foot of a young maiden. He saw her run and admired the grace and ease with which she appeared to float over the land. He watched her balance water vessels on her head that seemed far too large for her frail frame. He saw the sandals wear so thin that they finally had to be discarded.

Shifting his inner vision, he moved through nature's memory looking for evidence of the ancient ones' insight into life's purpose. Instead he saw the ancient ones positioning themselves approximately one hundred paces apart in a line that stretched for over a mile. The sun was still shining on another part of the world when they settled down into their places of concealment.

With the dawn, a small herd of bison began to stir as the younger animals enclosed in their protective circle lurched to their feet. An old bull sniffed the wind. He was uneasy. He snorted and trotted off a few yards. The bulls and cows ceased grazing and stared in the direction of the hidden warriors.

At that moment, twenty hunters sprang from the concave depressions they had dug in the earth. They ran screaming, waving their arms. In a second, the old bull's tail came up and his head lowered. Spinning around, his powerful quarters bunched then uncoiled, driving his body forward. Within a few strides the mighty leader was in a full sprint. Behind him thirty cows and calves labored to keep up.

The hunters trailed far to the rear. The men moved leisurely, apparently enjoying themselves. About a mile away, the bison slowed to a stop. The shaggy animals stood, breathing heavily. After a few minutes, following the old bull's lead, the herd began to graze. It was then that a second group of men ran from cover. Once again the bison broke into a run, only this time the herd did not run quite as far, or as fast. All morning long this cycle of panicked flight continued. Eventually exhaustion began isolating the old, the weak, and the very young. The animals were driven up a steep incline into a box canyon. The weak and the old were culled. Hides were taken and bison meat was bundled for the trip home.

Kuntamba was impressed. The cliff dwellers did not kill more than they needed. They let the strongest and youngest animals live, assuring themselves of a harvest in the future.

Moving ahead in time, the dark runner soon discovered change was blanketing the thriving and widely scattered communities of the ancient ones. The villages were joining together into a confederation. Their society had developed a type of caste system. Individuals' wealth and ownership of land had replaced egalitarianism. Strange tribes from the four directions of the compass carried goods, ideas, and new concepts on religion and slavery. All were embraced with capitalistic enthusiasm, but trade brought more than wealth: it brought those who craved the riches and easy lifestyle of the Indian people who lived high above the land with the vultures and the eagles.

From the west came the drum, seashells, tanned hides, archery, and slaves. Out of the south flowed copper, strange brilliantly colored birds, and a religion that practiced human sacrifice, and more slaves. Travelers from the north brought wood cravings; homes made of buffalo hides, the scalping of enemies, and ancestor worship.

With an inner sight that transcended the visual, Kuntamba saw wealth transformed to power. He watched the powerful crush the weak and the dominant drain the land of its vitality, sealing their nation's fate. Trying to look away, the dark runner shed tears that contained no moisture. Unable to retreat from his vision, he witnessed the bartering of human flesh. The dark runner's soul winced as a cane drove the helpless to build monuments to nothing.

His eternal heart, which did not pump blood or race to supply oxygen to laboring muscles, paused in its endless pulse. For an instant, his soul could not hear the music of the spheres or feel the vibration that set existence in motion. Kuntamba's spirit suffered as his inner eye watched children sacrificed to a nonexistent god. His spiritual pain became unbearable as he witnessed beating hearts ripped from young girls' chests by a priesthood that was blind to all spiritual things.

Kuntamba's spirit was exposed when he entered the realm of the past. As a result, he suffered the pain of the ancient ones had inflicted on themselves. Unable to endure the endless misery his inner vision had shown him, the dark runner returned from the region of nature where the past ruled and time was an illusion.

For hours he sat immobile, slowly breathing in the healing power of the universe. Gradually, his internal and external balance returned. From this balance came the ability to assimilate what he had experienced while maintaining a detached poise. Once again wisdom and truth were the fulcrums of his life.

Finally free of his self-inflicted ordeal, Kuntamba's attention turned to his homeland. A pang of loneliness gripped him. It was at that moment that he realized his feet would never again touch African soil. Shrugging his shoulders, even though there was no one to see, he accepted the revelation. From thousands of miles away and across months and years of time, Kuntamba was able to see Africa for what it was; a beautiful land full of potential, a land whose present and past were filled with courage, slavery, and pain.

Kuntamba thought of the Europeans who had been visiting Africa for hundreds of years. Even their advances in navigation, trading, and the manufacture of goods seemed to always end in carnage.

Times had changed. Different people walked the earth. Old lessons were forgotten, and the human race was still bound by spiritual blindness and an overpowering competitive drive to win what was essentially worthless. Kuntamba's introspection slowed, allowing wisdom to replace logic. The ancient ones had turned all of their physical and mental energy toward competing for that, which had only fleeting value. They starved their aesthetic and inner natures while reaching for what their hands could hold and their eyes could see. With no higher understanding to guide them, disaster and misery was inevitable.

Saddened, Kuntamba mumbled out loud, "When will we, who claim an intelligence that is cradled in self-awareness, realize the path to eternity has only one direction--inward toward our source." The dark runner stood, stretching his legs, preparing for the run that would take him from this place.

During the interval of his journey back into nature's memory, Kuntamba had forgotten the blue coats. He now recalled their leader, whose vengeance-driven pursuit was born in another time. The dark runner knew he was being pursued, and was positive he and the blue coat would inevitably confront each other. Kuntamba saw in the major what he would have developed into if he had consciously directed his mental force and physical energy toward the dark side of life.

Throughout his journeys, Kuntamba had witnessed thousands of men and women fulfilling destines, raising families, and living and dying, and conforming to their own understanding of right and wrong. In his travels he had observed less than a dozen individuals who were truly evil or beyond the reach of temptation. Most people were basically good until challenged or confronted.

Other times, under different circumstances, the same, easily aroused violence-prone, individuals might risk their lives to save a stranger from fire or drowning. Their physical, mental, and spiritual power was unharnessed and without direction. It rode the tumultuous tides of human emotion. The few dark souls whose presence caused fear and uneasiness in those around them had long ago vanquished their sense of right and wrong. Those who were unfettered by morality were able to project all the forces of their being toward personal gain, pleasure, and accumulation of power at any cost.

Kuntamba knew the blue coat major possessed an enormous reservoir of power. Most of it was oriented toward evil. Yet the dark runner believed the leader of the horse soldiers, a killer of Indians, could, if his higher nature had not totally abandoned him, use this power to change his ways.

CHAPTER FOUR

For the first time since his escape up the slope, the dark runner felt the negative weight of the major's presence. With the heaviness came a revelation. He had to bring about the transformation of the evil that thrived in the major's being. As a holy man, Kuntamba was bound by his nature to fight evil and relieve suffering. In the struggle, the only weapons available to him were wisdom, love, and truth. The contest between good and evil would take place in the world of objects and on the battlefield of the mind. Soon the major's phantoms of ignorance and viciousness would confront the African's pure flame of truth.

Abruptly Kuntamba flinched, but it wasn't an intentional movement. It was a reflex. He was responding to an object entering the energy that surrounded his body. The reaction twisted his body to the left as a lead ball sped by his head and buried itself in a wall of sandstone. Continuing his spin, he dropped to the ground as two more flesh-seeking missiles thumped to a stop behind him.

The dark runner immediately looked to his right and left. A very narrow ridge that provided an aged route up the cliff face was being explored, tested, and climbed by three blue coats and an Indian scout. Knowing the slave was unarmed and believing he was cornered high above ground in the decaying remains of the habitations left behind by the cliff dwellers, Feriluc and his men took their time. They moved slowly, gaining toe holds where moccasined feet once rested comfortably. Hands reached up, probing hopefully for the next concave depression that would anchor them to the wall.

Grey Eyes, the Apache army scout, led the way. He had the keen eyes and the instincts of a mountain cat. Where his hands and feet found safety, Feriluc followed. In another area, two young cavalrymen were beginning their ascent up the cliffs' southern exposure. They had inadvertently stumbled onto one of the very narrow and perilous passages that the ancients had laboriously hewn into the nearly vertical sandstone wall. The trail began about twenty feet above the land. It had been cut in such a way that, when standing on the ground regardless of the time of day, it cast no shadow.

The young blue coats scaling the wall had grown up in the cities of the east. They did not understand the significance of the piled sand blocking their path. They simply brushed the grit away before reaching for another irregularity in the stone surface as they climbed higher. They did not realize that when the trail narrowed, they could be entering an area where the underlying rock was weak. They saw the tiny grooves caused by desert rainstorms pounding the sandstone wall before it ran down and collected on the ledge that supported them.

They saw the trenches that rainwater pulled by gravity had cut into the path where it joined the wall. The inexperienced soldiers moved with caution, not knowing what to expect. Each soldier tried holding his rifle in one hand, but that proved to be awkward and dangerous. Even slinging the weapons across their backs made them less sure-footed. They did not think to push their rifles, canteens, and extra supplies ahead freeing their hands and distributing their weight on the ledge. The blue coats did not know that the ledge they stood on had been sculpted by and for a people who were smaller and lighter than they were.

When the lead soldier's feet slipped down as the sandstone ledge that supported him crumbled, his partner dropped to his hands and knees and watched in horror. Caught in one of the moments where intense concentration seems to slow the passing of time, the second soldier stared transfixed. He saw his friend's body twist in the air, his arms flailing and his fingers searching for a hand hold.

The remaining soldier flinched as the corporal's strangely acrobatic body plunged downward, striking a mound of sand and rock that had collected at the base of the cliff over hundreds of years. The debris changed the direction of the soldier's fall, sending his body rolling and tumbling to the desert floor. He landed badly scraped and bruised, but he would survive. High above, his partner was slowly and carefully retracing his steps.

Grey Eyes and Major Feriluc watched in detached fascination as the corporal's body thudded on the collected rubble at the cliff's base before bouncing head over heels to the ground below. The major was disappointed. His men would be unable to complete their assignment. He hoped the uninjured soldier would have enough sense to watch for and shoot the dark runner if he attempted to escape down the path the corporal had fallen from.

Feriluc was relieved that only the Indian scout would be left to deal with after he had killed the dark runner. The thought of avenging the horrors he had experienced at Baptiste's hands long ago made the major impatient. He urged the Apache to move faster, but the Indian scout could not be hurried.

The major fought to contain his fervor. Grey Eyes' lack of response was pushing Feriluc past the point of irritation, but the fact that he needed the Apache to complete the climb suppressed his hand. A feeling of almost irresistible anticipation compounded his anger. The closer he got to the slave that he believed to be the personification of Baptiste, the more obsessed he became. His hands began to tremble. His mind filled with thoughts of the pleasure he would gain by returning to Baptiste's embodiment what the pirate had given him.

Just ahead, with only about thirty feet left to climb, the Indian stopped. He knew the dark runner was trapped. He saw no point in taking unnecessary risks. He told Feriluc he wanted to turn back, letting thirst, hunger, and heat take their toll on the strange black man.

Even though Kuntamba was unarmed, Grey Eyes still feared him. He had seen the African run with the same ease as the wind blowing down a canyon. He witnessed the company's best marksman firing from a few hundred yards away and repeatedly missing. He believed the slave possessed the combined power of a mighty warrior and the greatest of medicine men. He saw no evil in killing an enemy who had invaded his land. In his heart, the Indian doubted the dark runner had committed the atrocities Feriluc described.

If the Apache could conquer the black man who seemed to be protected by the gods, he could claim the runner's invincibility to the white man's rifles and his spiritual power. Grey Eyes had visions of returning to his own tribe, of becoming a mighty chief and driving the white man from the land. The Indian envisioned succeeding generations petitioning for his help and guidance. He could hear his name being chanted around the campfires, children fighting to claim his name in their games of war and hunting.

When Feriluc refused to turn back and let time and the elements fight his battle, Grey Eyes slipped passed him and returned to the level ground below. The scout was positive the major would be helpless against the dark runner's power. He knew that pistols and knives could not harm an adversary who lived both in this world and the region of spirits. But the Indian had not seen the major's dark force nor felt its heavy weight crushing inward on his heart and mind.

Feriluc grimaced, nodding his head in agreement. Now he would be totally alone with the African. There would be no witnesses to his absolution, just as there had been no observers to his defilement long ago. His own screams never left him; they still rang in his ears. Over the years he had strengthened his power of concentration, enabling him to partially block old memories and the sound of his own voice crying out for help.

Since the first sighting of the dark runner, images of Baptiste had been breaking through his mental barricades. As he continued to climb, Feriluc envisioned the black runner screaming and begging for mercy, but the runaway slave's cries would summon no delivery, only the vultures. It was his vile passion, his desperate need to somehow reconcile his own lingering torment and repressed guilt with the African's blood that drove him, blind to everything around him, toward his goal of capturing the slave. Pausing, he watched the Apache retreat down the cliff face. He did not trust the Indian, but he would deal with the scout later.

Because Feriluc, in his years of self-imposed exile, had encapsulated himself in a world of darkness, he was able to gain access to the venues where violent and negative thoughts are born. This permitted him to feel the treachery in Grey Eyes' heart. He became convinced the Apache was preparing to ambush him on his return. Many times in the past, the major's own paranoia had read dislike and disgust for plots on his life. It was a blind spot born of fear and distrust that now filled his mind with thoughts of a second orgy of blood and pain, one where the Indian scout's voice would call out in terror.

Thirty feet above, and a hundred and fifty feet east of his position, Kuntamba felt the cold breath of absolute negativity pressing in on him from two directions. He looked down into the grey eyes of the Apache and acknowledged the Indian's presence and intent with a nod of his head, then he turned his attention to the blue coat's advance.

Slowly the part of Kuntamba's spirit, which would never experience absolute victory or defeat, flooded his consciousness with the guidance he needed to be victorious over the white man and still remain true to himself. The message was simple, and it echoed Grey Eyes' plan. The dark runner would hide in the hundred enclosures. He would move constantly, waiting for hunger, thirst, and the desiccating heat to soften the poisonous shell that enclosed what little remained of Feriluc's, higher nature.

With Kuntamba's inner guidance came lessons in truth. The teachings reminded him that every human being possesses and is possessed by a tiny flame, which like its infinite source is indestructible, incorruptible, and eternal. He knew this fragment of the infinite was the guide to every soul's evolutionary journey. Kuntamba had learned when he first attempted to reach out to others with offerings of wisdom, that his words were rarely understood. He quickly discovered that the minds of most of mankind were filled with wants, desires, and an incessant information stream supplied by their senses. He now understood what he had to do. He had to wait and let time, fear, and paranoia become his allies in the struggle for the major's soul. When exhaustion and fear of death smothered the voices of the blue coat's inner demons, truth would have one last chance to penetrate his consciousness.

CHAPTER FIVE

The blue coat had come after him, armed with a pistol, rifle, and knife, but he had failed to carry enough food and water to sustain him for more than a few days. The dark runner was more than two hundred feet above the desert floor. He was standing in the middle of a deserted community whose buildings reached upward three and four stories. Some buildings were round, while others were square. Many had subterranean chambers connected by narrow tunnels.

Not far away, the dark runner saw stockpiles of large rocks and small boulders. Kuntamba suspected the original inhabitants of the cliff dwellings had used the bigger stones as missiles of defense. He could almost see the ancient ones, standing at the edge of the precipice and hurling their projectiles down on invaders. He had a use for the piled rocks, as the blue coat would soon discover.

On his long journey, the dark runner had acquired many psychic abilities. But just like everything else that enters the field of existence, these extensions of the soul are dual in nature. If Kuntamba continued to use the powers to further his spiritual growth, they would increase in strength. If he were to misuse even one of his forces, it would become tainted. Because all spiritual strength flows from one source, the tarnished power would darken the others.

This meant that for Kuntamba, the use of violence was an impossibility, but it did not mean Kuntamba had to ignore his senses or his ability to feel the major's negativity. All of the information and impressions that caught his attention remained available to him. He did not have to turn away from his wisdom, or his understanding of truth, or even his physical ability to survive for long periods without food or water. If the blue coat chose to suffer hunger and thirst rather than retreat to the desert floor for supplies, the decision was his and not the dark runner's.

Standing where Feriluc could see him and using his best English, Kuntamba called out, "Leader of the blue coats, why do you hunt me?"

Feriluc looked at the African but only saw Baptiste as he responded. "Why do you run from me? Are you afraid I will repay you for your attentions one night long ago?"

"Whom do you think I am?" Kuntamba answered.

The major was irritated. "I know who you are! Tell me you have never set foot on a sailing vessel! Tell me you don't know the bow from the stern or a yardarm from a skipjack! Tell me you are not a liar!"

"Of course I know these things. I have been on a sailing ship, as have most of the Africans who walk this land," Kuntamba replied.

"Yes, that is true, but none speak the English language as well as you. None speak with the authoritative voice of command that you, Captain Baptiste, possess."

Kuntamba was confused. Was there another African who ran across this great land? Did the other African look like him? What had the look-alike done that had caused the blue coat major to want to take his life?

Because Feriluc seemed certain he had found the right man, Kuntamba doubted that words alone could convince the major of his error, still the dark runner wanted to try again. "Leader of men, if I am Captain Baptiste, why didn't I kill you as you clung to the cliff face?"

"Because you plan to indulge your sadistic sexual desires on my flesh one last time. But I say to you that before the sun rises tomorrow, you will cry out for death's cold embrace!"

Articulating his oath, Feriluc raised his rifle and fired. His intention was to wound rather than kill the black runner. But mysteriously, the black man in front of the rifle sights disappeared as the rifle's stock recoiled against the major's shoulder. Feriluc was standing only a few feet from the edge of the cliff. The rifle's recoil forced him to step back with his right foot. From the corner of his left eye, he saw nothing but space. Instantly the major's concentration shifted from the black man's impending death to his own survival. In the unexpected moment of vulnerability, Feriluc's reflexes confirmed his desire to live and his fear of death.

It told Kuntamba that the blue coat had at least one fear that was stronger than his desire to seek revenge. He now knew why the major wanted to torture and destroy him. Feriluc had been victimized and forced to participate in brutal sexual practices. The ordeal had scarred his mind and soul and filled the blue coat with a poisonous need to avenge and redeem himself.

From a distance, Kuntamba studied Feriluc's sullen body movements as his thick fingers struggled to reload the rifle. The dark runner studied the features of the man who despised him. He could not help noticing that even the sun was unable to completely dissolve the darkness that emanated from the major's glowering face. Not wanting to see more, and needing to collect his thoughts, Kuntamba turned and disappeared among the intertwining buildings left by the ancients.

Feriluc watched as the African's effortless steps carried him from view. From the major's perspective, the slave appeared to float over the ground. With his irritation growing, Feriluc began to nod his head as if talking to himself.

Suddenly he yelled vehemently, "So you want to begin where we left off long ago? Only this time I have weapons and you are helpless."

A hundred yards away Kuntamba watched the major from the portal of a three-story building. Waiting until the blue coat was out of sight, he responded from the building's interior. "Major, I am over here, waiting for you."

His voice reverberated within the chamber and took on a directionless quality that prevented Feriluc from pinpointing the dark runner's location. Hearing the slave's voice, Feriluc dropped down into a crouch and circled the buildings.

When he thought he was close to the area the sound had come from, he called, "I see you plan to outlast me by constantly moving about and hiding. You know I have only enough food and water to last me for a few days. But I know you possess no water or food. We can both endure far longer in these conditions than most men. Why don't we end this now, no weapons, just bare hands?"

Feriluc waited for a reply. After several minutes, he began to fidget. He was sure the African would wait until hunger or sleep deprivation claimed him. He muttered in agitation. "I am a military man. I should be able to devise a strategy that will defeat an unarmed slave."

It suddenly occurred to Feriluc that Grey Eyes and his two remaining healthy cavalrymen with their rifles controlled all movement on the cliff. When he ran out of food and water, he could climb down, gather supplies, and return. He would be able to last forever. He was back in charge and felt better. Only time stood between him and victory.

Relieved, he reverted to an old military tactic. He would seek the high ground. Climbing to the top of a cylindrical structure, he looked around before settling in. Half of the world stretched out before him. He did not see the beautiful sunset, the purple tinted hills, and the silver strip of a river flowing south, and he could find no trace of the dark runner.

Propping his rifle up against a wall, Feriluc waited, hoping for a crippling shot at his prey. His mind exhausted from its inner turmoil, quieted. Gradually silence enveloped the land and the grand community that an unknown people had carved and built high above the plains. It was mesmerizing. The silence had a quality that wove a spell of placid quietude, capturing the major in its embrace, holding him in the suspended world of nothingness that lies between wakefulness and sleep.

The dark runner's inner tranquillity did not let anger, fear, or desire divert his attention. He was able to see and feel the beauty that surrounded him. From the motionless warmth of the late afternoon, he drew the recuperative strength that comes from perfect rest. Looking across what had been rooftops, he saw the soldier's head nod and drop toward his chest. Walking out into the open, Kuntamba picked up a large boulder and aimed it at the place where the blue coat had completed his ascent up to the cliff dwellings.

"Blue coat, see what I can do with this rock," bellowed the dark runner, hurling the stone against the crumbling edge that divided vertical from horizontal surfaces. As the rock hit, a chunk of sandstone broke off from the face of the cliff and crashed below. The sound woke Feriluc. Clearing his mind, he felt for the rifle and took aim, but the African was nowhere in sight.

Feriluc heard the crash of rock against rock. At first he was unable to figure out what the African meant by, look what I can do. Like an epiphany, the major began to understand. In an instant, his daydreaming turned to rage and racing feet. When he got to the place where his quarry had thrown the rock, he did not see the dark runner standing in the shadows a hundred feet away. All he recognized was that his retreat to the flat land below had been cut off. He was trapped high above the ground beyond the reach of his reserve food and water.

Feriluc now believed if he tried to leave the sandstone cliff, rocks and boulders thrown from above would speed his journey downward and into the grave. His nemesis was trying to destroy the last few precarious hand and foot holds that made the completion of his climb possible. Even in his anger, Feriluc could not help but admire the brilliance of the African's strategy. By simply throwing a rock, Baptiste's likeness had left him with only two strategies. He could hunt the slave or guard his path to safety.

The major felt like he was back in Baptiste's quarters, vulnerable and helpless. A shudder went through him. Would he have to endure another night of Baptiste's debauchery? 'No,' he thought. 'I will jump to my death first!' Fear flushed old memories from the internal vaults he had forced them into. The vivid and unwanted visualizations solidified his choice to die rather than endure a second night with the pirate.

The significance of the renunciation caused the long-held fear of death to lose its hold on him. He did not comprehend it, but he was freer. Never again would the threat of dying force him to commit any act against his will. The vile mental pictures of his defilement partially faded, but the frightful memories had a life of their own. Time, pain, and repetition had vivified his fearful submission to Baptiste's passion. Self-loathing had dominated his life for too long.

When Feriluc vanquished his fear of death, his inner demons lost some of their power. The declaration that death was preferred to dishonor was a challenge to the self-created phantoms that roamed the paths of his subconscious. But the demons refused to be expelled. The ongoing mental struggle exhausted the major's mind. His body demanded physical release from the tension of the inner conflict.

"Now we both shall die here in the emptiness of this lost civilization," screamed Feriluc. "I cannot lose. If you kill me and try to escape, my men will shoot you. Either we settle this now or both of us will perish."

Kuntamba remained silent, but he recognized a change in the rhythm of the major's words and knew his pursuer was no longer terrified of death.

Frustrated, Feriluc paced back and forth. There had to be a way to end the stalemate quickly. Slowly he developed a plan. He would start at one end of the elevated city, carefully searching each structure. His hope was to gradually force the African into an ever- shrinking area. He understood that the task he was undertaking was flawed. His enemy could move easily and circle around behind him. Still, the activity would fill the hours and hopefully give him a shot as the slave ran from hiding place to hiding place.

CHAPTER SIX

The dark runner silently slipped to the back of a cavern where the sunlight never cast shadows. Feriluc began his search, moving from building to building. Sitting Yoga style, Kuntamba studied the blue coat as he jabbed at shadows, threatening the owls and bats that had taken up residence in the buildings' interior. He saw the soldier's methodical search become a series of pauses and backward glances. The dark runner listened to the white man's chaotic steps and watched perspiration collect on his forehead and run down his shirt.

Feriluc, like Kuntamba lived alone. The dark runner's isolation was by choice. The major's was an unwanted segregation born of fear and other people's dislike of him. But the isolation of the cliff dwelling was a different kind of loneliness. He was hundreds of feet above the desert floor and several days ride from the soldiers he commanded. He longed to hear the noise of human conversation, the sounds of his men eating and caring for their equipment. His mind hungered for change, for familiar voices, for something to show he was not alone with the African.

Feriluc began to deliberately bump his rifle butt against the walls instead of moving quietly from structure to structure. Occasionally he threw a stone just to hear it clatter as it skipped along the sandstone surface. The sun rose and set and was rising again when he finally sagged to the ground, rolling over on his back and surrendering to fatigue.

In his dreams, Feriluc chased phantoms that slipped through his fingers like a cold wind. He saw Baptiste staring down at him. When he turned away from the haunting pirate's face, he was confronted with the placid demeanor of the slave staring at him. One part of his dream body wanted to move closer to the dark runner. A second more fearful part cringed and pulled away.

In the dream-state, Feriluc felt as if he was intentionally being pulled apart. He was caught on the razor-sharp edge that divides pleasure and pain. If he pulled away completely, the feelings of peace and terror would cease. He hungered for the peace reflected in the slave's face and detested the cruelty he saw in Baptiste's eyes. He finally slipped into the uncharted world where body and mind are rejuvenated in deep sleep.

Nearby, Kuntamba waited for the blue coat's sleeping body to settle into the stillness that muffles the senses. Walking on soundless feet, the dark runner approached the major's motionless form. He picked up the rifle, easing the pistol from its holster. He intentionally left the knife undisturbed not wanting to leave the major with a feeling of total vulnerability.

Later, while the moon was dark and a thin layer of clouds obscured his view of the stars, Kuntamba slipped over the edge of the cliff and moved down. Below him, Grey Eyes and the cavalrymen slept fitfully. The uninjured soldiers were supposed to be awake but the endless boredom had temporarily claimed them in slumber.

Kuntamba inched down the cliff face on a narrow ledge no wider than the width of his foot. Although the ledge could not be seen from the ground, to a careful observer of shadows and light patterns from above it was discernible. Traversing the limited steep slope was no problem for the dark runner, but for Feriluc's large body, passage would be next too impossible. Kuntamba carried the bottom half of a receptacle fashioned by the long dead inhabitants of the cliff dwellings.

He was going for water but not for himself. The dark runner wasted no time. He had to return to his hiding place before the earth rotated another fifteen degrees, bringing dawn and wakefulness to the blue coat. An hour later, the coming of the sun's first light and the condensation of moisture from the night air on his body woke Feriluc. His hand came up to brush away insects that buzzed near his head. His eyes looked up at the sandstone ceiling, then out at the blue sky. His mouth was dry. His tongue tried to dampen his teeth and lips, but the long night of sucking great drafts of oxygen-rich desert air into his lungs had drawn all the wetness from his salivary glands.

Instinctively he reached for his rifle, pawing the ground, guided by eyes still thick with sleep. Rolling over frantically, he searched for a rifle that was not there. His right hand reached down for his pistol and found only an empty holster. His fingers circled his waist, seeking the leather sheath and the hunting knife it contained. Relieved, he removed the knife with its six-inch long blade as he said to himself, "African, you missed this finely honed weapon. Your carelessness may cost you your life."

Feriluc's conscious mind had not yet digested what the loss of his defenses meant, but his subconscious mind had. Panic, with roots embedded in the netherworld of unborn thoughts, tightened its grip on his chest and vocal cords. He wanted to curse and yell that he would cut his own throat before submitting to another night of bloodletting debasement, but the sound would not come.

The major stood, pulling off his shirt, displaying a swirling series of razor-thin scars on his back and chest. He wanted to exhibit himself as used goods. Feriluc wanted the African; the resurrected vehicle of Baptiste's dark soul, to know that he was no longer young and appealing. Struggling to regain his voice, Feriluc walked out in the open, inviting his imagined adversary to end his torment with a shot to the head.

Abruptly his attitude changed as he shouted, "I will survive!"

Looking for anything edible to sustain him, instead of crawling insects and beetles, he found a vessel of water.

Once again paranoia, and the past, stayed the major's hand, preventing him from drinking. Suddenly, Baptiste's cajoling voice was recalled, urging him to drink a sweet-smelling liquid. When he refused, the first scar was sculpted into his chest by the pirate's shaking hand. The beverage was aromatic, easing the pain and stripping away the veneer that civilization, schooling, and religion, had enclosed his lower nature in. The potion, and his actions after drinking the concoction, were the chief sources of his guilt, reducing him to a semi-voluntary participant in his own defilement.

Tentatively the blue coat touched his finger to the liquid's surface before placing it to his tongue. The fluid was not sweet. Still he waited for hallucinations and blurred vision to confirm what he suspected. When nothing happened, he swallowed a mouthful of the liquid and waited. Thirty minutes later, feeling no effects of being drugged, he picked up the container and drank half its volume. Refreshed, he hid the remaining water to keep Baptiste's reincarnation from drinking.

As the major piled rocks over the basin that contained his reserve water supply, he wondered where the water had come from. Who had put it near his sleeping body? There was only one conclusion, the African!

Seeking answers to why the slave had left the water, Feriluc's mind conjured up scenarios Kuntamba could have not imagined. The major believed with certainty that the African had somehow become possessed by Baptiste's spirit. The gesture of leaving water for his use could have only one meaning—the African wanted him alive, but weakened by days of hunger.

Reaching for his knife, the blue coat ran his fingers over the cold metal. He sought reassurance in the blade's sharp edge. He even fantasized of using stealth and the point of his blade to gain victory. Feriluc's bravado took on a shade of fear. The African had his weapons. The slave could kill him at any time. From this dread sprang an anticipation that envisioned Baptiste's face in every shadow.

Feriluc irrationally believed that the African had outsmarted him, intentionally leading him to the nearly inaccessible cliff dwellings. He chastised himself. How could a military man fall into such a trap? His judgment had been misguided, blinded by the need for revenge.

High above, the rock surface cracked as the sun drove the prior night's chill from the sandstone's outer face. Bits of sand and rock flaked off and fell near him. Startled, he jumped clear then tripped and fell. With skinned hands and elbows as a reminder of his trepidation, Feriluc leaned back against the cool wall, trying to relax.

In the nearly absolute silence of his solitude, his hunger intensified. His stomach growled and his mouth salivated as he thought of the rations stored in his saddlebag. Time, inactivity, and fear of the unknown were taking their toll on Feriluc's body and fragile mind. He began to agonize over when the African would attack. He saw the African's ability to survive without food and water as proof of his possession by Baptiste's dark soul. Ever so slowly his thoughts grew more frantic. Needing to vent the menagerie of imaginings that filled his mind, Feriluc began to shout.

"Phantom Demon, whose body runs with the wind and whose mind and face are one with evil, what do you want with me?"

Knowing that the blue coat's time of testing was near, Kuntamba decided to try to prepare him for his impending ordeal. Turning so the source of his words would be confused by the concave ceiling of the ancient city, the dark runner answered. "It is you who pursues and tries to kill me with your weapons! I am the one who hides from your rage. While you slept, I could have bound your feet, crippled your legs with a boulder or shot you with your own gun. The water you drank, I left for you. I brought you no food because it would only feed your hunger for revenge against an innocent man."

"It is my belief, and you have no choice in this. When a man is possessed by demons that live within, starvation can serve the good. By depriving your mind and body of the sustenance they need to function, the grip of the self-created spirits that thrive in the mental world can be temporarily weakened. This weakness occurs when the mind and body become consumed by the most basic need of all--survival."

"Unwillingly, you have begun a fast that will test every fiber of your being. If you persist and refuse to succumb to death's waiting call, you will acquire the power to enter the inner worlds where only truth survives. If there is even a latent spark of goodness within you, it will reveal itself to what remains of your soul. If you can let go of the past long enough, you will enter the presence of your own eternal flame of truth. If you have the power to stand still in its presence, it will temporarily dissolve your inner darkness."

"In that moment, which occurs as naturally as the rising sun displaces the prior night's darkness, you will discover, if only momentarily, the purpose of life."

Feriluc struggled to understand the meaning of the words the black slave had spoken. But he could not turn away from his need for revenge and his body's demand for food.

"Your words are gentler now," replied Feriluc. "But that is because you stand alone against me. If your men were here with sabers and guns, you would take me by force. When you think I am defenseless, your true nature will reveal itself. Beware! When I appear helpless, I am the most dangerous."

Kuntamba did not reply. He was waiting for time, thirst, and hunger to do their work. He knew when Feriluc's body started to lose its grip on life; his mind would flood with distorted images of the past. During his mental wanderings, the blue coat major would review all the events of his life. He would see the balance that measures good and evil, and would witness the net impact of his life on the world and people around him.

CHAPTER SEVEN

untamba waited in the shadowed recess of the cliff. He watched the major's steps grow weary, fading into floundering exhaustion. He listened as the repeated alternations of day and night changed the blue coat's vocalizations to incomprehensible mumbling.

The African stood nearby as chimeras filled the major's mind with confusion. On the tenth day, he heard the blue coat's screams for mercy echo through the vast chamber. The pain-filled cries for help told Kuntamba that the semi-delirious man was reliving a shocking secret. The blue coat's eyes no longer sought the slave-- instead his lids were shut tight as his mind's eye sought to gain a focus in the unchanging world of perfect truth.

Feriluc's arms and legs began to convulse in seizure-like spasms as his hands clenched and unclenched as if they were grasping something hot. Kneeling by the major's side, Kuntamba worked to prevent the major from harming himself. When the major's body calmed, the African relaxed and waited.

Slowly Kuntamba's head tilted back as if looking up at the sky, yet his eyes were closed. His inner vision sought the midpoint between his pituitary and pineal glands. He guided his spiritual energy in a pulsating rhythm into the tiny space that separated the two organs. Soon a living bridge was formed, calling the glands to life in the supernatural world.

It had taken Kuntamba a lifetime of meditation and abstinence to gain access to the wisdom he possessed.

It had taken him much longer to transmute all his appetites, fears, hopes, and even the right of self-defense, into spiritual strength. Even with the vast purifying labor behind him, Kuntamba was risking his life and all he had worked for. Just one flaw in his spiritual transmutation could cost him a lifetime of growth.

Kuntamba did not seek spiritual growth for any reason other than it was as natural to him as the sun in the sky. Looking back, it was clear that fateful day in Africa when he first sighted the *Ocean Breeze* that he was predestined to fulfill an important inner journey. The motion of the law was set. He was here in the arid land to assist the blue coat major. He would willingly enter the nonphysical regions without fear. If he was found wanting, he would gladly retrace the steps of his life, but his own testing time had now arrived.

The African began to chant. The intonation had a cadence that set the air around him vibrating to the melody. The song spread out in spherical waves, influencing everything nearby in its rhapsody. The pulse enveloped Feriluc in a harmony that filled his lungs, heart, and finally his entire body with energy. The major's expression slowly softened. Visions of a night long ago on the Barbary coast in the pirate's quarters faded as his suffering merged with the universe, letting his soul experience its first breath of true freedom.

Feriluc moved on a second sojourn into the past, guided gently by an unidentifiable shadow figure. He entered a subjective world where excuses and personal pain could not justify actions. He entered the regions where the full weight of past endeavors is felt.

The first of his inner revelations ushered him into the time of the ancients. Religion ruled. Human sacrifice was common and slavery encouraged. He looked into the eyes of the helpless and felt their fear, terror, and deaths. He marveled how people's minds had become so twisted that evil became goodness.

A shift of scenery provided a picture of massacred Indian women and children. He saw the shadows of the unborn hovering over bodies that would have been channels to physical life. The major's spirit contracted into a closed ball as chains of horror concentrated the immense negativity of his life, thoughts, and actions on the remnants of his soul. The sense of absolute freedom he had felt when his inner search began turned dark with self-revulsion. He was unable to look at the encyclopedic record of misery and pain he had so willingly forced on almost everyone he encountered.

He heard the sound of his voice ordering the lash because a recruit did not sit straight enough in the saddle or because a salute lacked crispness. He recognized his lack of compassion when the blood from wounds opened by the whip turned the sand red. He heard the cries of dead soldiers' parents and felt the grief his harsh discipline had caused.

His soul sagged and shriveled under the burden of his debt. He attempted to turn away, but he had entered an unseen current whose direction could not be changed. It carried his resisting essence through the slave quarters where he witnessed his own brutality on the chained victims of bondage. He looked into the dark haunted eyes that stared back at him, asking why his blows needed to be so well placed.

With each experience, the weight and the enormity of his regret grew. His body began to convulse involuntarily as his mouth opened and his diaphragm heaved in retching spasms. The muscles in his shoulders and arms bunched as his clenched hands pounded the stone floor in a blind flagellation that punished hands for past abuses his mind had directed.

But his ordeal was not over. The major saw a younger Feriluc sickening in body, mind, and soul. He felt Baptiste's embrace and was unable to pull away. He saw a small part of himself smile with pleasure as Baptiste's arms held him. It was a pleasure that lived on the threshold of pain. He stared into the pirate's eyes as Baptiste studied his face. In that exact moment, Feriluc discovered that deep in his heart, there existed an uncultivated appetite for sadistic sexuality. An extreme tide of disgust immediately welled up. On its crest was the realization that what Feriluc hated was not Baptiste, but an evil that lived within himself.

Like an ebbing tide flowing out to sea leaving behind the naked wet sand, the review of Feriluc's earlier life ended. As the events passed from the present into his memory, he felt an instant of bliss. The fleeting moment of indescribable peace gave him the strength to endure his last trial. It began with a feeling of compression. It grew in intensity until he felt like his body and mind were collapsing in on themselves. For Feriluc, time seemed to decelerate. In reality, only a few seconds had passed.

The blue coat encountered a paradox. His mind told him the force was pressing in from the outside. Actually it was his soul, activated by a moment of splendor pushing outward against the weight of negativity that his lifetime of violence had entombed it with. For the briefest period, the two forces found equilibrium.

In the fleeting passage of time, a part of Feriluc's soul escaped into a world of beauty. But off in a dark corner of his vision was a large cage. The enclosure was constructed of solid steel with bars thicker than a muscular man's arms. The major tried to look in another direction, but wherever he looked he saw the cage. Its magnetism called to him, an irresistible force that grew and drew him to the pen.

Feriluc's first steps were hesitant but soon his pace took on a compulsive urgency. He had to discover what strange beast the cage constrained. He ran headfirst into the bars then recoiled, expecting pain, but he was in a place where physical hurt did not exist. He strained to see in the darkness that veiled a most uncommon prison. He slipped his hand between the bars, but touched nothing.

Reaching deep to control his fear of the unknown, the blue coat called out, "What thing is so violent and so powerful that it must be confined with bars of steel?"

His words needed no answer.

The beast's heavy steps and sickening odor signaled its approach. The ground that was his spirit, his soul, and his individuality, shook. Feriluc's eyes, which were shared by the ogre, searched the darkness. As Feriluc met the gaze of his own lower nature, the perversion came into view. Its huge body was cloaked in long shaggy hair covered in oozing yellow-red blood. Immediately the major saw the outline of long muscular arms. From the creature's wrists and neck hung the skeletons of Indian women and children. Its snakelike, bony fingers held terrified slaves and the bodies of dead bison. In the depths of the ghastly abomination's eyes, Feriluc saw himself.

The major tried to look away, but turning his head only revealed another aspect of the frightening and detestable vision. He beheld a thick, wide chest heaving in the act of breathing. Only the creature's exhalations left the part of Feriluc that stood outside the cage gasping from the exhaled filth of the malignant beast.

Feriluc froze in place as the loathsome anomaly's bowed sinewy legs flexed and squatted. Suddenly the monstrosity jumped, crashing into the bars that separated the two parts of his psyche. Its sexual organ were large, engorged, and twisted into a knot. Feriluc sprang back as the aberration's pelvis pumped against the cold steel in an offering of sexuality.

Falling back in horror, Feriluc screamed out. "What have I created? How can I repair the damage I have committed? How can I call back the pain I have caused?"

In the silence that followed came a faint almost indistinguishable voice. The voice whispered, "The beast is part of you. You cannot shrink from it. You created it from yourself and it is contained within you. You have cultivated and nourished it with your thoughts and deeds, yet it stands between what you are and what you may become. If you continue to hate and kill, the beast will consume your soul and your individuality. Your eternal journey will end and a strand of infinite potential will remain unfulfilled."

"If you cease nourishing this Minotaur of self destruction that roams the labyrinth of your mind and the dark side of your soul, the beast will grow weak. Eventually when your spiritual light is strong and wisdom's truth fills you, a battle will be fought. Your lower nature, which is the beast fearing oblivion, will call on all the subtle nuances of its power and challenge its enemies--truth and wisdom-- in the battlefield of your mind."

"Either your lower nature will consume all that you are, or you will transmute the beast's power into the spiritual force needed to continue your eternal journey. The choice is yours. The ultimate nothingness of negativity, or an endless journey of expanding spiritual discovery awaits your decision."

Bewildered, the major's soul fell incapacitated. Either choice carried him down a road of pain. If he chose the dark side, his life would continue on its present course and end in nothingness. If he persisted, an incomprehensible expanse of existence waited for his exploration. Only the brave and strong could enter the hall of true learning. Feriluc's courage was being tested.

Calling out in a voice filled with indecision, the major implored, "How can I stand against the creature I have created? It has more power in one hand than my entire body possesses."

A voice, which rose from the tiny spark of the Infinite Absolute that each life possesses, answered. "As you empower your lower nature, so also do you disempower it. The source of all thoughts, words, and deeds rest on the mind's interpretation of experience and its reaction to stimuli from within and without. When you covet power, riches, and sexual excess, the beast gains power and the mind becomes a conduit serving the ego. Control your mind and you control your destiny. It is the work of ages but in the Infinite, all measures of time shrink to a relative nothingness."

As the words faded, Feriluc's essence became aware of an oppressive heaviness. It grew in intensity until it forced his spirit outward into the world where his body and mind waited.

For a full day and night he lay immobile, his spirit and soul hovering just above his weary form, waiting for the moment of awareness to arrive. On the second day, just as the sun pushed darkness from the land, Feriluc drew in a long slow breath simultaneously merging his mind and body with his spirit and soul.

He sat up, strangely refreshed and famished. Only his hunger was not for food. It was for change in his life. Calling out in a loud excited voice, Feriluc said, "Slave, I will hunt you no more!" Hearing no reply, he looked around. Not far away, cloaked in a morning shadow, he found Kuntamba.

CHAPTER EIGHT

The dark runner lay helpless, vulnerable, and barely alive. The major did not know it was the dark runner's energy that made his inner search possible. Feriluc had no way of knowing that Kuntamba had endured his suffering. He would not have understood why the African's pain had been so much more intense than his own. Feriluc sensed that somehow he was responsible for the African's condition. For the first time in his life, he dropped to his knees and wept tears of sorrow and regret. The tears dampened the ground, cleansing a minuscule part of his soul, allowing a ray of spiritual light to escape from him.

It was enough to recall Kuntamba from the realm between life and death. His breathing quickened then deepened. For hours he lingered in this recuperative state. The call of the night owl told him he was once more in the world of change. When his strength returned, Kuntamba's spiritual and physical powers would be at a peak, enabling him to complete his journey. Willing to give his own life force to Feriluc, the dark runner had received it back, multiplied.

When Kuntamba ultimately woke, he saw Feriluc sitting beside him. In that moment, he knew the major had begun the quest for his holy grail.

The blue coat spoke first. "I now know that you are not the reincarnation of Baptiste. In hunting you, I unwittingly pursued myself.

I have learned the evil I fear lives within me. I have only one question: were you the shadow that guided my steps into the region of the beast?"

Kuntamba nodded. "It was me. But it was your soul hungering for truth that gave me permission to enter your world."

Feriluc hung his head. "Then I owe you all that I will become in the future."

Kuntamba disagreed. "You owe me nothing. Your debt will be paid in time with interest. As I have helped you, others have helped me. Those who are able must go on helping until the human race raises its spiritual awareness to a point where it equals its intelligence."

The dark runner said, "Ahead of you lies an almost endless series of trials. If you call to me in a selfless plea for guidance, I will hear you. If you believe and listen with an unclosed mind, you will sense my reply. It will speak with a clarity that denies distance. My message will come, not on the spoken word, but on the sigh of intuition and with the flash of inspiration."

Feriluc remained silent, trying to understand all he had heard. It occurred to him that he and the slave were stranded in the land of the cliff dwellers. Without thinking he blurted out, "How shall we get down from this height?"

Kuntamba answered with two words. "Follow me."

Taking the major's right hand in his left, the dark runner led Feriluc out onto the narrow path. "Trust me. Have faith and you will be safe." Feriluc followed as a child heeds a parent.

Leading the way, the dark runner studied the ground below for the grey eyes of the Apache. When he finally located the Indian scout, instead of cunning, the dark runner saw surprise and disbelief. Grey Eyes had patiently waited to kill the survivor of the struggle between the blue coat and the African, but not in his wildest dreams did the scout envision the foes becoming friends.

Because Kuntamba led the way and was vulnerable to a push from behind, Grey Eyes knew it was the black man's power that had transformed hate to friendship. The apache's heart filled with admiration and a desire to claim the African's prowess as his own, but fear held him in check. Once on the dry canyon floor, the African holy man and the commander of the cavalry were plied with questions from the confused soldiers.

"Now it is time for me to go. I run south, drawn by a force that cannot be denied," Kuntamba said as he departed. Leaving Feriluc behind, the dark runner once again felt the pull of the unknown. Ever so slowly the pleasure of motion with its purifying cadence blended the forces and energies within him. His eyes saw far and near. He read the landscape, the sky, and the atmospheric forces of wind and rain. He felt the magnetism of his path as it pulled him toward his ultimate destiny. Far to his right and hundreds of feet lower in elevation flowed the *Rio Grande*.

For five days he paralleled the magnificent, flowing desert oasis. On the second day, Kuntamba felt the curious eyes of several young Pima warriors who had come to investigate the trespasser who dared to cross their land. The Indians were on horseback. They rode as if they were part of the horses that carried them. At first, they watched from a distance. Driven by curiosity and an eagerness to claim the right of first storyteller around the evening campfire, the Indians moved closer. Yet there was something about the dark runner that made them hesitate. He was unarmed and without supplies. He ran as easily as tumbleweed blowing across the land, and he seemed unconcerned with their presence.

The Pima leader, wanting to demonstrate his prowess, raced past Kuntamba and turned, urging his horse into a gallop. His intention was to knock the dark runner down, then ride around the fallen black man claiming victory over the intruder. But at the last minute, with only strides separating Kuntamba's body from a thousand pounds of horseflesh, the animal shied and nearly threw its rider.

The young Pima brave was embarrassed. Spinning his steed around, he decided to try another maneuver. He moved closer, driving his horse into a sprint. He intended to count coup by touching Kuntamba. But his mount again changed course at the last minute, denying him his moment of courage and his claim of being the first to touch the mystical dark mirage that drifted across the land.

The brave's followers were watching closely. They concluded that their leader had intentionally turned away at the last instant. Eager to show they were not afraid to touch the black man, one by one, they charged forward. With one hand locked on their horse's mane and the other arm outstretched, each Indian leaned to the side as far as he could, driving toward the dark runner.

One by one, each horse balked or pulled away just before extended hands and fingers could touch black skin. Unable to make contact, the Pima gathered together and followed Kuntamba at a distance. The warriors talked as they rode, wondering what power the African possessed over their horses. Several thought Kuntamba was a supernatural being that should not be approached.

As the Pima braves trailed behind the dark runner, they saw him raise his right arm and move it in a circle. To the Pima, the black man's arm motion was both a challenge and a request. The motion asked and dared them to run step for step with the dark runner as far as their stamina and willpower could carry them. Slowing, Kuntamba allowed the mounted warriors to catch up with him. After the Indians had dismounted and fallen in behind him, the dark runner held his pace allowing the Pima to approach and touch his skin. Hours later, with only a crescent moon illuminating his path, Kuntamba ran alone.

The morning sun rose, bestowing on the dark runner a shadow companion that never experienced fatigue or thirst. It always accompanied Kuntamba when there was enough light to give it definition. The shadow told its creator the time of day and whether the sky was clear or cloudy.

Hours later, Kuntamba was moving through waist-high grasses with roots buried under a thick mat of compost. His steps slowed to a walk. The world around him was teeming with life. He saw the great bison raise their heads and stare dully in his direction, and he watched red calves nudge their mother's udders.

The African looked up at a distant knoll where three wolves stood with heads held down as if in a discussion. The dark runner sidestepped nests of birds, befuddled cottontails, and an occasional snake. He moved through flower-adorned fields that shamed every rainbow he had ever beheld. He detected a hundred different scents that filled his lungs with their blended aroma. His mind reached back to Africa in search of a similar experience but he could recall nothing that was as untouched or that existed in the same perfect harmony.

Kuntamba's ears filled with the drone of clouds of insects toiling to fulfill their part in nature's unfathomable complexity. Stopping to enjoy the indescribable pleasure of being cloaked in a sea of multicolored butterflies, he marveled at the intensity of color their vermillion, purple, black, and powder blue wings displayed as they flashed their beauty all around him. As he moved across the vast floral display, avoiding the tiny thumbnail sized violets that dotted his path, he gently waved his arms, clearing a way through the swarming insects.

Out of the corner of his eye, the dark runner saw a long, thin-bodied creature with short legs and an elongated tail. The animal's feet were dressed in black boots that accentuated its light tan fur coat as it moved through the grass as easily as a serpent. A moment later Kuntamba saw a mouse, only its fur was silver colored. The small rodent stared straight back at the trespasser as it nonchalantly consumed a grasshopper.

Above the dark runner, drifting on the up currents of heated air and contrasted against a turquoise-blue sky, floated a pair of large hawks. The birds' white chests and underwings defined their location in the world of space. The five-foot wingspans enabled the birds to drift lazily on nature's breath as their eyes searched for a meal below.

For several minutes, Kuntamba was captured in the flow of the life force that animated the boundless variety of living creatures that swirled around him. It was as if he were basking in the fount of universal energy that is expressed by nature's all-permeating presence. Kuntamba reflected and recognized that this moment in his eternal journey was only possible because he had chosen a path of self-revelation.

He also realized that the land and the very spot where he stood were in perfect harmony, but would not always be. Because his body, mind, and soul were in balance, he retained a peace that was unshakable. This peace only existed when his entire being was without conflict and no tides of emotion, desire, or fear washed across his mind. It was his ability to find this internal point that made his glimpses of the future possible. He did not need to meditate or enter into a trance to see what the land he stood on would look like in a hundred years.

The entire world was entering a time of change and upheaval. The shadow of what was to come was on the horizon, readable by anyone with a sensitive nature. He saw a barren land. Gone were the butterflies, the birds of the air, and the animals that lived above the ground, he saw only flies, mosquitoes, and dry, sterile soil. Even the river that flowed south had become a dry wash.

Kuntamba's present pleasure clashed with the knowledge of what the land would endure. His inner balance teetered on the fine edge that divides that which is permanent and that which is changing. For just an instant, he found himself being torn between the disintegrating chaos of the future and the point of natural perfection he was currently enjoying. It was his ability to balance himself on the pinnacle of objectivity that enabled him to transcend the competing images of the world as he was perceiving it and as it would be in a hundred years.

He was relieved when the ever-present urge to move south recalled his thoughts to the present. In that moment, and for the first time since his odyssey commenced, he felt the fleeting touch of anticipation. It told him his southerly journey was nearing its conclusion. He felt no need to hurry his steps, but his mind tried to reach ahead in time, anxious to discover what power had called him from the other side of the world.

Kuntamba knew some unseen power had beckoned him from a faraway land. Why he did not know, but the moment of discovery was drawing near. As a flower opened to the morning sun without haste, he too would permit events to unfold in their appointed time.

The African looked down at the motion of his feet in a full stride. He knew his feet had no independent intellect, yet they fulfilled their mission with a perfection and efficiency that seemed impossible. He was aware his first steps began the process of training, not only his feet but a portion of his subconscious mind. At some point, the self that his efforts had created to perform the task of running took over, leaving his mind free to experience the world around him. He wondered if the force that called him from beyond the great ocean was cognizant of its magnetic attraction. Did the power know he was approaching, or was it like his feet, simply following a process ordained by repetition and the eternal unfolding of universal law?

CHAPTER NINE

With the sun pointing his shadow eastward, he looked upon the rise of mountains that blocked his path. From the outline framed against a clear blue sky, he estimated they were approximately seven travel days away. There was something friendly and inviting about the mountains. The closer Kuntamba got, the more he felt like he belonged to them. It was as if he were returning to his birthplace. His mind was flooded with fragments of memory linked to the rolling hills of his African homeland.

Instead of being overwhelmed by the steep mountain trails and treacherous passes, Kuntamba saw only beauty in the snow-covered peaks and verdant forests. Where the deep appreciation of the alpine world he was entering had been cultivated, he did not know. He searched his memory, questioning what this land of mountains, gorges, and high plateaus had in common with the earth that nurtured him as a child.

As he climbed the foothills, the land took on a strangeness. The dark runner saw plants and animals that had only a slight resemblance to life forms he had observed in the past. Beyond the plants and animals, he found a harmony that stirred memory tracings whose source seemed to have no beginning. In this ethereal world, Kuntamba felt at home. He had found a stream of consciousness that would guide him to his new life.

The hours quickly merged into days as he began an effortless ascent up the Sierra Madre Mountains. The air was clear and the land was untainted by the affairs and desires of men.

Two days later, and many miles deeper into the mountains, the land took on a new feeling. It spoke to Kuntamba of violence, death, and the devastation of oppression and slavery. Nature and a powerful neutralizing force had almost lifted the heavy cloak of violence from the mountains and valleys, but traces of the past still lingered for Kuntamba. They spoke, as always, of man's greed, insensitively and ignorance of inner truths.

Stopping his motion, the dark runner calmed his breathing before positioning himself on a prominence that provided a view of the trail he would follow. The area appeared to be devoid of human traffic. In contradiction, his senses told him he was entering a land populated by a brave people.

The tribes still inhabiting the nearly impassable recesses of the Sierra Madre Mountains had a painful history of slavery. The mountains and the surrounding country had been invaded and controlled by the people of another continent. Not only had the invaders enslaved the indigenous people, they had attempted to destroy the tribe's way of life and religious beliefs. From these intuitive flashes, Kuntamba gained an understanding of the mountain tribes he would soon live among.

Once again the dark runner ran with a rhythm that carried him to higher elevations. The sun had just passed its zenith and was casting the first shadows of the afternoon when Kuntamba noticed the footprints. The wind had filled the impressions with fine silt, leaving an unmistakable outline.

The imprints were not those of someone carrying a heavy load. They were the footsteps of a man or woman who ran with tireless ease. The stride was even, expending the same amount of effort with each motion. The placing of the foot on the ground left a record of conservation of energy and a precise positioning of the body over each foot as it landed and pushed off from the uneven surface of the path. There were no small telltale clumps of dirt behind or off to the side of the footprints, evidencing pronation of the foot or the use of too much force driving off the ball of the foot.

It was the only time in all of Kuntamba's travels that he witnessed evidence of someone else possessing a running skill that approached his. He could not help but wonder who the person was, or if most of the inhabitants of these mountains ran with the same proficiency.

The tracks led south.

The dark runner was curious. He wanted to meet the man or woman who was so well adapted to the art of motion. For two days he followed the tracks of the mysterious runner. He marveled at the person's stamina and ability to travel long distances without stopping to rest, eat, or drink. Kuntamba wondered if the person he was following had mastered the secret of controlled breathing. He hoped his suspicions were true, but logic convinced him that the possibility of finding someone whose spiritual journey paralleled his own was highly improbable.

Kuntamba knew that to truly master the ability to run indefinitely, or to do anything with near perfection, an individual first had to master all the forces of his physical, mental, and spiritual being. The energy consumed by desires, passions, hate, and greed had to be transmuted into spiritual power. To accomplish this degree of spiritual awareness took many lifetimes of dedication. He wanted to believe such an individual left the tracks, but he was not a man who lived in the world of hope. He would wait and let time reveal the identity of the person who had left the trail he was following.

In time, his questioning doubt turned to amazement. The tracks left by one runner were suddenly joined by the impressions of a dozen runners. A careful examination of the footprints disclosed that all the runners were skilled, but only one set possessed a running skill equal to his own.

The dark runner soon noticed individual runners were leaving the pack and taking paths that climbed toward the high peaks or plunged down into the deep canyons. Eventually he was once again following only one set of tracks. They were not as perfect or efficient as his first discovery. The footprints told a tale of aging bones and shrinking flexibility, pushed by a heart and mind that loved the physicality of feet striking the ground.

He felt a kinship with the traveler of the mountain paths who had found an inner peace in distance running's consummate harmony. To Kuntamba, attaining the transcendental state was a mystical experience. The belief that another person had acquired this level of transcendence was gratifying. It removed some of his feelings of isolation while giving him hope that in the fullness of time much of mankind would join him in the spiritual quest.

Kuntamba was convinced that an older man made the trail he followed because the old one's steps had the rigidity of advancing years, yet the stride was still powerful and undaunted by steep inclines. If he could find him, he might learn if the old one was in possession of the wisdom of self-perfection. Kuntamba ran faster, hoping to communicate with an equal on a level that needed no spoken words. He wanted to know the people who lived at the higher elevations where the clouds hung just above his head.

Everywhere he looked, the land sloped at steep angles. Many of the paths that wove through the pristine alpine forests were no wider than a man's shoulders. He wondered why the inhabitants of the perpendicular slopes had chosen such a harsh environment for their home, yet the raw beauty of the landscape, the tumbling streams, and the verdant forests clinging to the near vertical mountain sides had an appeal that his inner nature could not have conceived of a month earlier.

The nearly inaccessible region's remoteness had a purity that intrigued him. The climate extremes, the peaks, and the deep gorges plunging down for thousands of feet elicited a feeling that touched primeval senses. The conditions awoke an inner perception in him that eradicated the passing of years, uniting a part of him that lived long ago with the present. He found himself understanding why the people who inhabited this mystical place had migrated into the valleys and deep canyons. But what did they eat? Suitable land for raising crops or livestock would be scarce. The lack of productive soil would force individual families to live great distances apart, distances that running crossed quickly.

Stepping off the trail, Kuntamba climbed up to a narrow outcropping. Sitting comfortably, he stared down into the shadowed recesses of the valley below. Focusing his consciousness inward, he searched for the impulse that had guided him on his long southerly trek. The urging was quiet. For a moment, he felt disconnected and lost then he began to understand, he had arrived at his destination. Now it was up to him to find his way unassisted. The realization aroused emotions of expectation and anticipation. It also brought direction, purpose, and the promise of a new life waiting to be discovered and fulfilled.

His next thoughts merged quiet happiness with questioning puzzlement. What should he do next? He could wait, but for what? He could find and meet with the people of his new homeland, but how would he communicate with them?

Memories of the *Ocean Breeze's* long voyage came rushing back. Recollections of sitting and watching, learning the new strange language of the gruff seamen, lingered. After a brief period reflection, he decided to find a family and offer his help through the act of doing. But first he wanted to explore the mountains, learn where the meadows lay, search the depth of the caves, and feel the vibrations of the area's history.

CHAPTER TEN

During the ensuing months, the tribesmen who lived in harmony with the changing faces and conditions of their mountainous homeland occasionally glimpsed the African's shadowy form. The phantom runner was usually sighted when the moon was full. Superstitious natives thought a ghost moved among them, but when they found the dark runner's footprints next to their own, they knew the specter was human and not a myth. Once the Indians knew *el negro* was mortal, they tried to track the elusive runner, pursuing him for days on end, but his trail always seemed endless.

The Indians believed the mystical *el negro* possessed a dual nature, the physical one that left impressions in the dust of the trail and the spiritual one that faded from men's sights when they drew near. The belief took on the dimension of omnipresence when the unearthly runner's footprints were found near peaks on narrow paths and the dark recesses of rarely visited canyons.

The isolated mountain people were unaware that when the tribe gathered to harvest crops or to build the one-room log cabins that sheltered them from the rain and the night, Kuntamba was watching and learning. They did not know that he waited just yards away as they celebrated the bounty of their harvest with corn beer. In the morning, a few vaguely remembered but discounted the dark hand that dislodged a knife held with murderous intent. After a night of heavy drinking, others thought ancestors had protected them when they awoke in the morning, miles away from their cabins. Only the small children, who tottered too far from their mothers' sight, were allowed to see the dark runner's face as he carried them away from danger.

When the cold wind and the heavy morning frost came, it told the secretive mountain tribes that winter was approaching. The tribe members gathered the stock, driving them down the narrow trails to the warmer floor of the deep canyons. Once the tribes settled in, the women resumed working their looms and tending the children. The men returned to the soil, tilling the ground with iron plows pulled by oxen. The instruments of cultivation, both the irons that cut into the earth and the animals that pulled them, had been purchased with blood from the Spanish invaders.

Many generations earlier, Spanish soldiers had corralled most of the mountain people in central locations where the Jesuit priests tried to convert the Indians to Christianity. Some joined the Christian community willingly. Others had to be coerced. Whip drove the converts to the mines where they worked long hours extracting gold and silver for a government they did not know existed.

When a few individuals refused to be converted to the foreigners' religious beliefs or protested being forced to work, military tribunals took over and the rebels were hung or beheaded as an example to anyone who dared to defy the oppressors. For more than two hundred years, various elements of the mountain people resisted and challenged the military might of the foreign conquerors. The Indians had few military successes and they suffered horrendous losses, yet they persisted.

During the last two decades of the Spanish domination, the trespassers' forces had begun to withdraw as the strength of Mexico's armies grew. But in the mountains, the Tarahumara, Tepehuane, Concho, and Chinipa retreated deeper into the canyons of the Sierra Madre, beyond the reach of the Spaniards and all news of the people in the lower valleys.

The Tarahumara had many brave leaders during their long struggle with the intruders, but there was one name from the 13th century that was always evoked with pride. He was a farmer named Temporame. He and two thousand warriors fought the Spanish and won many small battles. In the final struggle, flesh and primitive weapons stood unflinching against metal, lead, gunpowder and armored men astride horses. Temporame's men died with courage, slaughtered like animals. In 1752, Temporame was beheaded and his head was placed on a sharp stake for all to see.

Kuntamba did not know the history of the land written in books, but he could still feel the scars that oppression had left on the people. It was a familiar experience for the dark runner. From Africa to America's southeast coast, on the *Ocean Breeze* and across the new country of the United States, he had followed a stream of consciousness that thrived on the domination of the less fortunate.

It was a weight that pressed in on him relentlessly. Seeking a moment of relief, Kuntamba decided it was time to meet with the venerable runner whom he was convinced possessed a wisdom few could comprehend. He had never seen the old man's face because he rarely left his abode, and then only at night to run on paths with eyes that could scarcely see the ground beneath his feet.

Members of the surrounding communities frequently visited the old man. The guests came bearing food and gifts. They always stopped about a hundred feet from his door, calling out in a respectful voice, requesting permission to advance. If there was no response, they waited silently for hours. Along with their offerings, the callers brought the ill and the injured.

For two days, Kuntamba observed the old man as he healed the sick and counseled the dying. When no patients remained, the African walked into the open, calling out in the language of the Tarahumara. "Temporame, I have traveled far. May I visit with you?"

When the dark runner heard no answer, he listened for the sound of shuffling feet or the rustle of garments as fabric rubbed together in the motion of walking, but he detected nothing. Closing his eyes, he called on his inner sight for assistance. It revealed the outline of an old man sitting with his head bowed in mediation. Withdrawing, the dark runner regretted his impatience and the invasion of the old one's privacy.

Standing in front of Temporame's cabin, the dark runner waited. An hour later a sharp clear voice called out, "Who invades my prayers without permission?"

"Just a friend who follows your steps on the dark nights when your feet seem to float above the ground," Kuntamba answered.

The old one did not reply immediately. He was revisiting the shadowless nights when his need to run was awakened by motion-hungry muscles and a soul that longed to bathe in universal energy. The omnipresent force seemed to flow along the mountain trails after the sun had relinquished its hot grasp on the steep inclines. He remembered vaguely feeling his nocturnal isolation was intruded upon, but the sensation was a positive one that added a dimension of security and well being he had not felt before. The black man in front of him radiated the same feelings of harmlessness and quiet power. The old one knew both experiences arose from the same source--the visitor who waited to see him.

Speaking in a barely audible voice the old one spoke. "For many years I have waited for your voice to call my name. Now I reply, how can I serve you?"

"It is not your service I seek. It is your counsel. May I approach and look at the spiritual guide that called me to these beautiful mountains? You are the only person I have encountered whose eternal journey has paralleled mine. Both of us share and participate in the enlightenment gained when our bodies find nature's harmony and the life force of the universe through the perfection of running."

"Your words and knowledge prove that my wait and my trials were not in vain," Temporame replied. "Please advance so that our conversation can be enhanced by the blending of minds across the bridge that eyes create when recognition is born."

A silent and spoken communication continued for hours. Kuntamba learned he and Temporame were among the few embodied souls that had entered the light of truth. In acquiring a level of spiritual growth, Kuntamba and Temporame had become the keepers of the truth's flame. Their labor would not end until the human race matured spiritually, stepping beyond the embrace of materialism and into the expanding field of consciousness that spiritual enlightenment makes possible.

He learned the old man was one hundred and thirty years old. The venerable and wise ancient one had maintained his hold on life until his burden of protecting wisdom's metaphoric lamp of truth could be shifted to an equally qualified seeker. It was not a weight that scales could measure. The heaviness was contained within the immeasurable and unfathomable depths of the mind and spirit. Only those who had acquired a high degree of self-mastery were able to assume the enormous responsibility.

Kuntamba's task, if he accepted, would be as a guide or teacher. His ultimate goal would require limitless patience. His labor of love would continue until an aspirant sought him out and eagerly accepted the responsibility of preserving wisdom's light. The future traveler on the path of self-enlightenment would need to accept his new role unconditionally, knowing the vigil would not end until another seeker had attained enough inner strength to become the preserver of the wisdom, which would free mankind from spiritual blindness in the future.

Outwardly Kuntamba was silent, but inwardly his mind was whirling in a turmoil that sought to comprehend his new mission in life. For years he had felt the increasingly urgent call of a power greater than his own. He knew he had to accept, and was positive that the new responsibilities would tax and finally exhaust his stamina and the spiritual limits of his soul. He understood that only after he had expended all his physical and spiritual forces in his task of preserving the light of truth could he call on those who had gone before him. Their strength, and his love for mankind, would empower him to call out in a voice only the purified could hear. In response, somewhere in the world another soul would begin the long southerly journey.

He looked closely at Temporame. The old man was breathing heavily. Each succeeding inhalation grew more labored. The muscle tone left his body as the years added their wear to his face. His vision failed and his body shrank into a decrepit, feeble, wasted form. The life force that had sustained him for so long was departing.

Kuntamba spoke with reverence. "With great joy I accept the mantle of preserving the truth. May I ask if this new life is one that must be lived in solitude?"

As the dark runner finished speaking, he saw the old one was trying to vocalize. Leaning close, the dark runner heard him whisper as the breath of death caught in his throat. "The footprints you followed that were as perfect as your own were my daughter's. Without knowing, she too has waited for you."

Temporame slipped from the confines of his frame, leaving behind the confining prison that was once his body. He entered a world of light and boundless freedom, a freedom that took ages of labor in the dense physical world to earn. He would undertake new burdens, but in the future the physical world would only be entered by choice.

As Kuntamba's wisdom matured, he had unknowing been preparing to assume Temporame's burden of love. His shoulders sagged, but not from the weight of his new responsibility. His pain sprang from loss and separation. It had taken him a lifetime to find Temporame only to lose him within hours of their first meeting. He felt incomplete. Gone was the only soul who had experienced the same truths and expanding consciousness, the only person who with just a look could fill his heart with universal love, a heart which in Kuntamba's lifetime of giving had grown lonely for the touch of an equal.

In his melancholy, he momentarily lost his spiritual balance. Then his inner voice whispered a message. "Your sadness springs from the seeds of selfishness that remain in your being. You should be happy. Temporame has suffered his labor for more than seventy years. He is free and you are the one who released him from his trial."

For an instant Kuntamba felt guilt and a sense of failure, but within seconds his inner consciousness prompted him. "First, I let grief blind me. Now I have let failure enter my domain and neither are welcome."

Kneeling beside Temporame's body, he began to meditate. Soon he found his inner balance and the ability to put his failings in perspective.

Standing up, he stared at the old one's corporeal vehicle. He was amazed that he had not noticed the same tightly twisted coils of hair on Temporame's head as he himself possessed. He looked at the full lips and slightly flared nostrils. Why hadn't he observed these characteristics earlier?

Thinking back over the last hour, he remembered looking into Temporame's faded eyes without seeing anything else. Kuntamba looked again at the old one's remains. He saw a lineage that reached back to Africa, but there was also another ancestral line visible. He could not be sure but he thought he recognized a Caucasian bloodline in Temporame's background. He recalled how the old one's blueish green eyes had held him with their near hypnotic stare.

He became preoccupied with the unknown. If the old one was one hundred and thirty years old, it would mean he was born in the late sixteen hundreds. Where had he come from? Had he been a slave? Who were his parents? Had he been drawn to the isolation of these mountains by the call of another wise man? Was he self-taught? Did Temporame's wisdom flow as a result of a hunger created on the other side of life? Who was his daughter and why wasn't she present when her father slipped beyond the reach of human hands?

Inhaling slowly, Kuntamba ceased the questions, waiting for meditation's calm to wash over him. From the tranquillity, he heard Temporame's voice. "Your questions will be answered in due time." And then the stillness returned. This time it carried an urgency that would not be pacified.

CHAPTER ELEVEN

The Tarahumara would soon be coming with offerings and the sick. They had to be told Temporame lived no more. It would be impossible for Kuntamba to spread news of Temporame's death by visiting the home of each family. Time was his enemy, not fatigue. Temporame's body had to be cared for. The mountain people would want to pass by the old one's remains.

Deciding to build a funeral pyre where he would lay Temporame's worn out physical cloak, Kuntamba hoped the cool dry mountain air would slow the disintegration of the body. He intended to let those who came for Temporame's healing touch spread the news of their physician and spiritual guide's passing.

For two days Kuntamba worked dragging deadwood up the steep forested slopes that surrounded him. On the third day, he placed Temporame's surprisingly light corpse on the pyre. As he stretched the frail body out on the straw mat that had supported his frame in life, he noticed that death's decay had not yet visibly claimed the old one's physical vehicle.

Taking the observation as an omen, Kuntamba decided to wait three more days for the tribesmen who lived in the far reaches of the mountains to travel their paths of respect and mourning before the cremation began.

Finally, the mourners started arriving. They did not leave. They sat on the ground. When the coldness that arrives with the setting sun wrapped them in its chilling mantle, they did not seek warmth. The hot alpine sun could not drive them to find shade. They did not eat or drink and no word was uttered. The dark runner walked among them prepared to offer words of solace or the gentle touch of passing fingers. When he looked into their faces, he saw a mixture of sadness and acceptance. He saw Indians from tribes totally unfamiliar to him and dark eyed deeply tanned men and women wearing turbans sitting lotus-style on the ground.

He watched yellow skinned priests with almond shaped eyes, whose expressions seemed to have a oneness with wisdom and peace, chant soundlessly. He saw Africans, Europeans, and people from areas of the world he did not know existed. Kuntamba was confounded. Where had these people come from? Surely in his months of exploring the region he would have seen at least a few of the strangers.

From the queries came answers that sprang from the powers that flowed naturally to those who have traveled far on the path of self-enlightenment. The African's understanding arrived as quietly as the rising sun.

In the past, he had communicated with others over the nonexistent distance that separates minds. The memory suggested to Kuntamba how the strangers from distant lands might have learned of Temporame's death. Still, two questions remained. How had the holy ones from the four corners of the earth trekked to the mountains of the Sierra Madre in such a short time? And why did they not eat or drink?

Extending his hand, Kuntamba tried to touch one of the saffron robed monks but his hand passed through the yellow orange garment and the man who wore it as easily as if moving through the mountain air. Once, during prolonged meditation, a part of the dark runner's spirit had slipped unbound from his body and wandered on the mind's highway back to Africa. It was a pleasant and revitalizing accidental sojourn.

Knowing it was a power that would flow to him when he was fully prepared, he never again attempted to use the power to travel or communicate. As his thoughts turned from the out-of-body experience, a new realization filled his senses. He was not alone in his quest. He was just beginning to knock on wisdom's door. The others who had gone before him had left a legacy. It was an availability of wisdom and a trail marked by the passing of those who preceded him. The African did not know how many unseen hands had guided him in his journey. How many would he reach out to in the future? Only the passing of time would tell.

With the expanded understanding came a feeling of exhilaration and a need for motion. The dark runner stretched his idle legs. He longed to run through the mountains, cross currents in a full stride, but he had to wait until Temporame's ashes were returned to the earth.

On the fifth day after the old one's death, a long procession filed into the clearing. Waiting individuals quietly arranged themselves in concentric circles around Temporame's elevated corpse. Silence still ruled. The holy ones who traveled without their physical bodies stood closest to the funeral pyre. Behind them Temporame's mountain people waited. Beyond the crowd, a circle was drawn in the dirt. It enclosed the mourners and the old one's remains.

When the sun was four hours past high noon, the shadows of those gathered connected in a series of spokes that terminated at the delineated outer ring in the grainy soil. The funeral fire was lit. As the dry wood ignited, the mourners started to move in unison. At first, they walked slowly following the unseen line that represented the circumference of their particular circle. As the flames grew in intensity, the living wheel accelerated. When the last of Temporame's remains were consumed, the crowd dispersed.

Only Kuntamba remained, alone and slightly confused. What had happened? Sitting quietly, he relaxed and after a time, entered a state of contemplation. With his head bowed and his eyelids tightly closed, on the screen of his mind's eye, he saw the strangers for what they were, ancient ones, who one by one, had preserved the light of wisdom for all of mankind. They had waited with the patience of Job for another seeker to rise up out of materialism to discover the eternal truths for himself.

Kuntamba saw the wise ones as equals, yet it was he who was yet to be tested by the relentless press of time. He saw the wheel of life and the final departure of the supernatural visitors accompanying Temporame's spirit, then it was over and he was alone again. The mountain tribesmen had departed. They had shed no tears and had made no sound of lament. All that remained was the hush that is experienced when an inexpressible loss is endured.

The dark runner planned to sit in front of the old one's cabin so all would know he was their servant. The funeral site was empty and the ashes cold. Succumbing to an inner hunger, Kuntamba began to run. Only the moon watched as he strode down narrow trials guarded by white mountain peaks.

In the first hours, his body recaptured the pleasure of motion while being recharged with the vital force that sustains all life. Abruptly, his mind entered the sphere of revelation where no language is spoken and the past, present, and future have a unity that transcends time and place. For the first time in his life, Kuntamba ran with a degree of consciousness that sensed the field of universal archetypes. It was a condition where creation sprang from the rising of divine desire, thought, and energy. Enclosing and permeating the first triad was an enveloping divine love.

The African did not know it, but his entrance into this field and the pure happiness he felt while in this region was a gift. In accepting his new role without conditions, he had committed himself and his physical and spiritual power to the community of guardians. His power would join with those who had gone before him in the Herculean task of holding back the darkness of evil. Only the unanimity of mankind's quest for truth could ultimately release him to continue his own adventure into the infinite. In his new responsibility, he had become a servant of mankind. It could not be otherwise. All life is connected and all men and women are part of a whole. What affects one affects all.

Through the night the dark runner ran, unaware where he was or what force guided him. Like the return of the sunlight that follows a fast-moving storm, his consciousness of the world about him returned. It brought an awareness that he was not alone. He heard no footsteps because the presence ran with a tempo that was identical to his own. Wanting to test the unseen visitor, Kuntamba accelerated up a long slope. He heard no sound, but he was positive he was being followed.

"Is it a human being who haunts my steps, or one of the ancient ones having fun?" he asked himself. Kuntamba stopped and studied the surrounding area. He saw no one. Sprinting across a small meadow, he looked back, hoping the open space would expose the entity that so perfectly mimicked his steps.

Strangely, when no one followed, he felt a sense of isolation. For a moment he longed for the company of the unseen presence that shadowed him much of the night. Worrying that the people might be waiting for his return, the dark runner hurried back to Temporame's cabin. The structure was the only physical evidence that the old one had ever lived. Kuntamba decided to preserve the shelter for his own successor.

When he arrived at his new home, Kuntamba felt wonderful; full of excitement and anticipation. The impulse that had called him to this land no longer spoke to him. His future labor lay before him and he was eager to begin, but his happiness was marred by a question that had plagued him for weeks.

The question returned, bringing doubt with it. Why did he have to guard truth when truth is indestructible? Why did he have to safeguard what his successors would discover through their own efforts? Before doubt could find full expression, the answer came. It did not arrive on the soft breath of wisdom. It crashed into his consciousness with the weight of regret, revealing his ignorance and commanding him to look beyond his logical disruptive reflections.

Remorsefully bowing his head, Kuntamba asked, "Why did I not seek truth where truth exists, in the realm of the real." Turning his energy of concentration inward, he began again.

"Are not all of those who seek enlightenment keepers of wisdom's flame?" This time his reply arrived with the softness of understanding. "The world of man is a spiritually dark place. On earth, the burden of negativity has blanketed all but the most remote locations. When an aspiring soul tries to rise above the shroud of spiritual darkness, failure is almost always inevitable."

"Some rare individuals do acquire the courage and strength to stand away from the entanglements of possessions, desire, ego, and their own lower nature. When this happens, they are ready to receive guidance. The channels of their minds are open and able to accept, metaphorically speaking, whatever spiritual food enters their upturned cup."

"Like most seedlings, those who enter into the quest are weak. They have not obtained the strength gained in the self-inflicted ordeals that await them. They have stepped away from the mass of humanity, but the effort consumes most of their energy. When they inwardly call out for help, those who live in the non-physical world hear and try to guide them. But the tangible world is dense and its oceans of negativity muffle the offerings of the masters. That is why links connecting the world of appetites with the regions of wisdom are needed."

"You are one of those links, your presence and those like you, who serve mankind, create an availability to wisdom that cannot be gained in any other way. You are conduits to the avatars. Remember this truth: without spiritual growth, existence becomes an exercise in futility. Your seclusion is important because in the past when holy ones walked among the people, they were discredited and killed."

The old *wisdom* flowed to Kuntamba as quickly and surely as light floods a room when a shade is lifted on a sunny day.

The timid voice of a Tarahumara woman holding a lethargic infant brought him back to the service of man. Asking for guidance, the dark runner took the child in his arms, looking deep into the mother's eyes. "Do not nurse your child anymore. Give him goats' milk and he will thrive," he said to her. With a nod of her head, the woman carrying the child hurried away. Kuntamba knew she had been drinking too much corn beer and its hold on her would not be broken until she wore out the pleasure it offered.

Walking back to the cabin, he slowed his steps. The same presence that had accompanied him the night before was near. A few paces more and he knew a visitor waited for him in the hut. It was no ordinary caller. The guest had great spiritual power.

The dark runner found himself hurrying although he could not explain why. As he opened the door, an overwhelming feeling of anticipation swept over him. Looking into the dim room, he made out the outline of a tall slender woman. A few streaks of light found their way into the chamber. The illumination entered through breaks in the chinking that sealed the gaps between the logs.

The longer Kuntamba's gaze rested on the figure before him, the clearer it became. He saw raven black hair combed out in long twisting spirals that shimmered with the beat of her heart and the tempo of her breathing. He looked at her face, discovering he could not turn away. The depth of expression in her eyes spoke of the primordial dust of creation, the stars in the sky, and selfless love.

The African remembered seeing the same twinkle in the heavens on moonless nights. He was not sure he had not seen the same dark eyes in his dreams most of his adult life. Her voice added to the spell. Its tone was filled with melancholy and compassion, a compassion that understood and felt the immense mountains and oceans of pain that had to be endured before mankind found its identity and purpose.

Kuntamba had also stood on the shore of mankind's sea of ignorance. Its enormity had taxed his faith in the law and almost ended his quest. Only after he had acquired the realization that all souls are fulfilling their place and moment in an eternity of time, was he able to find an internal balance that touched on the law's infinite infallibility.

The woman introduced herself in a soft voice. Her words were simple, yet spoken with elegance. "I am called Estrella." The syllables had a harmony that struck a cord within Kuntamba. He began to quietly repeat her name, trying to recapture the melody of her voice but its perfection eluded him.

Hesitantly he answered, "My name is Kuntamba."

"Yes, I know. I have run with you in the sacred trance on the mountain pathways."

Kuntamba was elated; Estrella was the force he had detected in the early morning hours. He remembered Temporame's death. The memory of his death and the sorrow his daughter must be feeling caused a wave of sensitivity to flow from him. It told Estrella he understood her pain and the loneliness that is born when a person who is truly one with you steps beyond the veil that separates physical life from the world of spirit.

The dark runner was surprised that Estrella read his feeling and replied without speaking. "I was with my father, as you were, when he died. Temporame and I communed for five days and nights in the place that separates the tangible and intangible worlds."

Kuntamba moved closer. Estrella's soft brown skin, the fullness of her lips, and an indistinguishable quality in her demeanor, told him that Africa still lived in her nature.

"We must talk. I have so much to learn. Your life with your father has blessed you with a wisdom few can claim. I have so many questions that need answering."

Estrella nodded. "Yes, we must talk of many things. The guidance accessible to me has also been yours. Temporame was your unseen instructor since before you left Africa. The wisdom you sought he helped to make available when you were ready."

Walking outside Kuntamba sat down and waited for Estrella. As she moved toward him, he marveled at her youthful appearance. His mental compliment brought to mind Temporame's age. If he had been one hundred and thirty years old at the time of his death, Estrella must be far older than she looked.

Smiling at him, Estrella said, "You have questions about my age and my parents. I do not know who my natural parents were. Temporame found me in the doorway of an empty building several hundred miles south of here. I was in a cardboard box, naked, cold, and hungry. I was three months of age and near death. Temporame did not find me by chance. In a trance, he learned that a soul with roots of wisdom that traced back through the ages waited for him. I am thirty-two years old."

It was his turn to speak. "I believe you and Temporame called me to this wonderful place where I feel a happiness that cannot be described." As he continued, he studied Estrella's face but her expression was unreadable. "My parents were captured by black slavers and sold into a life of misery and servitude. But the foreigners made a bad bargain. Neither of them survived their shipboard ordeal."

"I know this because in my youth I visited with them in the world of spirits. I was cared for and loved by my elder sister. To her I owe the debt of survival and the gift of guidance on the path of self-mastery. She was unable to travel as quickly as I was on the journey of self-enlightenment, but she has taken her first conscious steps into the infinite. We commune in the place where distance is nonexistent. As for my age, I am thirty-six years old."

As Kuntamba, a man far away from his homeland, finished speaking, a silence that could not be penetrated by the shrill call of birds or the howling of the wind through the trees enclosed them. The quiet held no element of awkwardness or embarrassment but it was not without communication. It was a meeting of minds, a touching of souls, and a hungry acceptance of this new and yet ancient relationship that existed on both sides of material life.

Each one found what neither had sought, a life mate. Each one received what both had prayed for, a teacher and someone who understood the language of truth. Each gained what neither dreamed existed on this side of life--the unspeakable pleasure that is experienced when kindred souls commune. These feelings were expressed in the undiluted realm of the real, a place where lies and deceit cannot exist.

The rising moon found two companions whose fingers had never felt the sensation of the other's touch running through the shadowed night in each other's spiritual embrace. Dawn revealed them caring for and healing the mountain tribesmen.

The years faded into the timeless sphere of the past, leaving no trace of aging on the bodies of mankind's two servants. The lapse of time, the co-mingling of toil and the attraction of souls whose paths had crossed and joined many times in their long journeys was a period of sublime peacefulness.

The magnetism of sexuality did not hold them together. Long ago, Estrella and Kuntamba had left the hungers of the flesh behind. It was the transmutation of the creative force that enabled them to live in the world of change. It made it possible for them to stand with the few in the ageless struggle of holding back at least fractionally the final darkening of mankind's spiritual light.

The two evolved souls had a oneness with selflessness. When their bodies joined in union, their magnified love carried them deeper into the regions of pure truth, wisdom, and divine love that neither of them could attain alone. During one of these moments of unconditional bliss, a child was conceived.

His birth was one of the extremely rare moments in mankind's history. For just a twinkling, the collective forces of the world's negativity retreated, allowing a flash of divine light to penetrate the darkness of ignorance that blankets the earth. It told those who were able to sense the brief lifting of the weight of ignorance from mens' minds that inner blindness was not permanent.

Kuntamba and Estrella would eventually be called to fulfill their final labor. They would go out into the world in search of those who had tired of materialism's demands and life's insipidness. Their son remained behind, serving the people, preserving the light of truth, and preparing for his final ordeal.

In their ultimate and most difficult expressions of love for the human race, Kuntamba and Estrella traveled separate paths. They taught those who would listen. They led the few who were ready to take their first steps on the road of self-enlightenment. They challenged evil wherever they went. They did not seek converts or to control others' lives. They refused gifts and wealth.

In time, religious zealots, fearing the prevailing interpretation of truth was in jeopardy, extinguished Kuntamba's light. Less than a year later, those who grew rich at materialism's fount, fearing a loss of wealth, sent Estrella home to her soul mate. Unknowingly, the powerful had not silenced truth with their murderous hands. They freed two souls to the higher regions where their power, unfettered by the confinement of physical bodies, would reach out to all who sought it.

Left behind, high in the mountains, or lost in the thriving metropolis of the world, or occasionally, in places of power, a thousand tiny flames grew into fires of illumination. In the world of spirit, Kuntamba and Estrella waited for the time when they would once again walk the earth, casting their beacons of light and hope.

Pray they are recognized and their words understood.